Acknowledgments

Thanks to Lisa Akoury-Ross and Sharon Honeycutt for their assistance in making this story become a novel. Special thanks to Ruth Buechler, Anthony DiPerna and Martin Foster for their advice on the courtroom drama contained herein, and to Peter Buechler for his advice on the computer technology. I would also like to thank all those friends who read and advised me as I wrote this.

To my wife, Mary, and daughters, Emma and Maria

Chapter 1

Dust and darkness filled the space around him, as did the sounds of shouting men and the sounds of falling rock landing on already fallen rock, but the loudest sound of all was his own scream. The pain was excruciating, streaking up from his foot to his thigh like electric shocks that flooded over him, each one more intense than the last. He was trapped. When he tried to move at all, the pain would come again in burning, pulsing waves ... wave after wave. He tried to stay still, but pain and fear drove him to pull again, to try to free himself, knowing that he could not and that pulling would make the pain worse again. He could not see through the dust and dark, but he knew what he would see if he could: his foot trapped beneath tons of rock. He was becoming dizzy from pain, or maybe from his impending death; he did not know. *Was this the way you died? he wondered. Was this what it was like to have your life slip away?*

A jolt of pain brought him back to consciousness as the men around him tried to move him and brought in bars and jacks to move the rock. He had done that himself when there was a roof fall in the coal mines and someone else lay trapped beneath it. The dust was settling a little, and he could see what they were trying to move. In spite of the pain, he realized their efforts would be fruitless. His foot was trapped. They could not get it out.

Another crash of rock from the roof of the mine raised more dust and startled the men working there. It drew Joe's attention toward another man who lay trapped beneath what had been, only a few minutes before, the roof of this coal mine. Joe thought it looked like Jeremiah underneath the rubble, but he couldn't be sure—only the man's waist and legs were visible. He could tell that whoever was buried there was dead. There was mute confirmation in the fact that none of the men were making any effort to free him. Freeing him would do no good.

Joe was in and out of consciousness now as the men moved around him, dirt and coal dust covering their faces. Lionel, the foreman, Joe's "boss," was the face he recognized first. Lionel looked at the pile of roof rock and then at Joe. "We got to get you out and soon," he said. Joe knew why. They were in a trap ready to spring. The roof that had fallen and trapped Joe had been the first fall. There would be others that could kill just as this one had.

To the rest Lionel said, "They're going to have to cut it off."

"No! Not my foot!" Joe screamed. One man in the group surrounding him looked at him, but the rest ignored his cry or looked away. They shared his pain, but their lives were at stake too.

Lionel said nothing to him. "Where's the doc?" he asked of no one in particular. Then to the group of men at the rock fall, "Y'all leave that be. You ain't gonna move nothing with them bars and all. You'll just bring it down on us."

A new face appeared in front of Joe, a clean, unfamiliar face. He pushed past Lionel and asked, "What's his name?"

"Joe," replied Lionel. "Joe Nelson."

"Joe," the clean face said. "I'm David Franklin, the doctor, and we are going to have to give you some meds. Some fluid and some pain meds. Don't pass out on me, do you hear me, Joe. Don't pass out."

The doctor moved fast. He took a blood pressure, wrapping the cuff around Joe's arm. Joe heard him say "Shit" beneath his breath. He looked at Joe's leg, pulled a tourniquet from his bag, and wrapped it tightly around the leg above the knee. He looked up at Lionel and said, "He's bleeding and getting shocky. We've got to get him out fast. Can you free that leg?"

Lionel looked again at the pile of rock as if to confirm what he already knew. "Not a chance."

"No!" screamed Joe. "I'd rather die here than live a cripple!"

The doctor stopped for just a second, but he quickly went ahead with the intravenous line, piercing the vein in Joe's arm and attaching a plastic tube and bag of fluid to it. He pulled out a syringe and injected it into the running fluid in the line. "That was morphine. It should help with the pain, Joe." Then to one of the men he said, "Here take this bag and squeeze it to get this fluid in as quick as possible."

Joe began to feel dizzy again. Maybe it was the morphine, or the shock, or the thought of losing his leg; he didn't really know, but the next face he saw was his father's. He looked at Joe as someone said, "He don't want to lose his leg."

His father looked around—the dirty, dusty face of an old miner scanning the scene and taking it all in. He looked around the way miners do, moving his head to point the light on his helmet toward what he wanted to see. Everyone could tell what he was looking at: his son, the pile of fallen rock, the foot trapped beneath it, and then at his son again.

"No time for foolishness, Son. You keep your leg and you'll die here with it."

"Pa, I can't ..."

His father cut him off. "You gotta fight back. Better to be shot running than standing still, Boy. Cut it off, Doc."

David Franklin looked at the father and then at the son. Joe closed his eyes, and then he nodded and began to cry.

It took only a minute and it was done. They carried Joe to the "lizard," the compressed-air-powered truck that carried them in and out of the mine along with the coal, the need for which had brought them all to this place ... all except the doctor. He had come to cut off Joe's leg. There was not enough room for all of them on the "lizard," so Lionel picked two to drive Joe and David Franklin out of the mine and told the rest to start running.

"We'll be back for you," one of the drivers said.

Lionel shook his head. "No use to that. Leave everything but your lights and respirators here, boys, and run for it. We only got a half mile at most and I'll skin any who can't do that in under five minutes. And I'll buy beer all around tonight for them that gets out. Now get going."

They did and they all got out, leaving only Joe's foot and Jeremiah behind. Twenty minutes later the roof fell where they had been, and it would be six months before either was seen again.

Chapter 2

Joe had been twenty years old when his foot was cut from him in that mine, and almost twenty years had passed since that had happened. While it was not surprising that the event had shaped his life, how it had shaped his life was beyond what anyone could have imagined. As Joe sat outside the court building waiting for his lawyer, he thought about how his life had unfolded since that day. It surprised even him every time he thought about it.

He had been depressed after that day in the mine—to the point of suicide he thought—but there had been no counseling, of course. Twenty years ago, seeking help for something like depression was not as common as today, and did not happen at all in his family. He had visitors—that was what people did up in the mountains of Eastern Kentucky. He had a "girlfriend" whom he had thought he might marry. She visited him twice, and on the second visit left him as a "good friend," no longer a "girl friend." It would be a year before he saw her again.

A couple of the men that worked with him in the mines "smuggled" in a six-pack of beer one night under their coats. No one from the staff seemed to notice, but they stayed conspicuously away. Lionel visited as well but had nothing to say except that Joe would be "all right."

A couple of his father's other friends visited just because he was their friend's son. They tried to distract him with stories about their lives and plans. They brought some beer too, but they just gave a couple of cans to the nurse and the aide to drink at the end of their shift, and that made it all right. One of those men,

Hank Morgan, a large African American, was a police officer too and that helped. He was planning to join the state police, which was a big career move for a local cop. AJ McPherson was leaving the mines to open a service station with a loan from his mother. Joe was polite to all of them, but their visits really made no difference. They had lives to live and he was crippled and nothing would change that. His father and mother had been supportive, but mostly just patient, waiting for him to "snap out of it," as if losing his leg was something like having a bad cold. Injuries like that were not uncommon for miners. The irony to Joe was that he *had* "snapped out of it."

The doctor, David Franklin, came by to visit one day. He asked how Joe was doing and told him he would get better. He said that the foot could not have been saved even if he had been able to leave the mine with it still attached to his leg. There was too much damage to it. The bones were crushed; the vessels and nerves were too badly damaged to be saved or to ever function again. Joe's recovery started with that visit.

That day he began to wonder about David Franklin. He expected the other miners to help when he was trapped in the mine even though it was dangerous. A miner who didn't try to save another miner after an accident didn't work long in the mines. The distrust or outright hostility was enough to drive him to other mines and usually to other occupations. Joe had gone into mines himself to help after roof falls or explosions, and he expected the other miners to do the same for him. You did that for others, partly in anticipation they would do it for you. He also expected Lionel and his father to be there, even though they had to come down to the scene of the accident because they were not there when the first roof fall happened. But as he thought about it, he realized that David Franklin was different. He came down just to help. He must have known it would be dangerous to do so. Neither Joe nor any of the other miners would ever be able to "repay" him, and he had known that too. He had been willing to take that risk and though he didn't die or even suffer any injury, the risk was still very real. David became the real hero in Joe's eyes.

When Joe began to recover, physically and emotionally, he did so in part because he decided he wanted to be like David Franklin. He knew he couldn't return to the mines, so the goal of becoming a physician became, for him, his reason to recover. In the strong religious nature of his family upbringing, he came to believe that this was why God had spared his life even as He made returning to the mines impossible. That belief was the drive behind his recovery.

He was fitted with an artificial leg—a prosthesis he learned to call it—below his knee, and he had to learn to walk and then run again. It was easier than he thought it would be, but it was still a lot of work. In the beginning he took pride in himself that he could walk and run as if he did not have a prosthesis at all. He even played on a basketball team until one of his friends, fortified by a couple of beers, explained to Joe that he wasn't a very good player. He hadn't been a good player in high school before the amputation and losing his foot hadn't turned him into a good player. It hadn't made him any worse, his friend explained, he just wasn't very good in high school and still wasn't any good. They shared another beer and Joe left the team.

When he gave up basketball he was in college full-time, and giving it up was probably a good thing for him. Joe no longer thought that it was important to appear as if he was like everyone else. From force of habit, he still minimized the evidence of his injury, and many people were surprised when they learned he had lost his foot. Some didn't believe him until he showed it to them.

He had thought his father, a high school dropout, would disapprove of his going to college, but he was actually very pleased and proud of his son. "Make something of yourself," he would say. "Don't forget where you come from, but do your family proud." In his senior year of college, his father died of lung cancer, and shortly thereafter, he heard that Lionel had died as well.

When he was home for the funeral, he took time to visit David Franklin again and was pleased that the doctor was happy to see him. David's own son was going to medical school and David thought that Joe should too. He offered advice and would have talked longer except the nurse in his office finally insisted he get back to work. His waiting room overflowed with patients. David told Joe to let him know where he was applying and said he would send letters or talk to the admissions people if he knew them. When Joe asked, David did just that.

As Joe left the office, David said, "Make something of yourself, Joe," echoing his father. He knew that David and his father had probably never talked much and especially not about college or medical school. He was surprised that they should have the same advice. To Joe, this was further evidence that it was his mission to become a physician.

Joe had done that, and four years later he started a residency in pediatrics, not surgery as David had done. Joe visited David whenever he returned home and one final time when he came home to bury his mother. That was the same year that David retired and moved to Florida, to vegetate he said, but he really sounded like he was looking forward to it. That was the last time Joe saw him alive. Five years later Joe attended his funeral.

Sitting outside the court building, Joe still believed that somehow God had a plan for him. The years had softened this belief, but it was still within him even on this day, which many would consider the worst day a doctor could face.

He looked up to see a beautiful, blond-haired woman walking toward him. She was smiling and Joe smiled back. He had always thought she was pretty, but when she was wearing a dress, as she was today, he thought she was truly beautiful.

Chapter 3

She came and sat next to him on the bench outside the court building and leaned over to place a kiss on his cheek. "How are you doing?" she asked.

"I'm okay," he replied. "Just waiting for Walter."

"But are you okay?" she asked again.

"Yeah," Joe smiled at her. He was glad she had come although he was a little surprised too.

She looked at him and finally said, "Malpractice cases are really hard on physicians. You were pretty depressed when this all started, Joe. Are you okay now? Now that the trial is actually starting, I mean?"

Joe shrugged and looked at the court building. "The trial doesn't really bother me that much. I was depressed when poor Linda Murphy died, and more so when I couldn't understand what happened. I don't think I did anything wrong, but I still don't understand why she died. That bothers me—that she died and I can't see how it happened."

The woman in the dress looked at the court building for a minute. "I can't believe you did anything wrong." She let the words linger.

Joe looked over at her and smiled. "Thank you, Carolyn."

"I know you didn't, but …" she continued, "… but everyone else seems to think you might."

Joe shrugged as Carolyn went on. "Little Linda was only four years old, and she did have a serious heart infection, a viral cardiomyopathy. But the path report showed an overdose of

Lidocaine. You were the only one who gave her any Lidocaine, Joe."

"I know," he replied. "But I didn't give that much. The tox report showed a level that would have been possible only if a full adult dose was given. More than a full adult dose, according to the tox report. I used a pediatric syringe, and I remember calculating the dose. They're different. I didn't use the adult syringe. They're all preloaded. I know which one I picked up."

"There was an adult preloaded missing from the code cart, Joe." She shrugged now. "I'm not saying you gave that, but that's what the plaintiff attorney is going to say. You picked up the wrong syringe, and ..." She let the sentence hang there again.

Joe shook his head. "Even if the adult dose was given—the full hundred milligrams—the level shouldn't have been as high as it was."

"I don't think that's going to convince anyone."

"That's what the defense attorney says too," said Joe.

"Walter Mosby? Your attorney?" Carolyn replied. "I told you he was a loser. Even Douglas says he is."

"Douglas?" Joe replied. "You mean my soon-to-be ex-brother-in-law? If Douglas thinks he's a loser, he probably is."

Carolyn was quiet for a minute before she said, "I told Douglas to postpone the divorce until after this is settled."

"That's not necessary."

"That's what Douglas said too."

"So what did you tell him?"

"That it was none of his business." Carolyn shrugged.

"Well, Douglas is only your attorney and your brother. I'm the one you're divorcing." Joe smiled at her. "Do I get a better reason?"

She smiled back at him. "No," she said. "At least not now. I'll pick you up after my shift at the ED and take you out to dinner. We can talk about it then." She smiled again and added, "Remember, until the divorce is final, we're still married so who knows; we could end up in bed together tonight. You're still the best I've ever had."

She paused for another minute. "The first day of these things is just jury selection anyway."

She stood and kissed his cheek again. "Ah, here's Walter now. Shall I tell him he's a loser or do you want to?" Carolyn did not wait for an answer but turned immediately and walked away. Carolyn and Walter walked past each other without a word or even a nod. Walter knew Carolyn and probably knew what she thought of him already.

Chapter 4

Walter didn't look nearly as charming or as happy as Carolyn had appeared. Joe thought he only had two faces: grim and grimmer. Today, he had a third one though: grimmest of all. "Are you sure you don't want to try for a negotiated settlement?" he asked as soon as he was facing Joe.

"No, let's see what they have to say," Joe replied. "I thought you said they wouldn't offer anything reasonable anyway."

"Well, it might be worth trying." Walter looked grimmer still if that was possible, frowning with furrowed brows and narrow eyes. "I should remind you that a judgment is likely to exceed your malpractice coverage, and that will place all your assets at risk."

"Except my retirement, you said."

"Well, yes," replied Walter. "And they must leave you with reasonable means to continue to practice—to earn a living and so on; but your savings and home are not protected."

Joe shrugged. "There's very little savings to lose and Carolyn's getting the house in the divorce, so I really don't have that much at risk."

"The house would be disputed since the malpractice case was filed before the divorce was," Walter said, frowning either at Joe's ignorance of the law or at his willingness to give Carolyn the house. Walter had been appalled by the ease with which Joe had settled all his common property to his wife instead of fighting every step. He had become almost angry when Joe told him, as if it were a personal affront. Joe had explained that there wasn't much to divide except the house and he really didn't want it. Walter was not satisfied at all with his attitude and had repeatedly said so.

"I don't think Douglas will give it up without considerable 'dispute' himself." Joe smiled. For some reason he thought that sharing the details of Douglas' plan with Walter was neither necessary, nor was it necessarily a good idea. "In any event I will not get to keep it. No, Walter, I think I want to hear what they have to say. I've never been satisfied that this death occurred in the way that everyone thinks it did."

"The evidence is rather convincing, Joseph, and I think the jury is going to have little hesitation in rendering a judgment against you," said Walter in his grimmest voice. "Your own malpractice carrier is very much in favor of a pretrial settlement."

"Yes, I know," replied Joe, and just waited for Walter.

He finally shrugged and said, "Well, let's go on in. It's just jury selection today. We'll try to avoid young mothers or any parents, I suppose. Or even grandparents. I'm not at all sure who would be sympathetic in a case like this." Joe wondered if Walter had taken a special course in law school on how to instill optimism in his clients. If he had, he had probably flunked it.

They entered the courtroom. Few people were present at this point: a couple of court officials and the plaintiffs and their attorney, Ronald Craft. Walter and Ronald greeted each other cordially and exchanged inquires about family and vacation plans. They were associates if not really friends, and this was business to them that involved no real emotion. Their camaraderie had surprised Joe the first time he had seen it at his deposition when Ronald asked him a series of questions that established his qualifications and his actions on the day of Linda Murphy's death. Joe had found it stressful and thought he should be offering explanations as to what might really have happened, but Walter had told him just to answer honestly and without any detail. What he said might well be used against him, Walter advised.

While Walter had advised that Joe use a cautious, laconic approach to the plaintiff's attorney, he had himself been friendly and even vociferous. Joe had come to realize that this could be no other way. Two physicians who were at odds over committee positions or a directorship of a department would still be friendly at meetings or other official functions. An opponent today might well be an ally tomorrow.

While the lawyers could talk back and forth, Joe had been told under no circumstances was he to have any discussion about the case with anyone except his family or his attorney. Ironically, Joe recalled, he was allowed to talk to Carolyn because she was still his wife, even though she was associate medical director of the emergency department where the death had occurred and that they were proceeding with a divorce. She could not be called to testify. Some of this made little sense to Joe.

The plaintiffs, Linda's family, looked more anxious than their lawyer. They had been told not to discuss the case as well, Joe was sure, and this would be hard on them because they had lost their child. There were three members of the family there today: Linda's parents, Lucinda and Peter; and Linda's aunt, Lucinda's sister, Gloria.

Lucinda was the youngest child of Lorraine Murphy, the matriarch of the Murphy clan, who had been dead almost ten years. Lucinda had, by all accounts, been the baby of the family and treated as such all her life. She had adapted to the position by becoming even more awkward and shy and had stayed as much as possible out of any social situation. She looked very uncomfortable there today. Her husband Peter was much the same and appeared equally uncomfortable. Rumor said they had married out of loneliness and desperation, and, looking at those two made Joe believe that rumor was true.

Lorraine, the matriarch, dominated Lucinda even to the point of "requiring," at the risk of disinheritance, that Lucinda's husband Peter allow her to keep her family name and give it to all her children. The "Murphy" family name would be carried forward by her daughters, and thus her granddaughter, Linda, had been a "Murphy" when she was born, and when she died. Lucinda was under her mother's control even with her mother now in her grave. Joe also understood that Lucinda and Peter had not wanted to pursue the malpractice litigation, but other family members had prevailed.

The principal "other family member" sat next to them. Gloria was Lorraine's middle child and had grown up rough and tough. She had delighted in defying her mother and living the "wild life" to her mother's continued distress. She had avoided "carrying on the Murphy name" by never marrying or having any children. Her public life was more sedate now, but the rumors had it that her private side was still suitable for tabloid cover stories if it had been available to those writers. It was Gloria who had seen to it that the litigation had been pursued. She was convinced that her niece, Linda Murphy, had met an untimely end and that someone was responsible and should be punished. Gloria had been present when four-year-old Linda suffered the cardiac arrest from which Joe had been unable to resuscitate her.

Joe sat there now, trying not to stare but also feeling empathy for these three, as well as sorrow at their loss and pain. He was even inclined to agree with Gloria that Linda's death left things unsaid and unanswered. He disagreed that he was in any way responsible, however.

The third and oldest of Lorraine's children was Reginald Murphy and he was not present. Joe had not expected him to be there at the sordid affair. He was second generation wealth and ran his affairs by delegation. He was never party to the activities that required association with ordinary people. Joe realized that while this was the prevailing opinion of many, he had never had any interaction with Reginald and therefore had no real basis upon which to judge him.

What was beyond question was that, along with her three children, Lorraine had left an immense fortune. The exact size was not known but estimates ranged from huge to gargantuan.

Reginald looked after this fortune and his siblings and, by all accounts, did very well with the fortune management, but he received mixed reviews when it came to managing his siblings. Many felt his sisters were spoiled and inclined to abuse their positions of wealth and power. That they were unhappy was uniformly held to be true. Lucinda and Peter had two other children, a boy and a girl both born after Linda had been born, the youngest having been born after her death.

Lorraine had disposed of her fortune to her children and expected grandchildren; there were no grandchildren at the time of her death. Nonetheless, her will instructed that they were to be provided for with sizable sums but only at the time of their majority, their inheritance being held in trust until that time. Also by the provisions of her will, if any were to die before that time, their inheritance would be given to several charities assigned by Lorraine. She had made this last provision known, as well as the list of charities, well before her death "in order to protect them" she had said. She had not said what she was protecting them from, but clearly it had not protected Linda Murphy. Her inheritance had all gone to charity at her death with no individual gaining any of the money at all.

The only others present were the attorneys. Walter had a reputation for thoughtful and solid defenses in malpractice cases. He had been assigned to Joe's case in part because the insurance carrier felt they were at significant risk: a young child dead and a difficult defense at best. The company had eventually come to the conclusion that the case would probably go against them and for far more than the amount of Joe's coverage, one million dollars, and that their best interest lay in a negotiated settlement to decrease the trial costs—Walter's fees, that is. Joe had been forced to essentially refuse to forego the trial, which had not pleased his insurance carrier.

In contradistinction to Walter, Ronald, the plaintiffs' attorney, was a dynamic and competent attorney. He had been chosen by the Murphys for this trial based on his personality and past record of success; however, Walter had pointed out that Ronald had little experience with malpractice cases. That might or might not be important. Ronald had a great deal of money at his disposal and could seek advice from many experts. Walter had expressed surprise that additional attorneys had not been brought in to actively participate in the trial, but Ronald was to be the sole plaintiff attorney. Joe wondered if he had proceeded in this way to avoid sharing the victory laurels.

Walter broke away from his cohort to return to his client. What might have passed for conviviality disappeared and was replaced with a frown. "Jury selection will likely take up the whole day. Maybe we'll get to opening remarks, but I think that will not start until tomorrow." His frown grew darker. "Ronald is planning to bring in an ED expert first. Establish that only you and the nurse had access to the patient. Then he will call Francine Hayes, the nurse that day, to establish that she did not give any Lidocaine. He may try to identify her as a hostile witness, if he can. That way he can ask much more aggressive questions. He will then call their own pathologist, and he will finish up with the toxicologist to speak about the Lidocaine levels and all of that. He may call someone else, possibly Gloria Murphy.

"After that it will be our turn. That will be really just you and maybe Francine on redirect. We'll have to see how her first testimony goes before deciding that. We have our own pathologist to counter any of the findings that are worth disputing." Joe nodded. He had discussed bringing in their own toxicologist to point out the significance of the Lidocaine level and the dose that would have been necessary to achieve that level—more than an adult dose—but Walter had decided not to do that, on the basis that it would only confuse the jury and still not point to anyone except Joe. No use discussing this again at this stage anyway as it was past time to bring in another witness.

The day proceeded much as Walter had predicted. A panel of prospective jurors was brought in and several offered reasons why they should not surrender a week or two of their time to ensure the fairness of the judicial system of the Commonwealth of Kentucky. The judge disagreed with most of the reasons and selection proceeded. Each attorney in turn asked a few questions and then either agreed to empanel the juror or offered reasons why they should not be included. These were done in whispered conversations at the judge's bench, presumably to avoid embarrassing the juror, or perhaps to avoid embarrassing the attorneys. The judge ruled on their objections, usually declining them, but each attorney could dismiss a limited number of jurors without stating any reason, so the arguments were really about whether they had to use one of these preemptive strikes or could talk the judge into dismissing a juror for them. When the jurors were finally empanelled with two alternates in case a juror was dismissed or otherwise had to leave after the trial started, the mood was one of smoldering annoyance, particularly evident on the judge's face. There would be no more done today, he said, and no one argued at all.

Chapter 5

Walter walked over to Joe.

"Opening arguments will begin tomorrow," he reiterated. "Ronald will go first and then I'll present our defense. We'll probably get to the first witness tomorrow as well, but we may not finish with that testimony." With that, he departed and so did Joe, the two men leaving in different directions.

Joe knew that Carolyn would be finishing her shift in about an hour although it would probably take another hour or so for her to finish everything up, sign out, and transfer her patients' care to the doctor relieving her. Despite the fact that the events of Linda Murphy's death took place in the emergency department, Joe felt comfortable there. Medicine was different than the law. The enemy was disease not a plaintiff or defendant. When he arrived at the ED, he found he was correct: Carolyn had just been relieved but would be a "few minutes" getting things wrapped up to sign out. A "few minutes" was likely to be an hour, so Joe went to the lounge to wait. He had thought of making an excuse, but he really had nothing to do this evening and really did enjoy Carolyn's company, divorce notwithstanding.

In the lounge were a couple of nurses who greeted him with smiles, but they were on their way out. Nurses generally left at the end of their shift while many, although not all, of the doctors required some time to finish up things before handing the patients over to the incoming doctor. Carolyn was somewhat compulsive about this. In fact, she was compulsive about most aspects of her job and career. While Joe was waiting, Lawrence Marshall, the CEO of the hospital, came in.

"Oh, hello, Joe."

"Hello, Lawrence. How goes the battle?"

"Always a battle, you know," replied the CEO. "Did your trial start today?"

"Yes."

Joe was a little surprised that the CEO would know this. The hospital had been named in the suit as was the habit in these cases. The plaintiff generally named everyone who had had anything to do with the malpractice case, just to see what information was forthcoming, and would then drop the people that would not be worth pursuing. The hospital was a "not for profit" organization and therefore had a very limited liability. It would have been hard to build a case that the hospital was at fault in any event. Joe was an employee, working the pediatric area of the ED at the time of Linda's death, but to prove the hospital shouldn't have hired him would be difficult at best and not worth the effort. Their policies were all appropriate, there were no apparent breaches of those policies, and Joe's record had been outstanding prior to the episode.

Lawrence Marshall was quiet for a minute before continuing. "We all hope you do well, Joe," he finally said. Joe thought that this was an odd way to put it—not an assurance that he had done nothing wrong, but that he should "do well" regardless of whether he was guilty or not. No, Joe decided, he was letting the paranoia get the best of him now.

"You were here that day weren't you, Lawrence?" Joe asked.

Lawrence seemed a little embarrassed by this comment. "Yes," he said. "I just happened to be here when Linda came in. I was talking to the family when she arrested."

"Yes," said Joe. "You were the first to notice the second arrest, weren't you?"

"Yes," replied Lawrence. "I sent that nurse—what's her name?—to get you."

"Francine," offered Joe. "That was a good pick-up on the rhythm, Lawrence. It looked like artifact on the monitor at the desk," said Joe, remembering that day now. Linda Murphy had come in quite ill with fever and a rapid heart rate. There was difficulty getting an IV—an intravenous line—started, so Joe had put an interosseous line directly into the bone in her leg. It had worked well, and Joe was preparing to draw blood studies and do a lumbar puncture to make sure it was not meningitis that was causing Linda's problems. Then things had happened quickly.

Linda had a cardiac arrest, a ventricular tachycardia, and Joe had given that dose of Lidocaine though the interosseous line. Linda had responded well initially with return to a normal rhythm, and Joe had decided that an immediate transfer to the medical center was the best course. He had gone to make those arrangements, leaving Francine, Lawrence, and Gloria Murphy, as well as several other staff members still in the room. Those others had left quickly too, and he had been making the calls in preparation for the transfer when Francine came to get him. Because there would be a transfer, everyone was trying to get the chart in order, including Francine, who was still in the room but working at the computer terminal, when Lawrence noticed the change in rhythm and sent her to get Joe "Stat!"

"Well, I was a paramedic, you know," Lawrence went on. "Still am, really. Kept my certification current, I mean."

"That's a good thing," Joe said. "It was just you and Gloria and Francine in the room when Linda arrested the second time." That was a silly thing to say, thought Joe, because it was that second arrest that had ended in Linda's death. It really made no difference who was in the room because they had not been able to resuscitate her.

"Oh, lots of people were coming in and out, weren't they?" asked Lawrence. "Never really alone in these situations. Any number of people were there. I don't think I was ever alone, anyway." Maybe it seemed that way to Lawrence, thought Joe.

People who were not in these situations every day always thought they were chaotic, more chaotic than they in fact were.

Carolyn came in at this point and ended the conversation, "Oh, hi, Lawrence," she said. "Ready, Joe?" She had changed out of her scrubs and back into her dress.

Lawrence cast a look of doubt at them and then just shrugged. "Better get about the CEO business. See you at eight sharp tomorrow for ED committee, Carolyn. Oh, and good luck, Joe," he said as he went out of the lounge.

Chapter 6

"Prick," said Carolyn as they walked out of the ED.

"Me or Lawrence or some other poor, unsuspecting man?" asked Joe.

"Not you, Joe, and don't assume all pricks are men, you poor excuse for a chauvinist piglet."

"I'll remember that in the future. I may refer to any woman deserving that epithet by its proper name. So if not me, perhaps Lawrence?"

"Yes," she replied, pointing toward her car. "Let's take mine. It's closer. You should park in the doctors' lot even if you're not working. Everyone does."

"Okay," he replied with no intention of taking the advice. "So what's wrong with Lawrence?"

"Have you ever sat on a committee with him?" Carolyn replied, clicking her remote to unlock the doors of her car. It was new and expensive as opposed to Joe's older and ... well, less expensive by half, even when it had been new.

"I've been on a couple. Committees that is. Lawrence is the CEO and has to worry about financial things. When did you get this?" he asked as he got into her car.

"Oh, just a week ago. You like it?" she smiled. "Lawrence is just such a 'bottom line' man. And sometimes I get the feeling he's more interested in his own 'bottom line' than the hospital's, the way he sets up the contracts for work here. Take the new ED. It's positively Byzantine the way the contracts were handed out. He would just show up with signed contracts and tell everyone that this is how it will be."

"It's nice. The car I mean. Lawrence's bottom line hasn't affected yours, has it?"

Carolyn smiled again. "I have good credit. The car won't be mine for another five years, and by then I may be in another place altogether. Did I tell you I'm interviewing in Las Vegas at the end of the week?" She shrugged and started the car. "It's just that Lawrence always has a friend who can do the job for a good price and then the good price turns out to be 'good' for the friend and not for the hospital."

"Las Vegas? Do they have hospitals there too? Buckle up, young lady," said Joe. "The ED turned out pretty well, I think."

"Oh it turned out great, but at thirty million it should've been super great. I usually do, buckle up I mean. Set a good example, I always say."

"I don't know much about it. Is thirty million a lot for these things?"

She shrugged again. "Maybe it's not the money. Maybe he just annoys me because he's a prick. It's not his fault really. He was probably born that way." She paused for a moment and then continued, "You remember back two years ago when he cut his leg and made me suture it up at no charge? I mean, he had insurance to cover it, so what was the big deal?"

"I remember you insisted that a medical record was generated to document it all," said Joe.

Carolyn just smiled. "Of course I did. And they do have hospitals in Las Vegas and probably people like Lawrence, but not people like you, Joe. So where do you want to eat tonight? Fancy or really fancy? You're in a suit, or sport jacket anyway, and I'm in a dress. How often does that happen?"

"Oh, I don't care where we eat. Not too expensive unless you're paying," smiled Joe.

"And I am paying, so spare no expense. Cloth napkins and tablecloth and a menu with only the dollar prices listed on it. Does that limit our choices too much?" She paused and then continued, "Maybe it's the 'financialization' of medicine that bothers me. Now I'm sounding like Joseph Nelson, aren't I?" she said with a frown.

"Well," said Joseph Nelson, "If you want more than one choice in restaurants, we may be talking about air travel here. Bruno's would be fine with me. We could even split the tab, but I'm not sure 'financialization' is a real word." He shook his head. "The difference between you and Joe Nelson, of course, is that you intend to do something about it and he'll just talk."

"You don't think you'll do anything?" She turned to smile at Joe, who was smiling back at her. "Maybe you're just waiting for the right time to make the move. Bruno's is where you took me on our first real date, remember?" Her smile broadened and she reached over and squeezed his hand.

"I was just trying to impress you. My plan for the future of medicine is to help this really smart lady I know get to be surgeon general. Do you think that idea has a chance?"

Carolyn shrugged. "I don't know about the surgeon general. I'd like to, but only if there's a woman president. I'm tired of the 'male-dominated glass ceiling' thing. I thought you were just trying to get me into bed."

"I didn't think getting you in bed on the first date would be a possibility," said Joe. "How many surgeons general have gone on to become president? Bet you haven't thought about that one, have you 'smart lady'?"

"It wouldn't have been possible. Getting me into bed that easily, I mean." They parked at Bruno's and Carolyn turned to him to say, "You're the only person I know who could use the proper pluralization of 'surgeon general' while discussing seduction, Joseph Nelson. And I intend to try my hand at getting you into bed tonight, so be forewarned. This isn't our first date after all."

She kissed his cheek and turned to get out of the car. Joe smiled after her and said, "I don't think 'pluralization' is a real word either."

Chapter 7

It was not busy at Bruno's and they were seated immediately. The *maître d'* was courteous and their waiter recognized them, inquiring as to why they had been so long away. They made only a vague excuse and ordered drinks. Non-alcoholic for both for differing reasons. Neither inquired what the other's reason might be and neither offered to explain. The server did not seem to mind either. It was a good start to the evening although there was a bit of silent tension until Carolyn finally asked how things had gone in court that day.

"Just jury selection as you suggested," replied Joe. "The plaintiffs' attorney will speak tomorrow, suggesting that I am beyond being considered a human being at all, and that the trial is a mere formality. It's what I've come to expect. You can't try a malpractice case by saying the doc is a really nice guy who just made a little mistake, after all. Walter will speak tomorrow, too, and suggest there's no reason to be there at all since, obviously, no mistake was ever made. Then I'll get to hear what they're really going to say. What they think happened that day."

She shrugged, "So what do you think happened that day?"

"I don't really know," answered Joe. "There seem to be pieces missing. The Lidocaine level was elevated, high enough to account for her second arrest, but I'm the only one who gave any. She wasn't there that long, less than an hour in the department. She didn't even have any other meds running." He shook his head.

"Well, the trial really doesn't matter, Joe. You're still the best doctor I know," said Carolyn.

"You're the best doctor I know too, but you're right; the trial doesn't matter as much as the fact that a poor little four-year-old died. You know, the malpractice system would work better if the emphasis was on learning from the cases instead of assigning blame. Some fund made up of the malpractice insurance payments to compensate the injured and an inquiry to determine what steps to take to avoid a repeat of the events." Joe shrugged now.

"Is this the part where you explain that there's no 'medical malpractice crisis'?" she asked.

"Well, it isn't a 'medical' crisis, really. Obesity and HIV are medical crises, but malpractice is a 'legal' crisis. It's the lawyers who have to clean up that mess, don't you think?"

"Now that's the Joe Nelson I love and admire. Let's order something to eat before I start gnawing on my arm ... or your arm maybe." Carolyn smiled at him.

He looked first at her arm and then at his own. "Let's order," he said.

The server was there almost immediately as if he had been waiting for them to be ready to order, which he probably had been. "Something more to drink or perhaps an appetizer?" he asked.

"I think we are ready for the real food," replied Carolyn. "The salmon for me and rice and the vegetable. Joe?"

"I think I'll try the chicken piccata. And a baked potato and vegetables."

"And if I remember, Sir, you like just butter on the potato?" the server said to Joe.

"Um ... yes. Just butter," an amazed Joe replied.

"Very good. I will put that in right away," the server said and left immediately.

"How did he remember that?" asked Joe. "What I wouldn't give for that kind of memory."

"Do you remember what you ordered our first time here?" asked Carolyn.

"Um ... no. Do you?"

"Chicken piccata," replied Carolyn. "And I had the salmon. The same things we're having tonight. Have we changed so little, Joe?"

"Perhaps not that much," he said. "Perhaps just older and wiser, but not much different. Not much older either. You look lovely tonight, Carolyn."

"And you look handsome. As in *tall, dark and ...*" replied the lovely lady, showing a bit of embarrassment. "Are you thinking we should not be divorcing after all, Joe?"

"I don't know. I don't think so. Maybe sorry it didn't work out is all but ..." He left it hanging there.

"I do love you, Joe. And I respect you more than anyone I know, and if I wanted to be married, it would be to you, but ..." It was her turn to leave the words hanging.

"And for my part, I have always loved you, Carolyn, but you're right. You want to be surgeon general, and I want to stay here in the 'little pond.' Just a pediatrician adding to the health and happiness of the people here in the mountains where I was born, where my parents were born." Joe seemed saddened by this truth.

Carolyn sighed and looked at him. "You wouldn't be happy in any other place, and I'd be miserable here if I couldn't move on to the bigger things I want to do. You'd grow to hate me if I made you move and I to hate you if I stayed. I'd rather keep a good friend than a miserable husband."

He smiled at her and raised his glass to toast, "To good friends. Forever," he said.

"Good friends." She raised her glass as well and added, "And occasional lovers if that suits you tonight." Joe made no objection. He never did.

The food arrived and in spite of all the reasons the two should be miserable, they were not. Good food and good conversation and, of course, the very best companionship can turn the worst of times into the best.

Chapter 8

They finished the meal, and Carolyn paid the bill—at her insistence and Joe's acknowledgment that it was not worth fighting over. "We can drive home in my car and ... well, in the morning I can drop you off at the hospital to pick up yours when I go to that damned meeting with Lawrence. Is that okay?"

"Yeah," he said taking her hand. "I still have as many clothes at the house as at my apartment. You don't mind, do you?"

"Keep the clothes there as long as you need to, Joe," she replied.

"I meant about having me stay tonight."

"No, of course not. Don't tell my brother though. Douglas thinks we're both crazy and that we're giving 'divorce' a bad name as it is. I mean, you don't even have a lawyer, Joe."

"That's one of the pleasant things about all this," said Joe. "Driving Douglas close to the edge."

"He thinks you're certifiable for not fighting for every knife and fork. Can't seem to understand why I'm getting the house without any fight at all. Why is that anyway, or is it really just to drive him absolutely crazy and deny him the pleasure of a good legal battle?" Carolyn questioned.

"Like I said earlier, I'd rather have a good friend than a ... well, than a house." He shrugged. "Besides, where would we be driving to tonight if I were fighting for that mortgaged, tax-burdened place I'm trying to force you to take off my hands?"

"To your apartment, of course. Ain't no house nowhere worth a night with you, lover. You know what I'd like to do, Joe?" she teased.

"Something obscene, I hope?" he replied. "Just a guess."

"You men are all alike. Maybe later, but now I'd like a fire in the fireplace and to cuddle up with you and drink ginger ale out of champagne glasses and pretend to get drunk and see what happens, okay?"

"You've been reading my dirty little masculine mind, you vixen." He smiled and asked, "Do you have enough ginger ale?"

"It won't take that much," she replied and it didn't. The ginger ale was hardly touched and the fire died down to embers alone.

In the morning Joe got up, leaving her asleep in the bed they had shared and took his shower. The shower was still equipped with the grab bars necessary for him to comfortably shower on the one leg the mining accident had left him. He dressed for the day, looked in on her resting peacefully and then went down to fix coffee and some breakfast, which is what he was doing when she joined him.

She was wearing a bathrobe and it looked to Joe as if that was all she wore. She kissed his cheek and said, "That was fairly adequate last night. I do enjoy it better when I'm not drunk."

"Adequate only? That's because I don't get enough practice," replied Joe.

She turned serious and said, "You have never been 'adequate' Joe. Never anything less than spectacular, for me anyway. Are you seeing anyone? The rumors say that you're not."

"The rumors are true," he replied. "Coffee's ready and I found some eggs to scramble if that suits you. Are you seeing anyone? I haven't the advantage of access to rumors as you do."

"If you did, they'd say that I occasionally go out with Carl Summers from operations, but just for the company, and no, I haven't gotten in bed with him and may never for all I care right now." She looked out the window at the rising sun and finally went on. "I really do think that I need to do something to correct the health care mess this country is in and well ... I can give up a lot of things to do that. You may call me egotistical, but I think I can make a difference."

"Honesty is sometimes mistaken for egotism, but not by me and not in this case," Joe replied. "I believe you will make a difference. I only hope you don't have to give up too many things to make that happen."

"Well, do you know what I hope?" she brightened. "I hope you remain my closest friend and that you find someone to 'practice' with even if it means that we won't have another night like last night, which, knowing how you feel about fidelity, will probably be true if you do find that 'someone.'"

A few tears formed in her eyes and she said, "I wish you happiness, Joe. And for me, scrambled eggs would be great." She sighed and added, "I'd better get ready to go, but first, a cup of coffee. One of the other things I miss is that no one can make coffee as well as you can."

Joe could not find anything to say in response, so he poured a cup and she took it and left the kitchen to shower and dress for her day. When she returned, the eggs were ready and the sadness had passed. They chatted and then drove to the hospital for committees and cars and courts.

Chapter 9

Carolyn parked in the doctors' parking lot after dropping Joe off at his car. She commented that it looked older than the last time she had seen it—a week ago. He replied that hers looked older than the last time he had seen it too. That had been yesterday. When he arrived at the court building, Walter was waiting.

"We'll trade opening remarks this morning, with Ronald going first, and then get their first witness on the stand. He's a hired gun, billed as an expert on emergency department procedures. He'll try to establish that only you could have given the Lidocaine is my guess, but they could be planning a surprise." The term "hired gun" was new to Joe in this context. It referred to that group of physicians who were professional witnesses, who made their living testifying in malpractice cases.

Walter was wrong, of course, because the egocentric nature of the attorney in him disregarded the opening remarks of the judge as being unworthy of mention. The judge, a grey-haired, sixty-year-old man named Stevens, was the first to address the jury after they were sworn in.

He thanked them all for participating in the judicial process, saying that they were the people who made it possible. He reminded them that this was a privilege as well as a duty, but that it *was* a duty. They owed it to the plaintiff and defendant to pay close attention to the arguments they were about to hear. He then got down to the specifics.

He told them that this was a civil case, not a criminal one; therefore, the jury had only to determine that the defendant was more than fifty percent responsible in order to return a guilty verdict. He reminded them that this was different from "beyond a reasonable doubt," which was required in criminal cases. He then instructed them not to discuss the case with anyone—even among themselves. Discussion would take place after all testimony and arguments were presented and then only with the other jury members. They would hear testimony from persons involved in the case as well as experts brought in by the attorneys. If the jury had questions, they could write them down in notebooks provided and hand them to the bailiff to give to the judge who would decide if they should be given to the witness to answer. He concluded by reminding them once again of the seriousness of their responsibility and then proceeded to the opening arguments by the attorneys.

Ronald presented the outline of his case, stating that Linda Murphy was a healthy little girl who had presented with an illness that she should have survived and, instead, had died as a result of the negligence of Dr. Joseph Nelson. He did not go into any detail, apparently leaving that for the testimony that would follow, but dwelt upon how tragic the death had been. The defense attorney, Walter, followed and simply said that the death of Linda had been tragic indeed and that no one knew this better than the very capable Dr. Joseph Nelson, but that he was in no way responsible for her illness (he emphasized this several times) or her death. Their speeches to the jury were longer, but the essence was just this: Joe *should* have saved Linda or Joe *couldn't* have saved her. All so black and white in a grey world.

The first witness was Dr. Phillip Sparks. He was a man of about fifty; dressed in a dark suit, white shirt, and bright red tie; and looked like a man anyone would trust to be their doctor. The initial questions established his credentials, which appeared impeccable. There were holes in his practice experience, however, and he did not seem to have a recent affiliation with any medical center, but Joe doubted this would be noticed by the jury. The testimony proceeded in that slow way that courtroom testimony did, with well-rehearsed questions and answers.

"And now, Dr. Sparks," said Ronald, "can you tell us what a 'red zone' is?"

"Yes," said Dr. Sparks. "The area around a critically ill patient can sometimes become crowded, often with unnecessary people, so most facilities have instituted a 'red zone.' It is an area of three or so feet around the patient, inside of which are allowed only the direct providers. This is usually a physician, a nurse and a tech or EMT, and then lab personnel and respiratory therapy as they are needed, but no one else."

"And do you know if that was the policy in this case?"

"After reviewing the policies and procedures manual provided, I have concluded that that was, in fact, the policy," replied the witness.

"So, in your opinion, could anyone except Dr. Nelson or the nurse have given any medication to Linda Murphy?"

"No," the doctor replied. Joe thought that he was more certain than the evidence allowed him to be, but that was apparently not going to be disputed. The jury might look unfavorably on such an argument, pointing the accusing finger at someone else.

"Now, as regards the Lidocaine dose, Doctor, in your opinion, would there have been any sound medical indication to have given a dose sufficient to raise the level to a toxic range?" Joe sat up slightly here. Ronald was getting into territory he hadn't established yet. The jury hadn't heard anything about Lidocaine or toxic doses yet.

Dr. Sparks was obviously prepared for this question, however. "There is no therapeutic reason to give a toxic dose of Lidocaine. This could occur if an incorrect dose had been given. If, for instance, an adult dose were to be given instead of the pediatric dose."

There must be something Walter should be objecting to here, Joe thought, but he wasn't sure what it was. Walter sat without any apparent concern, however, while Ronald and even the judge looked at him as if to ask if he wanted to say anything. He said nothing.

"And who could have given such a dose, Dr. Sparks?"

"In my opinion, only the nurse or Dr. Joseph Nelson could have given the toxic dose of Lidocaine. They were the only ones who could give medications who were also allowed inside the 'red zone.'"

"Do you have an opinion as to how such a toxic dose could have been given, Dr. Sparks?"

"Yes, I do. There was an adult, preloaded Lidocaine syringe missing from the code cart. It seems likely to me that someone picked up the wrong syringe and gave it to the patient." Walter remained silent and even Ronald began to look uneasy with his silence. Maybe he was beginning to feel that he was setting himself up for a trap at this point, but he had accomplished quite a bit with this diversion and now was the time to get out and nail it down.

"Do you have an opinion, Dr. Sparks, as to whether the management of Linda Murphy's care was below the level she had a right to expect from her physician?"

"Yes, I do. It was unquestionably below the standard of care."

"I have no further questions," said Ronald.

Judge Stevens looked at Walter, and with a somewhat quizzical expression asked, "And do you have any questions for the defense, counselor?"

"Yes, I have a few," replied Walter. He then took a few minutes to introduce himself again to the jury and explain that he would be trying to find the truth, as everyone there was. They would hear conflicting arguments, and they would have to decide who to trust and who not to trust. He then began to demolish Dr. Phillip Sparks.

First, he questioned the doctor's lack of affiliation with any medical center. He had none. Or any other hospital? Yes, he did have that although he seemed a bit nervous about the answer.

41

"Active privileges?" asked Walter.

"I am on leave right now," replied an increasingly nervous doctor.

"May I ask why that is?" Walter said.

He was already turning toward Ronald when that attorney stood and said, "Objection, your honor." Walter had him boxed, however. To disallow the answer would leave the reason to the imagination of the jury, but to answer it had to be worse.

"This is badgering the witness, your honor," was all Ronald could manage.

"We have a right to know the qualification of the witnesses—"

The judge's gavel cut Walter short. "Why don't we approach the bench, gentlemen?" The jury would not hear the discussion and a couple of them looked disappointed.

The discussion was brief and when they left the bench, the judge said calmly, "I will allow the question. You may answer, Dr. Sparks."

"Well, I don't actually recall the specifics," he stammered. Even Joe knew this was a bad answer. Better to have just said it—or maybe it was not, depending upon what those "specifics" were.

"Ah," said Walter. "I have a report from the hospital if you would like to refer to that. To refresh your memory."

"Those allegations are still under investigation," said Dr. Sparks. Ronald did not appear to know about this and looked about in dismay to try to stop the avalanche.

Walter must have known he had time for only one more question before Ronald would manage to come up with an objection. "The allegations of sexual misconduct? Are those the allegations you—"

"Objection, your honor!" shouted Ronald. "Counsel has no right to refer to these investigations as 'allegations'!"

Walter practically danced now as he turned to the court stenographer. "Perhaps you could read back the witness' answer.

\The one he gave right after I asked if he wished to consult his hospital's report."

"That is not relevant," Ronald stammered.

"Oh, but it will help resolve this so much better than our arguing over it," replied Walter. He was looking at the judge now.

"Yes, Miss Barns. Read it back," Judge Stevens replied.

The stenographer looked at her spool of paper, only a single page back. Everyone remembered what had been said. Walter was doing this to *reinforce* what had been said in the jury's minds, not to *remind* them.

She began to read: "Attorney Mosby: 'I have a report from the hospital if you would like to refer to that. To refresh your memory.' Is that where you would like to start?" The judge and Walter nodded. Ronald grew pale.

"Dr. Sparks: 'Those allegations are still under investigation.' Do you want to hear any more?" She knew they didn't. She was smiling now too.

"No," said Walter. "The witness referred to the ..." He cleared his throat as if it were distasteful to have to even talk about this. "... the situation as an 'allegation.' I merely continued to use the term."

Walter did not return to the question of sexual misconduct, however, but he did continue the slow discrediting of Dr. Sparks.

"Do you practice now?"

"When was the last time you actively practiced in an emergency department?"

"Have you ever given Lidocaine?"

"How long ago was that?" When Dr. Sparks answered this last question, Walter pointed out that he had said he last practiced four years ago and now said he last gave Lidocaine three years ago. Walter didn't ask a question, just pointed that out. Ronald made no objection. And so it went. Walter finished with a question about the doctor's website.

"Do you have a website, Doctor?"

"Yes."

"And on it, did you advertise yourself as an expert witness with a list of your fees for such services?"

"Well, I did. I took that off two years ago."

"And why did you drop that from your website?"

"Well, I thought it was unprofessional."

"Do you recall being asked that same question on August fourteenth of 2011?" asked Walter. "It was during a trial in Kansas City. Perhaps you could read the answer if you don't recall." He held up a piece of paper.

This roused Ronald from his dejection. "Objection, Your Honor. I fail to see how this is at all relevant to the case at hand."

"I withdraw the question, Your Honor. Your witness, counselor," Walter said to Ronald as he sat down. It sounded like an accusation.

"No questions," replied Ronald. Joe thought that if Dr. Phillip Sparks were to be found dead this afternoon, the police would look first at Ronald Craft.

"It is lunch time," said the judge. "Reconvene at one thirty."

"All rise," said the bailiff, and that was the end of the first morning of testimony.

Chapter 10

The courtroom emptied with the jury leaving by their own exit to eat at the expense of the state. Joe went over to Walter to congratulate him, but he simply shook his head and cautioned silence with his eyes.

When they were outside, he said, "Ronald has good hearing. Anything you say he will hear."

"I was about to say you were brilliant in there this morning," Joe replied. "Ronald couldn't have used that against us."

"It was exhilarating, wasn't it?" said Walter. "I pity the poor jury trying to eat lunch and not mention Phillip Sparks' sexual misconduct." He shook his head.

After a minute Joe had to ask, "What was that about?"

"The sexual misconduct?" said Walter. "Nothing really. He knocked up one of the nurses, and the papers got a hold of it when it went to a paternity suit. The events happened on hospital property, so, of course, the hospital was obliged to act horrified. Dr. Sparks agreed to go on leave to avoid further notoriety. He already had a fairly lucrative business testifying, so he thought that was a good idea. The hospital apparently didn't want him back. He's not very good at the practice of medicine, I understand, and his personality makes me wonder how he got the nurse in bed in the first place. Anyway, the hospital has kept the file open and 'under investigation' to prevent him from trying to get back on staff." Walter shrugged. "If he'd just said that, he would probably have gotten away with a few scowls, but with his credibility intact. As it is, he probably lost his future in there today. No one will want him to testify again."

Walter shrugged again and added, "It may not have been that big a loss, actually. Many states are going to the 'three in five' law."

"Three in five?" asked Joe.

"Oh," said Walter. "Yes. It requires that an 'expert witness' actually practice three of the past five years and usually in the specialty that he is asserting his expertise. If widely accepted, it may be the end of 'hired guns' in this business."

"And the website?" asked Joe.

"Oh that," said Walter. "He told a lawyer in that trial in KC that he took it down because he wasn't getting any 'hits.'"

"And you knew that? Walter, you amaze me."

"What do you think I do on the lonely nights, Joseph?" Walter smiled for a moment. They had arrived at one of the local sandwich shops, and Walter opened the door for Joe. "This afternoon they're scheduled to call Francine Hayes, the nurse from that day. Is there anything I should know about her? Any sexual misconduct on your part?" He winked at Joe.

Joe thought of Carolyn now, and very pleasantly. "None," he replied. "Least of all with Francine. She's ... well ... fifteen years younger than I. I'm a pediatrician, not a pedophile."

"She's only thirteen years younger than you, and well beyond the age of consent," responded Walter. "They may be rough on her though. Will she support you?"

"She'll tell the truth, and I can ask no more. She may not bear up under pressure though."

"She'll be asked if she gave any Lidocaine," said Walter. "Will she answer as she did in her deposition?"

"Yes," said Joe. "I don't think she did give any."

"Then that will leave only you who could have given it. That's unfortunate." Walter sighed.

"You're not considering implicating Francine to save me, are you, Walter?" asked Joe.

"No," he replied. "That would make me look bad to the jury."

Joe wished Walter had added something about being honest or ethical but he didn't. They ordered sandwiches and talked about the weather. When it came time to leave, Walter asked Joe if he could pay. "A little short of cash today," he said.

Chapter 11

The trial reconvened at one forty. Walter had predicted a later start, but had insisted upon returning early. Ronald looked as if he had recovered and greeted Walter amiably. Walter returned that greeting with equal friendliness. It still amazed Joe that they could act as they had an hour and a half ago and return as if nothing had happened. He realized that they must have emotions beneath their appearances, but they had those emotions so well controlled that they never showed. Courtroom law was "performance art," he decided.

They all rose for the judge, and the jury returned, and the battle was set in motion again. Francine was called and sworn. She was a tall and rather pretty African American lady who insisted, when asked, that she was American. Not necessary, just interesting.

Ronald began slowly this time. Her qualifications and training were reviewed. Her employment status at the hospital, as well as her past employment history, were covered in detail. The questioning eventually got to the purpose of the current trial. Had she been there on the day in question? Did she recall the events? What was she doing when the cardiac arrest occurred? What about the second arrest? It was at this point in the questioning that Joe noticed the Murphy family. He hadn't noticed them earlier although they must have been there. The parents seemed distracted, while Gloria followed every word.

"And did you give any Lidocaine, Miss Hayes?" Ronald asked.

"No," she responded. Joe was surprised again that no real testimony about the toxic Lidocaine had yet been given. *Will the jury be able to follow this line of argument?* he wondered.

"Then the only other person who could have given it would be Dr. Nelson. Is that correct?"

"Yes," replied Francine. "But I know he couldn't have given too much. He's too careful."

"Were you watching him constantly, Miss Hayes?"

"Well, I couldn't do that, but—"

"So he could have given anything when you were not watching?" Ronald cut her off. "Is that correct?"

"I know he—"

"*You think*, Miss Hayes. If you were not watching every minute, you can only guess." Ronald looked ready to attack. "You weren't even in the room the entire time, were you, Miss Hayes?"

"Well, just for a minute," she was getting stressed. Joe could tell from her frown and the way she clasped her hands, although others in the courtroom who had not worked with her might not have noticed.

"You were the only person in that room with any medical background when Linda Murphy arrested a second time, and you left the room, didn't you?"

"Well, Mr. Marshall told me to—"

"Mr. Marshall?" asked Ronald. "That would be the CEO, right? Administration, not a professional. Not a medical professional, I mean. You took an order from a non-medical—essentially a lay person—to abandon your patient and you did just that."

Francine dissolved into tears. Walter finally rose, albeit slowly, and said, "Your Honor, is this really necessary? Badgering one of his own witnesses? I am appalled." He looked appalled too. No question, Walter was a good actor.

"This is clearly a hostile witness," Ronald said.

Walter ignored him. "May I approach the witness, Your Honor," he said, but he did not wait for a reply, walking over to

Francine to offer his handkerchief. Francine continued to cry as Walter turned back to the judge's bench.

"May I request a recess, Your Honor?" he said.

"You may," said the judge. He looked at Francine and added, "I know it is only two thirty, but I think we will adjourn for the day." He did not wait for a reply but banged his gavel and stood. The bailiff was taken by surprise and barely got the "all rise" out before "His Honor" disappeared through the door to his chamber.

Walter walked to the witness chair and said, loudly enough for the jury to hear, "You may keep that, Miss." He motioned toward the handkerchief and walked away, shaking his head. The jury watched this scene closely as they filed out.

Chapter 12

Everyone seemed at loose ends by the abrupt cancellation of the remainder of the afternoon session. Joe turned to Walter as they left and said, "What now?"

"Well," said Walter. "We will have to finish with Francine Hayes tomorrow. She's done some damage to your position, but not irreparable. Ronald lost on her too, of course. He seems to be off his game right now, but his case is still pretty strong."

Joe frowned. "How did Francine hurt my case?"

"First of all, she said she didn't give any Lidocaine and secondly she defended you. She is not projecting herself well."

"But you said Ronald lost too?" Joe went on.

"Yes," said Walter. "His treatment of her was really quite appalling. Did you notice the ethnic makeup of the jury? Five of them appear to be African American. They are likely to see the scene we just witnessed differently than, say, a white person—you or I, for instance—would. It may not be 'just part of a trial' to them." Walter smiled. "I selected those five partly in anticipation of this situation."

Joe nodded. "So what will happen tomorrow? Besides Francine, I mean."

"Ronald will call his pathologist to testify. I hope I can establish that Linda had a serious heart condition, and if not implicate it as a cause of her death, at least raise that question." He thought for a moment. "We have our own pathologist who will be able to dispute the cardiac findings if necessary. He'll say they were very serious; if I can't get Ronald's man to say they were, that is. The Lidocaine is the key still. I wish we could show them that it would have been impossible or at least unlikely that you could have given too much."

"Don't we have to show that someone did give it?" asked Joe.

"Not necessarily," Walter said. "If we can just raise some doubt, confuse the jury as to what to believe, they might just throw their arms in the air and say they can't decide."

"Well, I know I didn't pick up the wrong syringe," said Joe. "They're so different."

"Really?" asked Walter. "You mean the adult and the pediatric syringes? How different are they?"

"One is twice the size of the other. You can't really mistake one for the other if you're used to them both, and I've used them both," said Joe, realizing that Walter had never seen the different syringes. Joe assumed he would know they were different because Joe knew they were very different himself.

Walter looked at him. "You've used them both? You've used the adult size too, even though you're a pediatrician?"

"Yes," said Joe. "A hundred pounds is the adult size and obesity is one of the main problems in the younger population. More than half my 'pediatric' patients are 'adult' size for meds."

"You know, Joe," said Walter. "Maybe if we can show the syringes to the jury and let them see how different they are ...?"

"I can probably pick them up tonight and bring them in tomorrow," Joe said.

"Maybe just bring them by the office tonight if it's not too late so I can see them and decide what to do. We might get to it tomorrow." Walter shrugged, and they parted to go their separate ways, Joe to the hospital and Walter to his office or wherever he was going. For some reason, Joe was not sure it would be directly to his office. Walter had demonstrated just now that he could be very competent, but he also had been secretive about his plans.

Joe tried never to use his cell phone while driving. Pediatricians had become aware that young people were exposed to the risk of accidents, and as a consequence, he spent a large amount of his time lecturing younger patients on the use of helmets when bicycle riding, and older, but still pediatric-aged patients, about seat belts and not using cell phones while driving. He never could tell his patients to avoid doing something he did himself. He, therefore, sat parked in his car and dialed the emergency department.

"Hello, Stacy," he said when the phone was answered. "How are you today?"

"Oh, fine, Dr. Nelson," she replied. Joe always thought the secretary's job was one of the most stressful in the department. Everyone came to that desk, from nurses and doctors asking to have their calls made or orders entered, to patients and their families asking when they would be seen or if they could get something to eat. He wondered how secretaries could ever say they were "fine."

"Who's on charge today, Stacy?" he asked.

"Robin. You want to talk to her?"

"Yeah," said Joe and was immediately put on hold.

He expected it to take a few minutes, but Robin picked up almost immediately. "How's my favorite pediatrician doing today, Joe?"

"I don't know how he or she is doing, but I'm well," he replied. "Got a favor to ask you."

"What can I do for you?"

"I need a couple of the preloaded Lidocaine syringes. One pediatric and one adult. Is there a code cart open, or should I go to the pharmacy?" Joe asked.

"Do they need to be loaded or can you use the empty ones? They do counts on the cart, you know, so if you need the loaded ones, you really will have to go through the pharmacy."

Joe thought for a minute. He could always fill them with water if need be. All syringes came without needles now as part of the effort to avoid accidental "needle sticks." That was the leading risk for HIV and hepatitis transmission to healthcare workers. "No, the used ones will be fine. Do you have any right now?"

"Oh yeah," said Robin. "We had two codes earlier today. Saved them both as a matter of fact. We have some from yesterday too that the pharmacy hasn't picked up yet. One of each, you said?"

Joe smiled. He knew that the odds of surviving a cardiac arrest that arrived in the ED were well below ten percent and to have two survivors in one day was an accomplishment. "You had a pedi code too?" he asked.

"Just a tachycardia, but they pulled the meds from the code cart. I'll get them ready for you."

"Yeah, one of each would be great. I'll come over and pick them up now, okay?"

"Always love to see my favorite pediatrician, Joe."

Joe was flattered, but he knew that every doctor was Robin's "favorite" when she was talking to that doctor. He put away his cell phone and pulled out into traffic. It was sometimes a long ride from downtown to the hospital if the traffic was heavy, but court had adjourned so early that traffic hadn't picked up yet. While driving, he thought about his attorney.

Walter was an interesting man. He had really been impressive in court today, anticipating Ronald's moves and countering them with ease. With Dr. Sparks it had been as much a matter of knowing his history, and then leading him in so smoothly that he was trapped in his own words, by his own denial. Walter had known when to expose the facts and when to leave them to the imagination of the jury. With Francine, he had been all about letting Ronald trap himself, waiting just long enough to make Ronald look like an "appalling" monster and then acting like the rescuing "knight in white armor" come to save her. Ronald villain. Walter hero. That was what the day came down to.

The case, on the other hand, might not hinge as much on heroes and villains as on facts. Phillip Sparks had made the point that there were a limited number of people that could have given Lidocaine to Linda Murphy, limited to two really, and Francine Hayes had asserted that she didn't. That left only Joe, and while Walter felt he could introduce enough doubt in the jurors' minds, Joe was not at all sure that would be possible. Joe knew he hadn't given an overdose of Lidocaine, but he couldn't figure out how one had been given.

The other thing Joe considered was what Walter was really all about. He clearly loved the "game" and the performance in court. Joe wished he would say he loved the ethical and honest part of the law too, but he didn't say that and Joe acknowledged that it wasn't necessary to say it, but he would have been happier if Walter had. He also seemed to dwell on the "sexual misconduct" a little more than was necessary. Not in court, but in his conversation with Joe. The only time he had actually been chatty was when he was describing Phillip Sparks "knocking up" a nurse. Yes, Walter was an interesting and a complex man.

Chapter 13

Joe parked in the remote lot, hoping he wouldn't have to admit this to Carolyn, and went into the ED. He saw Carolyn and waved, but Robin came over at the same time and said, "I have them in the med room, Joe. Larry from pharmacy is here too. If you really want the new ones, he can maybe get them for you."

Lawrence Marshall was walking around, too, with another man dressed in jeans and a flannel shirt. They turned when they heard Robin speak, and Joe recognized Bert Wilson as the father of one his patients. "Oh hi, Dr. Nelson," he said.

"Mr. Wilson," replied Joe. "How are you and how are Jennifer and her mother? Over the ear infection, I hope." He nodded toward Lawrence as well.

"Oh yeah," said Bert. "Postponed the ear tubes 'til the next time."

"How goes it, Joe?" Lawrence said. "At the trial, I mean?"

"Okay, I guess," Joe shrugged. "Walter wanted me to pick up some Lidocaine syringes though."

"Walter Mosby?" asked Bert. "He's my lawyer too. Great guy."

"Yeah," said Joe.

"He wants Lidocaine syringes?" asked Lawrence.

"Yeah," shrugged Joe. "Wants to look at them to see how different the adult and pedi ones are."

"Why would he want to do that?" asked Lawrence.

"We're trying to figure out how an adult dose might have been given that day," Joe replied.

"I remember that day," said Bert. "It was pretty wild. I can see how a mistake might've happened."

Joe looked over at him, but it was Robin who spoke. "You were here?"

"Well, yeah," Bert said, looking a little embarrassed. "The day that Linda … Anyway, Gloria and I were just checking out some of the work. We'd had a meeting here that morning. I didn't go into the room with Linda or anything. Not my place, but Gloria was in there, wasn't she, Lawrence?"

"Yes," said Lawrence. "We better get back to work, Bert. I'm leaving for a conference on Friday and I want to have this done by then."

Robin shrugged and said, "I remember that now, Bert. You standing outside the room, like you wanted to go in, but feeling you had to stand outside. You really looked nervous, but I guess everyone was."

Things seemed awkward now, with Joe listening to his malpractice case being discussed, but he seemed to be the least nervous of all of them. Larry, the pharmacist, came out of the med room at this point, breaking the awkwardness. "Got your syringes, Joe? I can give you the new ones if you want to walk down to the pharmacy with me. You just have to sign for them. We're keeping close track here, Mr. Marshall." He nodded and smiled toward Lawrence.

"Oh," said Lawrence. "Of course you are."

"How close track are you keeping, Larry?" Joe asked.

"We know where every one of these goes." He nodded toward the syringes. "When one is misplaced, we have to look around for it until we find it … or someone remembers throwing it in the needle box or something. You're supposed to save them for me, ya know?" He looked at Robin now.

"We do pretty good on that, Larry," she replied somewhat indignantly.

"How do you know it's the same syringe that was missing?" asked Joe. "I mean, do you only have one missing at a time?"

"No," Larry smiled and added, "Robin and the nurses do pretty well, but there are usually two or three unaccounted for." He winked at everyone and said, "Probably the doctors are the ones screwing up, ya think, Robin honey?"

Carolyn had walked over now and said, "I think it's just the pharmacists trying to play games with our heads, if you want my opinion."

"But we don't want your opinion, Dr. Prentiss," rejoined Larry.

"But how do you know it's the right one if it does show up later?" persisted Joe.

"Oh, I'm sure they can't really know," said Lawrence.

"Ah, but we can come pretty close," Larry replied. "*Just in time inventory*, people." Larry was beaming, while everyone else was bewildered. Larry was enjoying this and took a moment to savor it.

"The Japanese invented it, ya know. We used to order large amounts of our routine drugs and stock them here. They took up space and often went out-of-date, which cost us money." Larry smiled at Lawrence Marshall, his boss. Yes, this was obviously a good moment for Larry.

"The Japanese had the same problem with cars and TVs and all that, but what they did was to start keeping real close track of everything, figuring how much they used and when they would run out, and then ordering it *just in time*. If you do it right, you use the last of the old stuff just as the new stuff arrives. All the big chain stores do that now. We can't tell the exact syringe, but we can know the 'lot number,' and there is usually only one missing in each lot because we buy small amounts frequently. The manufacturer's 'lot numbers' are different for each order, so …"

Joe frowned and asked, "So you could tell me if the adult syringe that went missing three years ago was ever accounted for?"

"Probably. Ya want to look?" smiled Larry. "I've got to stock the other station, but then we can go down and look it up. I can give you the new Lidocaine syringes at the same time if you want those too. I'll just be a couple minutes."

"Yeah," said Joe. "I'll wait here for you." Joe was not sure whether Larry wanted to be helpful or to show off how great his system was, but he wanted to see that system and would be grateful for any help right now.

Larry pushed his pharmacy cart off, and Lawrence turned to Bert and said, "I have to leave on Friday, so we better keep moving." They headed off too, an animated conversation taking place, but beyond the hearing of anyone else.

Chapter 14

"They're not lovers are they?" asked Carolyn. "I mean when this place was being built, Bert was the favorite contractor, and now those two are here every other day it seems. Fixing this or that or whatever didn't get done right the first time."

Robin disrupted Joe's private thoughts when she said, "More a *ménage à trois*. Lawrence and Bert and money make three. Hence Gloria, I guess."

Joe stared at her. "You *are* kidding, right?"

"Only a little," replied Carolyn. "Lawrence and Bert are wrapped real tight around the dollar sign, and Gloria, well, her second best work is done in Bert's bed. Her best work was getting Bert the contracts here."

Joe's disbelief grew more evident on his face with each word she spoke. This only encouraged Robin, who smiled and added, "Yeah, that's what I heard too. The smart money is betting that's why Bert is a 'friend' to Gloria: to get the Murphy's family influence here and elsewhere. They also say that Gloria demanded she be a 'consultant' for him on this project. To keep an eye on him. Like she knows the first thing about any of this." Robin waved her hand at the surrounding ED and her face registered more than a little disgust.

"I heard she was an EMT once," asked Carolyn. "Is that true?"

Robin smiled a conspiratorial smile and leaned in toward the other two. "Well, I heard that's how they met. Bert was teaching a CPR course and Gloria signed up for that course, and love, or lust anyway, blossomed."

Carolyn winked and added, "That's what I heard, too. I also heard that she studied really hard *with him* and got an EMT certificate. Bert's a nurse, right?"

"Used to be," said Robin. "That was a while ago. Before he and his brother, Andy, inherited his dad's construction business. I don't think he kept his license active though. He's the one that runs the business."

Joe shook his head in bewilderment and said, "Bert and Gloria? But Bert's married."

Both women stared at him. Finally Robin reached over and ran her hand along his check. "You are so adorable, Joe," she said. Then, turning to Carolyn, she asked, "Are you sure you want to give him up, girl?"

"I'm not giving him up," Carolyn replied. "I'm just divorcing him, that's all." With this, both woman laughed and walked away, Robin to her desk and Carolyn to the secretary's desk.

"Stacy," she said, "where's that CT report? They've had it long enough to translate it into five foreign languages by now, and I need the written report to send with the patient to her referral."

"Well, I can call again, doc, if you really think that will make one bit of difference," Stacy responded.

"Oh, save your time, Stacy. I'll walk down there and threaten them myself, as if that will do anything." Carolyn headed off down the hall, waving to Joe as Larry came back.

"You ready, doc?" Larry asked.

"Yeah," said Joe.

As they headed out of the department, Lawrence and Bert were deep in conversation near the exit. "Just get it done, Bert. And make sure the door is fixed too." They stopped talking as Joe and Larry walked by, but began again as soon as they passed. "There are only a few other minor problems here that you have to take care of before we can sign off on the construction and get you the final payment."

Bert nodded, "Okay, I'll take care of my part. I could use that final payment too, Mr. Marshall."

Joe and Larry went to the pharmacy and Joe signed for two preloaded Lidocaine syringes, one adult and one pediatric. They were in boxes and Joe didn't bother to take them out. Walter could do that; Joe already knew what they looked like. The medication would be in a clear plastic barrel marked along the side in milliliters and milligrams to make calculating the exact dose easier. At one end would be a closed hole which could be opened to let the Lidocaine out of the syringe by screwing it onto a needle or an intravenous port designed to receive it; otherwise it would stay closed. The handle to inject the medication also came separately and had to be attached to a plunger at the other end of the barrel by screwing it into place. This was not easily done by someone with no experience, but if one had done it before, as Joe had, it would take only a few seconds to put one together and deliver the medication.

Larry went over to his desk while Joe signed the form. "So let me show you how it's done and then we can track down your 'missing,'" he said. He pulled a book out of the drawer he had just unlocked and opened it. "I still keep everything in this book and transfer it to the computer when the 'lost' are found."

"Each cardiac arrest, each code, or more accurately, each time the code cart is opened, it gets sent first to us and then to 'supply' to get restocked. If we just send up a request for what was used, you're never sure that everything that's supposed to be in the cart *is* in the cart. The only way to be sure is to check the carts each time they're opened and make sure. We replace the meds and 'supply' replaces the instruments and kits—you know, intubation stuff and all that." Joe knew what was supposed to be on the code carts and nodded.

Larry went on, "I have the code sheets that tell me what was given, or what someone thinks was given, and usually they check. I also have the empties and can check that against the other two. They all have to agree."

"Yeah," said Joe. "That all makes sense. A little obsessive-compulsive, but logical so far."

"Obsessive-compulsive is not always a bad thing. Anyway, when they disagree, I enter the missing and the date and the lot number, like I said upstairs. I record it even if I find it a minute later—speaking of OCD." He smiled at Joe when he said this. Joe thought Larry probably pitied others who were not obsessive-compulsive.

"Then when I have a chance, I call around and ask what happened or where the used syringe is. Most of the time someone just forgot to enter it on the code sheet, and if I have the empty, that's all I need. It's really a billing problem in that case, not that that's insignificant." He frowned as if to say that was not nearly as significant as keeping the records straight. "If it's recorded and missing from the cart but I don't have the empty, it usually shows up when the room is cleaned, or I look around in the nurses' station. If the lot numbers match then it's all cool." He smiled at this. "Sometimes someone will remember throwing it away in the sharp box." He referred to the box where all needles and other 'sharps,' like scalpels, were placed to be disposed of safely.

"The problem is when it's really missing. Not on the cart and not on the code sheet and not an empty. Then I have a problem. We're supposed to account for it. Sometimes someone remembers they gave it and where the empty is, but sometimes not. Once we found a nurse had picked up one to give to her kid for some high school class or something. Big trouble over that one." He shook his head. Joe had not heard of this episode and wondered if it had really been "big trouble."

"So, how often does one really go missing?" asked Joe.

"Maybe three or four times a year. That's all." Larry shrugged. "When was the one you were interested in?"

Joe gave him the date and Larry looked it up in his book. "Nope," he said. "That one's never shown up."

Larry turned to the computer at his desk and pulled up a screen, punched in a date, and said, "That's funny. The pedi one went through, of course, but it looks like someone entered the adult as being given too. That's strange, isn't it?"

"What do you mean, 'entered the adult one as given'?" asked Joe.

"Must be an error. No 'lot number' or anything, so it must've been an error. I'm not the only one entering this stuff on the computer. The routine stuff is done by the pharmacy secretary. They're not as compulsive about all the details as I am." He shrugged, and Joe thought that no one was as compulsive as Larry.

"But it wasn't really given?" asked Joe.

"My book is accurate. This computer is not. Only I can make entries in my book. Anyone can get into the computer," Larry asserted.

Joe just looked puzzled. Finally Larry said. "Well, let's pull up the code sheet." He went to another screen and pulled up medical records. After a minute he had the medical record for Linda Murphy and then went to the "code sheet," the record of the cardiac arrest that had ended in her death. "See!" said Larry in triumph. "Only one pedi Lidocaine listed as given. Epinephrine given and IV fluids, but only one Lido. It should never be entered as 'given' in the computer unless all three were verified somehow. Missing from the cart, listed as 'given' on the code sheet, and an empty syringe too, with a lot number, or at least someone saying they tossed it into the sharp box or something. I should have that all in my book and I don't."

Joe had seen the code sheet already and knew only the one dose of pedi Lido was listed as being given. The issue in the trial was whether he had accidently given an *adult* dose that had been listed as a *pediatric* dose in error, or that he had given another adult dose that was never entered on the code sheet at all. The toxicology report seemed to indicate a larger dose was given, even if the code sheet didn't, but the code sheet specifically said only one dose was given.

After a minute Larry added, "This is strange too." He then switched screens back to the document entry screen and clicked on "properties" under the record in question. "It looks like someone tried to get into this record about two years ago to change it. That's really strange, isn't it?"

"Yeah," replied Joe. "Really strange. Are you sure someone tried to change the record?"

"Well, the dates it was opened are all listed and the one two years ago lists a 'denied addendum' to the chart. Chart was locked, probably because of your trial," he added in a matter-of-fact voice. No judgment or pity or embarrassment at all.

"Who?" asked Joe.

"Doesn't say," replied Larry. "Just an administrative code for the entry and anyone can use one of those. The vendors and drug reps sometimes have those so they can restock stuff. Sometimes they have to if the 'just in time inventory' thing is going to work properly. They're not supposed to be able to enter anything, but sometimes someone leaves a chart 'unlocked.' That's not supposed to happen, but … well."

Joe must have looked surprised because Larry went on, "You know Joe, security on these systems just means that getting in is too difficult for congressmen or administrators to figure out. Their egos make them think that if they can't get in, no one can; but … well, every system can be broken into and usually very easily if you know how."

Larry looked at Joe who still looked puzzled. "I know you wouldn't give the wrong dose. Besides, I was there when the code was going on. I didn't see any adult Lidocaine given."

"You were there, Larry?"

"Yeah. I was just doing routine restocking." Larry shrugged.

"And you saw me giving the Lidocaine?" Joe asked.

"Well, no. I didn't see you give any Lidocaine, really. But I didn't see you give any adult dose." Larry seemed to think this verified that Joe had given a pediatric dose although Joe couldn't quite follow this argument.

"You think someone tried to alter the medical record, but you can't tell who it was?" Joe asked.

"Well, it looks like someone did, but I can't tell who. Like I said, getting in to view the chart's easy. Almost anyone could do that, but altering the chart ... well, no one could alter this chart. Even by adding an addendum." The tone of Larry's voice said this was a finality. No room for any question.

"One more thing, Larry," said Joe. "Are all pharmacists as obsessive as you are?"

"They should be," replied Larry. "That's the trouble with the world. They're not!"

Not just pharmacists, thought Joe. He didn't think anyone was as obsessive as Larry.

Chapter 15

When Joe left Larry, he was more puzzled than satisfied. An adult dose of Lidocaine either missing or found? Probably missing still, if obsessive-compulsive Larry was right and Joe thought he probably was. What gave him a bigger pause to think was that someone wanted the record altered. Well, maybe someone did. Joe had to take Larry's word for that too, and he couldn't get that to make sense. Still, Larry had no obvious reason to mislead him, which made it all so curious.

Joe was tempted to dismiss it, but somehow it kept nagging at him. Probably it was just someone trying to straighten out the records, maybe trying to protect the hospital when they were named in the malpractice suit, even if listing the adult dose as "given" would have been very damaging to Joe. That shouldn't have been done, of course, but he knew it sometimes was, and a colleague had actually suggested that he alter the record when he was named in the lawsuit. He remembered being surprised and embarrassed by the suggestion. Though he couldn't recall exactly who had made it, he seemed to think it might have been Lawrence, the hospital CEO. Joe had never falsified a record in his life and couldn't even bring himself to consider doing that, but maybe someone else had tried.

The other thing that struck him was how many people had been in the ED that day. He had thought there were only a few, but now everyone he met seemed to have been present that day. He had already known about Lawrence and Gloria, but now Bert and Larry turned out to have been there as well.

Joe stopped by the ED on his way out, partly because it was on his way and partly to thank Robin. He saw Carolyn again, but she was busy and just waved. Robin looked busy and Joe was about to wave and leave when she gave the chart in her hand to one of the other nurses and came over to him.

"So how's it really going, Joe?" she asked as she approached. "The trial, I mean."

"Oh …" Joe shrugged. "It's an education all right."

"Francine called a few minutes ago," Robin said. "She was pretty upset."

Joe winced at that. "Yeah. It was brutal. It will probably be easier tomorrow. I can't talk to her, you know, but you can tell her."

"I will, but she's really upset. She swears you didn't give anything except the pedi dose, but she's spinning about the whole thing. She was upset about it when it happened and more so now. They gave her a hard time about leaving the room to get you when Lawrence Marshall told her to get you 'stat'?" It was more a statement of disbelief than a question. "She couldn't have been out of the room more than ten seconds!"

"Yeah," said Joe, thinking of Walter's remark: "*She is not projecting herself well.*" Francine was being discredited because she was defending him.

"She's worried they're going to ask her about the missing adult Lido and the missing needles, and … she's really falling apart," Robin said.

"The missing adult Lido is just missing, that's all. Tell her to say she doesn't know where it went and stick to that regardless of what they ask her." Joe was feeling truly sorry for Francine, all the more so because he was the reason she was going through it. "What needles is she worrying about?"

"The needles?" said Robin. "Oh, you remember. You were going to do the lumbar puncture before the first arrest because she was febrile and looked so bad. You thought it might be meningitis, but you didn't get to it. The tray was out but was just pushed aside when Linda coded. When Francine was cleaning up, all the needles were gone. We reuse the special pedi lumbar puncture needles, and *supply* was pissed that they were missing. Probably someone just threw out all the sharps off the tray, but no one remembered doing that. Francine was so upset about Linda dying that everything seemed important. She stayed two hours after her shift just looking for those needles."

Joe shook his head again. "Just tell her it will all be over tomorrow no matter what she says or does, and I will survive as well, no matter what happens. Do you want me to ask Carolyn if she would prescribe a little something to help her relax?"

Robin shook her head. "She probably wouldn't take anything—afraid they would accuse her of being on drugs or something. Can I tell her you really do think she's doing okay and you still like and respect her?"

"What?" Joe asked.

"She's afraid you're going to blame her if you're convicted, Joe. She wants you to respect her the way we all respect you. That's what's really upsetting her."

Joe was surprised. "I can't talk to her, Robin, not during the trial. But if I could, I'd say I've never had more respect for her than I do after seeing her in court today. Tell her that for me, will you? This trial's not going to alter the truth one bit, and that's all she has to tell them. The truth."

"That's what I'll tell her. Thanks Joe." She squeezed his hand and added, "Gotta go." As she turned to leave, Joe thought he saw a tear forming in her eye but couldn't be sure. These were special people he had the honor of working with.

Chapter 16

When Joe arrived at Walter's office and saw his attorney's dark windows, he realized that he had forgotten to call and make sure Walter would be there. The office was on a one-way street, and he parked right in front of it even though it required a couple of passes to parallel park between two already parked cars. Joe prided himself on his ability to parallel park and remembered that Carolyn had always been impressed by how well he performed that task even in a manual shift with his prosthetic left foot.

Once he was parked, he noticed the neighborhood. It was the first time he had seen it when it wasn't daylight, and he realized it appeared a little run-down in the diminished light of evening. He was parked next to one of the few street lights on that street. Walter had had his office in the high-rent section of the city until six months ago, and this area was definitely a step down from that address.

Joe tried Walter's cell phone but only got a message service. Someone else was talking to Walter or the phone was turned off. He didn't bother to leave a message. He could do that later if he didn't find Walter tonight. He could talk to him before court tomorrow anyway. He tried the office phone which rang unanswered, and he left no message on it either.

He got out and went to ring the office buzzer, just in case Walter was up there and busy in the dark. It was unlikely, but Larry wasn't the only one who could claim obsessive-compulsive bragging rights. There was no answer to the buzzer either. Joe looked up at the windows and thought there might be someone in the office. It occurred to him that there were things to do in a dark office that also would make answering the phone inconvenient. Things that could be done with the right companion. He shook his head. His imagination was getting the best of him. He got back into his car and was trying to decide if he should wait a little before leaving when a shot punched a neat little hole in the driver's window, spidered the rest of the glass, and paralyzed Joe where he sat.

He heard the sound a second later and instinctively threw himself onto the seat. He looked at the hole and realized it must have been a bullet that made it. A second later he realized it had to have been meant for him. Even if it was not the high-rent neighborhood, it was not one for random shootings either. Someone had shot at him for some reason, and someone was still out there waiting to shoot again—maybe coming over to his car to shoot again at that very moment. He couldn't chance sitting up for a quick look, much less to try to drive away. Damn his perfect parallel parking job!

He listened intently. There was no sound from outside. He knew he had to do something, but he might not have time to do much. *Think straight, Joe,* he told himself. *Make the time count.* He managed to contort himself into a position that would allow him to open the driver's door just enough to kick it open if anyone came up to the window, but not enough to turn the lights on inside his car. Then he lay down on the seat again with his feet against the door. With this accomplished, he pulled out his cell phone and dialed 911.

When the dispatcher answered, Joe gave his name and said as loudly as he could that he had been shot at and that he knew the shooter was still outside and then gave Walter's address. He said he would stay on the phone until the police arrived so that he could tell them who was coming if the shooter approached his car. When the voice on the other end asked why he was shouting, Joe merely replied that he wanted to make sure the shooter heard everything he said. There were no more questions before a face appeared in the driver's window. She held a gun in one hand and a police badge in the other.

"I am Sergeant Moore," she said. "Are you all right?"

No, thought Joe. *I would be all right if I were in bed watching TV or even in that damned courtroom, but lying on my back in shattered glass is not all right.* "I think so," is what he said. "I'm unarmed and would very much like to get out of this car and stand up. Is that okay?"

"Yes," said Sergeant Moore, but she did not lower her gun. "Slowly," she added.

He did so, slowly as he had been told, and when he was out of the car, he stood and raised his hands. "I'm not really familiar with the procedure here, so you'll have to tell me what to do. I'm Joseph Nelson and I called when I was shot at." He motioned toward his car window. "And I want to thank you for coming so promptly."

Sergeant Moore only nodded as she was joined by a man with a badge on his belt and an attitude on his face. Joe thought that this was only going to be slightly better than facing that shooter would have been.

The police checked Joe for injuries and weapons, took a brief report, and asked Joe to come to the station to finish the report. Two uniformed officers had arrived and were left to investigate the scene.

Joe rode to the station in the back of the patrol car with Sergeant Pierce driving and a barrier between Joe and Pierce. Joe thought sarcastically that this must be to protect him from the sergeant as he was unarmed and cooperative and the sergeant was neither. Pierce was the man with the badge and the attitude who had joined Sergeant Moore. It annoyed Joe that they knew his first name and he did not know theirs, but that was one of the least annoying things that night. Sergeant Moore drove his car to the station. At least she had asked his permission although he got the impression it wasn't really necessary that he give it. She looked as if she would have found another reason to do so if he hadn't agreed.

At the station he found himself in a glass-walled cubical, waiting for half an hour before the two sergeants joined him. Sergeant Pierce was outside talking to another police officer who was dressed in a shabby suit as the sergeant was. They were obviously talking about him because there were frequent nods and looks in his direction. Finally Sergeant Pierce left the other and joined Sergeant Moore, and they both came into the cubicle where Joe waited. Sergeant Pierce would be questioning him while Sergeant Moore was watching … frowning actually. If this was going to be the "good cop, bad cop" routine, Joe would have trouble identifying which one was the "good cop."

"So, tell me again what happened, Mr. Nelson," said the sergeant. Joe knew Pierce was aware that he was a doctor, and therefore he must have chosen to address him as "Mr." to prove something. Joe didn't usually mind being addressed as "Mr." outside of his work, but he did mind the antagonism. He was the victim after all.

"I went to meet my attorney, but he wasn't at his office. I was about to leave when someone shot at me. There is a hole in my car window to prove that." Joe hoped he didn't sound as antagonistic as he felt.

"Meeting your attorney at this time of night? A little late, isn't it?" asked Pierce.

Joe sighed. He had been through this already. "We are in the middle of a trial, a malpractice trial, and he wanted some examples of the medications given to the patient. I picked them up at the hospital and was dropping them at his office."

"But he wasn't there. Why would he ask you to meet him and then not be there?"

"I don't know," replied Joe, and he was sure he would ask Walter when he saw him again.

"We couldn't reach him on the number you gave us," said the sergeant, challenging Joe with the look on his face.

"Neither could I," replied Joe.

"I can't understand that," said the sergeant. "Can you, Natalie?" He looked at Sergeant Moore and Joe looked as well. Natalie looked annoyed, and, for the first time, Joe thought that it might be with Sergeant Pierce. She just shook her head. Joe looked a little longer at her then, noticing that she was not shabby, either of clothing or of person. She had dark, neat, shoulder-length hair and a face that bore little makeup and that could have been pretty if it were not frowning.

Sergeant Pierce spoke again. "So, someone shoots at you, for no reason you can tell us, and you just lie down on the seat of your car and wait for … for the shooter to get there before the police? Is that right, Mr. Nelson?"

"As I said before: I had a plan," said Joe patiently. "I thought it would be dangerous to get out of the car or even to sit up and try to drive away. I opened the driver's side door enough for me to kick it open if he came up to it, and I then called the 911 operator and made sure I spoke loud enough to be heard. The shooter would have known you were on your way and would therefore be encouraged to leave before you arrived, which he apparently did."

"Pretty cool under fire, Mr. Nelson," replied Sergeant Pierce. Joe said nothing. Finally the sergeant continued. "We're going to look into this. We need to keep your car for a few days to do that. Will that be a problem?"

"I don't think so," said Joe.

There was silence for another moment and then the sergeant asked, "The address on your license is different from the one you gave us on the report. Which is correct?"

Joe had been through this before as well. "The one on the report is correct. My wife is at the old address. We're getting a divorce."

"Yes, you said that, didn't you?" At this point a uniformed officer came in and handed Sergeant Pierce a note. He read it and stood.

"Tell them to wait there for me. No one is to go inside until I get there," he said to the messenger who then left the room. Turning to Joe, he said, "Well, that will be all, Mr. Nelson. We can have an officer give you a ride if you wish—to whichever address you are going to tonight."

Joe stood as well and said, "A cab will suit me fine." He took his bag of Lidocaine and started to leave the room.

"We'll be in touch," said Sergeant Pierce.

Chapter 17

Joe was annoyed as he rode to his apartment. He would make no calls tonight, just settle in and get some sleep and hit the morning as early as possible to find out what happened to Walter. At least he would not be on the witness stand tomorrow.

His annoyance was duplicated back at the police station. "What the hell was all that about, Peter?" Natalie asked Sergeant Pierce. "A doctor gets shot at and you act like he's the criminal."

"Well, first of all," replied Peter, "he was way too cool for someone who had just been shot at—not how your average pediatrician would act, ya think?"

Natalie just frowned. Peter went on, "Then there's the fact that I don't see the exit for that bullet. Just the one going in, like the door was open when the bullet was fired so it never went into the car at all."

Peter paused for a moment and then continued, "Ya know what I think? I think our pediatrician shot that hole in his own window somewhere else, before coming to the nonexistent meeting with his attorney just to get attention. Maybe to take the heat off himself over this malpractice case he's going to lose. Maybe he thought he could get a mistrial or something, ya think?"

He smiled and Natalie scowled. "How do you know what's going on in his trial, Peter?"

"I read the papers, Nat. I'm more than a handsome stud you know."

Natalie scowled again. "I think he's telling it straight, Peter. And I don't know why you can't look at this objectively without speculating about all this bull. There was a bullet hole in his driver's window, and there was glass on his front seat and on his clothing. He's either really clever, or that door was closed and he was in the car when the shot was fired. You haven't even looked for the bullet inside his car."

Peter didn't seem bothered by his partner's accusation. "Ya know what else I think, Nat? I think you've been too long without a man in your bed. Every tall, dark, and handsome guy has you all hotted up so you can't see straight. That's what I think."

Natalie scowled again. It always came down to this with Peter: her miserable love life and his chauvinistic views. All she or any woman needed was a man in her bed. He knew he could shut her off anytime he wanted by bringing up her past failure to "get a man" and the divorce she had been through. Yeah, her love life was miserable right now and no, she did not want to discuss it with Peter Pierce.

"And another thing," said Peter. "I just got a note about a 'breaking in and entering in' situation," he said, mocking the police jargon. "Notice the address?"

He handed the note to Natalie and she looked at it. "That's Dr. Nelson's address. The one on his driver's license."

"Yep," said Peter. "The one he's not staying at, but his divorced wife is. You want to see your competition?"

Natalie's scowl mixed with curiosity. Not about her "competition" but about a strange coincidence. A very strange coincidence.

They drove over to Carolyn's home in silence and found her waiting in the driveway. Two uniformed police were there already, but Peter had told them to wait until he and Natalie arrived. "Nelson is the name on the address," Peter said. "You must be Mrs. Nelson." After this preliminary introduction, he asked Carolyn to show them the break-in, and she took them around to the back door where there was a broken pane in one of the six panels that made up the door's window.

"No one has been inside, have they?" asked Peter.

"No one except me," said Carolyn, "and the burglar, of course."

He looked over at her and she added, "I went in the front door and didn't notice there had been any break-in at all until I went to the kitchen."

"And then you called us and waited outside?"

"After I checked around inside, of course," said Carolyn. Peter stared at her and finally she continued. "I wanted to see what was missing."

"And what is missing?" asked Peter.

"Nothing that I could find. The silver is all here as are the TVs and computers and everything else as far as I can tell."

Peter did not look pleased as they went through the back door into the kitchen. "No need to worry about fingerprints if there's nothing missing," he said to the uniformed officers. There was broken glass on the floor, which they all took care to avoid. "The 'burglar' could still have been here, Mrs. Nelson."

"I didn't think that was likely," said Carolyn. "And it is *Doctor* Prentiss."

"It's chilly in here, Dr. Prentiss," said Natalie. "What time did you get home tonight?"

"About one o'clock."

"Was the kitchen door closed when you found it?"

"Yes," replied Carolyn, looking at her.

"Did you open it?"

"No," replied Carolyn.

"And where is the thermostat located?" Peter turned to look at Natalie at this point.

Carolyn looked quizzically at her as well and said, "In the hall. Just one on this floor." Carolyn nodded toward a closed door opposite the one through which they had entered.

"And," said Natalie, "the hall door was closed as it is now, is that correct?"

"Well yes, but ..."

Natalie smiled. "This room is cool, which means the heat from the hall didn't get in here to warm it. The hall door must have been closed. The hole in the window is pretty small, and it's not too chilly or windy outside so the kitchen would have taken a while to cool down. That means the break-in was probably a few hours ago."

Everyone smiled now, even the uniformed officers. Everyone except Peter. "We can finish the report," he said, frowning. He turned to the uniforms and added, "You can have a look around, boys."

"Mrs. ... oh, I mean, *Dr.* Prentiss," said Peter, "you're sure there's nothing missing. No jewelry or perhaps a firearm?"

Carolyn looked puzzled and replied, "The jewelry isn't worth much, and it all seems to be there. We do have a gun. I didn't think to check that."

"Maybe you should," offered Peter.

Carolyn went to a desk in the living room and opened a drawer. "It's still here," she said, reaching for it.

"Let me get that if you don't mind," said Peter, taking out a glove and putting the gun into a bag. "May we keep this to check it? We'll return it to you."

"Well, I guess," said Carolyn. "If you want to. I never use it anyway."

"Guns are one of the things people steal when they break into a home, you know," replied Peter, putting the bagged weapon into his pocket.

"Does your husband live here with you?" he asked. "Or maybe another gentleman?"

"Neither husband nor anyone else."

"There is some men's clothing in this closet," Peter said, looking into the hall closet.

79

"My husband and I are getting divorced—an amicable divorce—and he still has some of his things here. I'm sure he had nothing to do with this. He has a key to the house."

"So your husband, not ex-husband yet, and you are getting along well, are you?" asked Peter.

"Yes," replied Carolyn. "He had nothing to do with breaking in here tonight, Sergeant."

Peter ignored her. "When did you see him last, Doctor?"

"Today at work. Why?"

"And before that?"

"Last night."

"No threats or arguments or anything, Mrs. ... I mean, *Dr.* Prentiss?"

Carolyn scowled at Peter now. "We did have one argument last night, Sergeant. The second time we made love he wanted to be on top and so did I. It ended amicably enough though. He got to be on top the third time." She looked at Peter and added, "I'm sure you know how that goes, Sergeant."

Carolyn had had enough of the man and his attitude, and she knew that challenging his male ego was the quickest way to end it, but she had a backup plan just in case. She pulled out her cell phone and hit a speed dial number and then looked at Peter. "My attorney," she said. "He's my brother as well, so he won't mind getting called this late at night."

She went back to the phone and a voice could be heard on the other end. In a moment she said, "Oh Douglas. I have two police officers here who think they can question me without a lawyer present. I thought I should ask you about that."

Peter looked a little pale. "We're pretty much done here, Doctor, right Natalie? We'll be in touch, okay? Come on, boys," he said and was the first one out the door.

The uniformed officers followed quickly and Natalie was left to politely say, "If you do have any questions or think of anything, let me know. And when you have a chance, go through everything to make sure nothing is missing. Burglars don't usually break into a home and take nothing, and it looks like he had time to take whatever he wanted. Here's my card and I'll call you in a couple of days. I'll have the patrol car drive by a couple of times tonight too. Have a good night, Dr. Prentiss."

Carolyn had been holding the cell phone against her chest while she listened to Natalie and put it to her ear again when she had gone. "And when you get this message in the morning, Douglas, give me a call and tell me your friggin' personal cell number so in case there ever is an emergency I can reach my friggin' brother. Have a good day, Douglas," she closed the phone. *Damned message machine and damned Douglas—Mr. 'so important attorney'—and damned Sergeant damned Pierce,* she thought to herself. She looked at the card: Sergeant Natalie Moore, it said. This, she would keep.

She stuffed a towel in the broken window and went up to bed. She'd clean up the glass in the morning and maybe call Joe to come by and repair the window; and maybe they could try for that third time again. They'd been too tired last night.

Chapter 18

Meanwhile, Joe was just beginning to fall asleep, but he still had a lot to think about. Mostly he was wondering why anyone would shoot at him in the first place. Maybe it had been a random shooting after all. No one really knew he was going by Walter's office, and he didn't think anyone was following him around. His apartment building had some security—a buzzer entry system from the street and a remote entry system for the garage, which he hadn't needed tonight, thanks to the police. Those security measures made a casual entry to the complex inconvenient, but even he could think of ways to get past them. If someone were really going to shoot at him, his apartment would be more likely.

The police officers' attitudes bothered him too. Why had they, especially Sergeant Pierce, jumped to the conclusion he was lying? He wished he had someone to talk this out with but he didn't. It always made more sense when he talked about something than when he just thought about it. He would have called Carolyn, but even though she hadn't been relieved at the ED until eleven that evening, he was sure she would be asleep by now.

He thought back to the police again, specifically he thought about Natalie. He realized he was thinking of her by her first name, not as Sergeant Moore. Pierce was clearly his antagonist, but he wasn't sure Natalie shared that feeling. It was she that he was thinking about as sleep overtook him.

Across town, sleep was not coming easily to Carolyn Prentiss-Nelson. She was sputteringly angry at burglars, police sergeants, and her brother. She thought of calling Joe but decided he would be asleep, and she didn't want to bother him. She could not make any sense of the break-in. Nothing was missing, and she had to admit that Natalie was probably right: the burglar had had plenty of time to take whatever he wanted. Maybe he had taken something and she just didn't realize what it was. A thorough inventory would have to be one of her priorities.

She smiled as she thought of Sergeant Pierce. She sincerely hoped she'd put him in his place, and she laughed to herself when she found she was hoping he tried and failed to perform on his third attempt when he next got a woman in his bed.

As these thoughts faded, the rest of the evening's events returned to her and anger replaced the mirth. Yes, she was angry now and anger always helped her to sleep, unlike what everyone seemed to think should be the case. She did, however, think that Natalie was a good cop and decided that if she wanted to talk to the police about what had happened that night it would be Natalie she would call.

At that same moment two police sergeants arrived back at their station after a very quiet car ride. Natalie wanted to think, not talk, and Peter was not eager to admit that "Dr. Prentiss" had cut him down as completely as she had. He'd had the idea that she was attracted to him before that last exchange. As they entered the station, Natalie finally broke the silence.

"Why did you take her handgun, Peter?"

"Oh," he replied, "Just a hunch. Bullet hole in the doctor's car window and gun in his wife's home. Break-in with nothing missing. These dots seem to connect to make a picture of a doctor shooting at his own car with his wife's gun, don't you think? Then there's that whole 'break-in' thing. Did Mrs. Nelson act like someone who had just had her home, where she lives alone, broken into, or did she act like someone who wanted the police to come by and maybe document a break-in?"

"I think it's a bit of a reach, Peter. I also think it's late and I'm going home to get some sleep and get ready for tomorrow," Natalie replied.

"Well, you go on home to your lonely bed, Nat. I'm going to get this gun to the ballistics guys tonight and put a rush on it for morning," said Peter as he walked away.

Carolyn Prentiss must have really stung him, Natalie thought. She couldn't remember the last time Peter had made the slightest effort to rush anything except getting a female out of her clothes and into his bed. This whole department was more than she could take and she resolved once again to move on as soon as she had put in enough time there to make her "work history" look good. There were just too many people who seemed to be able to do whatever they wanted and never get called on it.

When she was new to the department, she had asked about the "gifts" that seemed to show up. No one made any effort to explain these, but no one made any effort to conceal them either. Peter had simply said there was nothing wrong with letting people "show their gratitude." She just had to make sure some of the "gratitude" got shared with her captain. He also advised her not to "make waves" or it might be her boat that got swamped. Most police officers realized that eliminating crime was a dream and that controlling it was the best that they could hope to do. In her department, it looked more like it was "supervised" crime. It looked to her as if there were drugs being sold and stolen property being trafficked throughout the county with little or no interference. *Can't do anything about it, Natalie,* she thought. *Put in your time and move on.*

As she drove home, she turned her thoughts to what had happened that evening. Odd, no matter how she looked at it. A pediatrician got shot at—and she was sure that he had been shot at, even if Peter was not. Then there was the break-in at his wife's home with nothing missing. Maybe when Carolyn looked over the place again something would be missing, but still, it was not your usual burglary. And then there was Peter with all of

his theories about faked gun shots and faked break-ins and …
and staying late to rush a ballistics test when he never rushed
anything. There was no reason to rush this ballistics report at all.
They could sort it out tomorrow or two weeks from tomorrow
and it would make no difference. It would particularly make
no difference if the shooting and the break-in were all faked.
As unlikely as their stories were, Natalie decided that Joe and
Carolyn were telling it all straight and that something else was
driving Peter that evening. Testosterone was the only thing she
knew of that drove Peter, but there could be something else.

She began then to think about Joe and that he seemed honest
in a way that would make it obvious when he tried to lie. He
also had not changed his story at all throughout the questioning,
which usually meant that it was the truth. Liars instinctively tried
to edge their story one way or the other when the police weren't
buying it. They would try to change it or "remember something"
or suggest something to convince the police it was the "real"
thing. Joe had not done that even with the parts that made no
sense.

Carolyn, on the other hand, did not seem interested in having
the police believe her enough to lie about it. She told them what
had happened, and Natalie was sure that "Dr. Prentiss" expected
them to take care of the situation. She had not tried to make
her story "believable," which liars always did. A liar wouldn't
have told the police she wandered around her house alone after
discovering a burglary, particularly when there was no reason to
say anything about it at all. She didn't find anything missing, and
she could as easily have said she came directly outside and then
looked around with the police present. If the gun was important,
she would either have said it was still there or never mentioned
it. No, the very nature of her story made it obvious it was not a
fabrication.

They were both doctors, too, and while that didn't mean
they wouldn't lie, the hospital seemed to be the only place that
wasn't involved in the county's sordid crimes. No one had ever

suggested that anything illegal happened there; it appeared to be above the criminal activities of the community. She had seen that sort of thing before in urban areas, where the hospital was treated as "neutral territory" by the street gangs because they all knew they would have to depend upon the hospital for their lives when they were the ones injured. The hospitals, and sometimes the churches, were "off limits" by mutual agreement.

Natalie smiled as she thought again of how Carolyn had shut Peter down. He had been obnoxious all right, but not as bad as he could have been. It was a "pre-emptive" strike on Carolyn's part. Natalie was also pretty sure there was no one on the other end of that cell phone conversation and that had been cool too, but the argument with the husband she was divorcing and the third-time solution had been brilliant—brilliant and so predictably effective on "Mr. Male Ego" Peter. Natalie wondered if that part was true and decided it probably was.

As she parked and headed to her empty house, she thought again of Joe, the pediatrician, and his wife. She wondered why those two were getting divorced, and particularly why Joe was letting a great woman get away if they were still friendly enough to have had sex the night before. Yes, thought Natalie, he might be telling the truth and he was even good looking, but there had to be something seriously wrong with him for passing up Carolyn Prentiss.

Chapter 19

Morning comes regardless of how tired people are or how busy the previous night has been. Carolyn could have slept later, but she wanted to clean up and take that thorough inventory to find out if she had overlooked anything that was missing from the night before. None of her things were missing, and she was pretty sure none of Joe's were either, although she wasn't exactly sure what was still in the house that belonged to him. He had clothing there and a few books—he still preferred books to the Internet—but all of his records were moved already. She was pretty sure he didn't have anything of value here. She would be at work by three that afternoon and Joe would be in court, but she knew he intended to have an evening session at his office today, and she would call him there to make sure.

Natalie was up at her usual time and decided that, in spite of the late night, she would make her usual stop at the gym before going to the station. She was sure the crimes would keep until her workout was finished even if it didn't turn her into the ravishing beauty that was on the cover of the advertising brochure for her gym. There was probably some violation of "truth in advertising" inherent in it, but to claim that, she would have had to admit that she was stupid enough to have believed it would make that transformation in the first place. Still, that brochure with the sweaty, smiling model on its cover annoyed her that morning more than it usually did. She did not realize that her stop at the gym made it possible for Peter to make it to work before she arrived, and that he would be waiting for her.

Joe was up early that morning too and thought of calling Walter but decided that he would see him before the trial began anyway. Coffee and a quick breakfast while he waited for the cab to arrive was all the time he wanted to take. The horn announced the cab's arrival, and Joe went downstairs to ride to the courthouse. He chatted with the cab driver about the morning's news and was pleased that his shooting from the night before was not mentioned at all.

Walter was already at the courthouse when he arrived and Joe went over to talk to him. Walter motioned that they should go outside where no one would overhear their conversation even though Ronald had not yet arrived.

Once outside, Joe handed him the bag with the Lidocaine syringes in it and asked, "Where were you last night? I thought you were going to be at your office."

"Oh, I finished up more quickly than I thought I would and decided to get an early night. Hope I didn't inconvenience you too much," Walter replied. He seemed a little embarrassed, and Joe decided not to mention his "inconvenience" of the night before just yet.

"Do you want to look at the syringes now?" Joe asked.

"We can do that later," replied Walter. "Today, we'll finish with Francine Hayes and that will probably take a good part of the morning. Is there anything I should be asking her?"

"Just that she doesn't know where the adult Lidocaine dose went. She'd say it would take a long time to inject that much Lidocaine through the interosseous line, a minute or two maybe; therefore she would've seen any given. And, of course, that was the only way it could have been given," replied Joe.

Walter frowned. "I'm not sure, but that might be too complicated for the jury to comprehend. What's the interosseous line again?"

It occurred to Joe that Walter might have meant that this was too complicated for *him* to understand. "The interosseus line is just an intravenous line that goes directly into the bone marrow instead of going into a vein. The bone marrow then goes directly into the circulation, the same as an intravenous would. It's a little slower, though, and would take at least a minute to give that much Lidocaine. A regular IV would only take five seconds."

"Hum," said Walter. "Let me think about that. It still might be more confusing than helpful. It's not really how long it took to give it, but who was responsible." He thought for a moment and then continued. "They have their own pathologist to go on the stand after Francine Hayes and then their toxicologist, but they probably won't get to both of them today. Today's Thursday and I'll have to see how things are going, but I may ask for a recess until Monday."

"Why a recess?" asked Joe.

"Oh," shrugged Walter, "mostly just to inconvenience the plaintiff attorney and his witnesses. But the judge has a camp up on the lake, and he'd love to get a long weekend up there with the warmer weather that's been predicted. If Ronald insists on making him stay, he'll be in a bad mood—at least toward Ronald."

Joe was always surprised at the "courtroom drama" and how truly tawdry it could be. On the other hand, he was also pretty sure Walter had no idea he had been shot at the night before if this was what was on his mind.

Joe smiled a bit and said, "While I was waiting for you last night, someone shot a bullet through the driver's window of my car."

The surprise on his face assured Joe that Walter had not expected this at all. "You weren't in the car, were you? I mean, were you injured?"

"I was in the car, but no, I wasn't injured."

"Who? ... I mean what? ... It's a very safe neighborhood. It must've been a random shooting or something. You're sure it was a gun shot?" Walter was actually stammering a little as Ronald walked by, looking very closely at them both. It occurred to Joe that Ronald would probably think Walter's reaction was to some revelation about the trial and that it might cause Ronald to alter his plans. Was he beginning to think like his attorney?

"You reported it to the police, I'm sure," Walter continued, oblivious to Ronald's listening ears.

Joe waited until Ronald entered the courtroom to reply. "Yes, of course. They took a full report."

"But you're all right. I mean, I could request a recess for the day if you need time to recover." Walter had begun recovering himself and was becoming an attorney again.

"No, I don't think that's either necessary or advisable." Joe was thinking of Francine and what she would do if her testimony were not completed today. He was not at all injured, physically or even emotionally, and a delay would not help him "recover." As he spoke, he became aware that the shooting, if it was really intended for him, probably had something to do with the trial. That was the biggest thing going on in his life at the moment, and the shooting had taken place in front of his lawyer's office. He could not see how the two events could possibly be related, but it was better to keep the trial going anyway.

"Well, then we'd better get inside," said Walter.

Chapter 20

There was only a brief time to wait until the bailiff announced they should all rise and the jury returned, followed by the judge. Francine was asked to return to the witness stand and was reminded by the judge that she was still under oath. Francine looked nervous and Joe thought the jury looked sympathetically at her.

The testimony proceeded with Ronald asking pointed questions, but with none of the aggressiveness that he demonstrated the day before.

"Did you see Dr. Nelson give Linda Murphy a dose of Lidocaine?" Ronald asked.

"Yes," answered Francine.

"Do you know if Dr. Nelson administered a pediatric dose or an adult dose?"

"No," said Francine. "Dr. Nelson removed the syringe from the code cart himself, and I didn't see which one he grabbed."

"Was there any other place that he could have taken Lidocaine from?"

"No," replied Francine. "All the medications and instruments that are used during a code—a cardiac arrest—are contained in that movable cart, the code cart, which can be moved to any room where it's needed."

"While you were in the room, were you able to watch Linda Murphy at all times?" asked Ronald.

"No."

"Did you see Dr. Nelson give Linda Murphy any additional Lidocaine after the first dose you saw him administer to her?"

"No."

"But is it possible, because you weren't able to watch Linda Murphy at all times, that Dr. Nelson could have given her more Lidocaine when you weren't looking?"

"Yes," replied Francine, and Joe knew it hurt her to say so.

Ronald repeatedly made her testify that she had not given Lidocaine or any other medication herself, that she did not see anyone else give any, and that she did not take any Lidocaine out of the code cart. There had, however, been several people in and out of the room that could have taken a medication out of the code cart, but Ronald managed to leave the distinct impression that only Joe could have given Lidocaine. Joe knew where Ronald's line of questioning was going, but he realized that the jury probably did not because it was yet to be established that a Lidocaine overdose was probably responsible for Linda Murphy's death. He thought that if he were a juror, he would be a bit confused by this even with his knowledge of medicine.

Walter followed with a friendlier demeanor, but his questions were just as pointed. Francine again testified she had not seen Joe give any additional Lidocaine and that, in fact, the only time—a very brief time, Walter emphasized, less than a minute—that she was out of the room Joe was not in the room either.

"If Dr. Nelson had given additional Lidocaine, would you have seen him do so?"

"Yes, of course!" Francine replied. Joe could see that she was eager to help him and happy that she might have that chance.

"Did you see Dr. Nelson give additional Lidocaine to Linda Murphy?"

"No, of course I didn't," Francine said, adding, "and he would have told me if he had so that I could record it on the code sheet."

"Could another nurse or doctor have given a medication such as Lidocaine?"

Joe saw that the question confused Francine, particularly the subtle point that someone *could* have given something, even if she had not seen anyone give anything. Walter was finally able, with some difficulty, to get Francine to say that any nurse, or EMT for that matter, would know *how* to give it and therefore *could* have given it, but she insisted that she did not think anyone *would* have given it or *did* give it.

"I didn't see anyone give anything to Linda Murphy except Dr. Nelson," testified Francine. With some reluctance and frustration, Walter finished on that note.

Joe, however, felt that Francine had told the truth and that is what he expected her to do. In the end, he thought the subtlety of the whole argument was probably lost on the jury. He did begin to understand the reasoning behind Ronald's slow build up toward establishing Lidocaine as the toxic agent that caused the death of Linda Murphy. Without any clear point to argue, Walter was left jousting with windmills, and the subtle arguments would be forgotten when the toxicologist finally told the jury what had caused the death of the four-year-old. Still, Francine's testimony ground on until finally Walter finished and Ronald, mercifully, had no further questions. Francine was dismissed and was possibly the happiest person in the courtroom at that point. She looked like she wanted to hug everyone in sight.

Lunch followed and Walter inquired again about the unusual events of the previous evening.

"Tell me again what time it happened," said Walter.

"Seven thirty."

"Why were you so late getting to my office?"

Joe thought Walter was trying to remove some of his guilt about asking Joe to come to his office and then not being there, while instead there was someone with a gun waiting. Joe was having trouble believing it had happened at all after the relatively mundane proceedings in the courtroom that morning and couldn't understand why Walter would feel guilty about the shooting—not keeping an appointment, maybe—but he had nothing to do with the shooting.

After lunch Ronald called his pathologist. Dr. Richard Michaels was questioned regarding his credentials, which were exemplary with no blemish apparent. His reason for being familiar with the case: he had been asked by the family to do a second examination because of their concern about the nature of Linda's death. Walter explained that *It* was not called an "autopsy" in order to avoid suggesting an unpleasant image to the jury, and Linda was referred to by name in order to "personalize" her to the jury.

"Did you know Dr. Dobbs, the pathologist who performed the first examination?" Ronald asked.

"Yes, I knew him."

"Did you have an opportunity, Dr. Michaels, to compare your findings to those of Dr. Dobbs?"

"No, I didn't. Unfortunately, Dr. Dobbs died of a heart attack only a few weeks after Linda's death."

Joe knew Frank Dobbs had died because he was the hospital pathologist, and they had known each other quite well. As a matter of fact, Frank Dobbs had died on the night of his own retirement party. He had had a bit too much to drink that evening, Joe remembered, and when it seemed that he would be unsafe to be behind the wheel of a car, or in the presence of any of the ladies at the party that night, the CEO had driven him home. He was discovered dead in his home the next day, and a heart attack was the presumed cause. There was no reason to question this.

Frank Dobbs had an extensive cardiac history as well as what many believed was a serious problem with alcohol, and it appeared that he had continued to drink after being dropped off at his home. Unlike Linda Murphy, the circumstances surrounding the pathologist's death were sufficiently clear that no one thought an autopsy was necessary. None of this was mentioned, or would be mentioned, Joe hoped, for the jury's consideration.

The questioning continued slowly in the classic trial testimony tableau. Each question was well constructed and leading from the preceding question; each answer was known in advance by Ronald and his witness. The jury might be surprised at some point, but it would likely be a "planned" surprise. All of the details were painstakingly presented, but Joe did have a few surprises as the questioning progressed.

Linda Murphy had not been his patient. She had a pediatrician in Lexington, Kentucky, the "medical center" for that region of Appalachia, as was often the case with the wealthier members of this community. He had known that she was thin, recalling this from the day she was rushed to the ED, and he had used her weight to calculate the doses of medication given to her. He was a little surprised when Dr. Michaels mentioned it again. At four years old she should have weighed forty pounds, but had, in fact, weighed only twenty-eight pounds. This was well below the standard and should have been investigated by her pediatrician. Her parents had not mentioned any such concern that day, but they were obviously upset. Joe had looked at the parents and noted that while Linda's father was rather obese, her mother was quite thin. He wondered briefly, but only briefly, whether there might be some familial problem.

Ronald made a point of telling the court that Dr. Michaels would not discuss the toxicology report, partly, Joe thought, to build anticipation for the revelations of the toxicologist. Walter's plan for a recess might throw Ronald off his plan. Joe knew that the Lidocaine blood level was very high—more than three times the toxic level—but the jury would have to wait for this information.

Dr. Michaels discussed the evidence of the attempts that were made to draw blood and to place an intravenous line, none of which had been successful. He frowned when Ronald queried about the pain Linda must have experienced. He replied that those procedures were painful perhaps, but he stated without reservation that they were necessary. He saw no reason to question them at all.

Ronald seemed both a little surprised and disappointed with the doctor's response and his volunteered opinion, but he proceeded to discuss the other external findings, which were all minor: a few blemishes on the trunk and a bruise on the knee. Nothing unusual, the pathologist asserted, but it established the completeness and thoroughness of the exam and would add credibility to the findings presented later. The heart would be the remarkable finding.

Joe had seen the report prepared by Frank Dobbs, so he knew this already, but he was interested in what Dr. Michaels would say. The heart disease was the reason Linda Murphy was critically ill and why she was brought to the hospital and given Lidocaine in the first place, even if the cause of death was Lidocaine. She'd had a cardiac arrest, ventricular tachycardia, and Joe had given the appropriate dose of Lidocaine. Linda had responded to this, her heart had returned to a normal rhythm, but then a second cardiac arrest had occurred while Joe was out of the room arranging the transfer.

Walter had not asked Joe to review the second pathologist's findings, saying they were the same as Frank Dobbs' and that the Lidocaine was the important finding anyway. Joe had thought this was a bit unusual but had been assured that that was true. Ronald had introduced the second pathologist into the trial proceedings only a week earlier, possibly to put Walter off his game. Two could play at courtroom drama, and Walter had actually asked for a postponement, but his request was denied. Even so, Joe was particularly interested in Dr. Michaels' testimony.

The testimony proceeded even more slowly, and Joe wondered if sleep was creeping up on the jury. The jurors, however, seemed intently interested in what was being said. Many physicians were of the opinion that juries were made up of "ignorant high school dropouts," but Joe thought these particular jurors were intelligent and interested in what was being said for the sake of knowledge as much as the relevance to the trial. Joe usually found people to be interested in medicine if it was presented in a way they could understand.

The questioning began to center on the internal organs: the heart was enlarged, more than fifty percent above what would be expected, and the walls were thin. Microscopic examination showed inflammation.

"Do you have an opinion, Dr. Michaels, regarding the significance of these findings?" Ronald asked.

"Yes, I do."

"And what is that opinion?"

"An inflammatory cardiomyopathy: a heart muscle disease usually caused by a virus." Dr. Michaels was clearly excited about this discussion and was getting ahead of Ronald.

"Do you have an opinion as to what caused the cardiomyopathy?" asked Ronald.

"No, I really don't." Dr. Michaels then discussed the several viruses that might have caused it and the lack of viral studies done at the time of the original autopsy. "It's unfortunate, but not important," the doctor said. Joe thought he was reluctant to unnecessarily criticize his late colleague, Dr. Dobbs, and, in the end, the cause of the cardiomyopathy was probably not important.

"Were there any other findings of importance?" asked Ronald.

"No," replied the pathologist. "The family had refused to have an examination of the brain, and the other organs were unremarkable.

"There was the intercardiac injection, of course," he said in passing, "but that was unremarkable as well." Joe was instantly alert, and his surprise must have been obvious on his face as he digested this revelation. No one had given an intercardiac injection, and he was sure it hadn't been noted on the report Frank Dobbs prepared.

Dr. Michaels continued without waiting for Ronald's question, and Ronald looked annoyed. "The track of the needle was subxyphoid, below the rib cage and through the heart wall into the left ventricle, directly into the heart. It was a typical finding for such an injection with no significant damage to the heart or any other structure."

"Thank you, Dr. Michaels," said Ronald. "Your witness," he said to Walter.

Joe tried to get Walter's attention, but the judge beat him to it with his gavel. "How long will your questioning take, counselor?" he asked Walter.

"I think it may be rather lengthy, Your Honor," replied Walter. "Two or maybe three hours."

"It is already three thirty, so maybe we should continue tomorrow, gentlemen," Judge Stevens said.

"I was prepared to ask for a recess until Monday to allow a witness the defense plans to call to be present for the testimony of the plaintiff's toxicologist," said Walter.

It sounded pretty thin, and Ronald was not about to be put off stride that easily. "Your Honor," he exclaimed, "I see no reason to delay this and waste all our valuable time." He looked at the jury, not at the judge, when he said that.

The judge looked around the courtroom and finally at Walter. "Your witness will be available on Monday, counselor?" he asked. It was clear that Ronald had lost.

"Of course, Your Honor," replied Walter.

Ronald looked as if he were about to speak, but the judge brought down his gavel first and said, "Adjourn until Monday then. Have a good weekend." This time the bailiff must have known how it was going to play out because he was already standing, asking everyone to rise for the disappearing judge … on his way to a long weekend at the lake.

Chapter 21

Ronald shrugged amiably in defeat, and Walter began sorting papers while the jury filed out. Joe was immediately at Walter's side, speaking far too loudly. "Walter," he said, "there was no intercardiac injection given." Ronald was clearly trying to hear without being obvious about it, while Linda's family stood next to him, paying no attention.

"Just one of the IVs or blood drawing attempts, is that right?" asked Walter.

"No," said Joe, becoming a little agitated and attracting attention as a result. "It's entirely different."

"Well, it wasn't important anyway," offered Walter. "At least that's what their pathologist said. We should talk about this later, I think." He glanced at Ronald and at Linda's family. The parents seemed oblivious to their surroundings, but Ronald and Gloria were paying close attention.

"It *is* important, Walter. Medication is given that way. Lidocaine is given that way, and no one did any intercardiac injection during that code. There wouldn't have been any reason to give anything that way since there was a functioning interosseous line. This doesn't make sense, Walter."

Everyone was staring at Joe, and Walter was getting nervous. "We should talk about this later—and in private, Joe. I have to attend to some important business right now, but call me later this evening. You won't be busy this evening, will you?"

Joe wasn't sure what this question meant or what "important business" Walter could have right then because he had no way of anticipating an early adjournment of the trial. Maybe it was all a performance for the "audience." Ronald and Gloria were watching his performance closely.

"I have office hours this evening. Seven to nine or so," said Joe. "I'll call you after that, but we have to talk about this, Walter. It's very important."

"Speak a little more quietly, Joe," admonished Walter.

Joe whispered so that only Walter could hear, "Walter, someone else gave medication during that code!"

"Be serious, Joe," said Walter. "No one saw anyone else give anything, and no one will believe you if you try to maintain that someone else did give anything. We can talk about this later. Call me tonight and don't … well, don't repeat any of this nonsense to anyone else for God's sake."

Walter scowled, and Ronald and Gloria looked away, pretending they had heard nothing at all. Joe looked around and noticed two more scowling faces, ones he hadn't expected to see here: Sergeants Pierce and Moore were waiting for him.

As soon as they made eye contact, they started walking toward him. At first Joe thought there might be some new information they wanted to tell him or a few more questions they needed answered, but the presence of both of them and their obviously stern demeanor made that seem unlikely.

"Can we ask you to come down to the station with us, Doctor?" said Sergeant Pierce. It didn't sound like a question, so Joe simply agreed. He was eager to get away from the "audience."

Sergeant Pierce seemed to sense this discomfort and spoke again. "It is in regard to the *supposed* incident that you reported last night. We are not sure you reported it accurately, Doctor."

He was trying to embarrass Joe, that was clear, and Sergeant Moore seemed embarrassed by her partner's behavior. "Why don't we continue this conversation at the station?" she said.

Her partner ignored her. "Some facts have come to our attention that cast doubt on your account, Doctor, and we do need to establish the reason for this discrepancy."

"At the station, Peter." Natalie was getting annoyed too. Peter smiled and nodded. The three of them proceeded toward the exit. Once away from the "audience," the conversation ceased as well. They rode to the station in the police car, two sergeants in front and Joe in the back with the barrier between them.

At the station Joe was placed in the same glass-surrounded office to wait while people milled about outside. Finally, the two sergeants came in, this time with the officer he had noticed talking to Pierce last night. It was obvious that this man was going to be the primary speaker today. Also obvious was the fact that he was the superior of both sergeants. He looked vaguely familiar to Joe, but not in any way he could place.

"Dr. Nelson," he said. "I am Captain Wilson, and I need to discuss the incident that occurred last night." He did not look friendly. "Can you tell me what happened?"

Joe patiently went through the same story again, giving the same answers to the same questions. Finally, the captain stood and walked over to him. "There are some problems with your account, Dr. Nelson, starting with the fact that we did find the bullet in your car. It was buried in the floor of the passenger's front seat. Does that surprise you at all?"

Joe thought for a moment and, while he was interested that they had found the bullet, where they found it didn't seem important. He did think it was important that finding the bullet should corroborate his account. "No," was all he said.

"We found the gun that fired that bullet as well," said the captain.

This did interest Joe. "Really?" he said.

"Yes," said the captain. After a pause he added, "It was your gun, Doctor."

"My gun?" Joe stammered. "I don't have a gun."

"This gun is registered to you, Doctor," said the captain, showing it to Joe. He recognized it as the one Carolyn had at her house.

"That's my wife's gun," he answered.

"Registered to you," the captain insisted.

"Well, yes. But it belongs to my wife. Where did you get that?" Joe asked.

"From a desk drawer in your home, Doctor," the captain smiled. "And the only fingerprints on it are those of your wife ... and you." He paused though Joe could not imagine what he was waiting for.

When he began to speak again, his sternness had turned to belligerence. "It looks to me as if someone tried to make it look as if there was a break-in there last night." Joe looked about the room. Pierce looked smug and Moore looked uncomfortable, but not as uncomfortable as Joe felt.

"Carolyn's house was broken into last night?" he asked. "Is she all right?"

"You haven't spoken to her today then?" said the captain. "Yes, she's fine. Let me not belabor this any further, Doctor. We do not believe there was a break-in at your house. We believe someone just wanted us to think there was. We think further that no one shot at you last night either. We think you shot at your own car with your own gun and then tried to make us believe that someone had shot at you." He paused while Joe sat, bewildered. Finally, the captain continued. "I would ask you why you did this except I don't really give a shit. I don't care what made you want to waste our time because I'm not going to allow you to waste any more of it. You've got no credibility here or anywhere else anymore, and I will make sure they know that at that trial of yours too. Now, you take your gun and you take your car and get out of here before I decide to charge your ass with some serious crimes. Do you understand?"

Joe just nodded, but the captain had left the room without waiting for his reply.

"I'll put him in his car, Peter," said Sergeant Moore.

"I don't mind doing it, Nat," replied a smiling Peter Pierce.

"I want to," his partner replied. "Get up and get going, Dr. Nelson." Joe got up and left the room.

Chapter 22

Sergeant Moore picked up the keys to his car and they walked to the garage in silence. There was a special section set aside for impounded vehicles and Joe had to sign for his car before he could take it. Natalie stayed with him, silently, throughout the process and he vaguely wondered why, but his head was spinning too much to give it much thought.

They walked together to his car and she stood facing the door they had come through into the garage. They were beyond being overheard by anyone unless they were yelling, which she was. "Now listen to me, Dr. Nelson, and listen very closely. Get in your car and get out of here and consider yourself lucky to get off with as little trouble as you're in right now." She faced him, and pointed at his car door. Her voice was suddenly much softer as she said, "I have to talk to you about what's going on here, and I don't think I can do that here at the station. Please meet me in fifteen minutes on that street where the shooting took place."

Joe hesitated a moment and then he turned back to face her, looking quickly at the door they had entered through. "You damned stupid police. You think you know everything, don't you?" he yelled. He grabbed the keys from her and turned to open his car door. If he was surprised by what she had said, it lasted only a second. When he was facing away from the garage entrance, he said softly, "Fifteen minutes may not be long enough for you to easily leave. Why don't I drive around a bit and show up there in thirty minutes?"

Joe "fumbled" with his keys. From Natalie's viewpoint it was clearly just a show, but from any distance it did probably look like he was frustrated and fumbling. She had to smile at his acting, but quickly scowled, putting her hands on her hips and hoping that her attitude looked more convincing than Joe's did. "You may be right," she said softly. "I don't think you'll be followed, but if you are, it will be Peter and I can keep him here long enough for you to get clear. Don't go to your house or your apartment, though, since he knows both of those addresses." She pointed at his car and yelled, "Get the hell out of here. Now!"

Joe opened his car door and yelled back, "With pleasure!" As he got in, he said softly, "Thirty minutes and I'll wait in case you have trouble getting away. And I didn't mean any of those things I said about 'stupid police,' you know." He didn't look at her, just slammed the door.

Natalie turned sideways so her venomous expression could be seen from the doorway to the garage. As Joe drove away, she was thinking that this pediatrician was pretty cool considering what he had been through that day: a malpractice case that looked like it was going badly—at least she had witnessed that heated discussion with his attorney at the court house—and then being dragged down to the station to be berated by her captain. He had carried off this scene in the garage pretty well, she thought, and had still taken the time and thought necessary to apologize to her about calling her "stupid police." Maybe it was Carolyn Prentiss-Nelson that was making the mistake, not her husband.

Natalie walked back toward the entrance to the garage and noticed that the door was slightly ajar. When she reached it, Peter opened it for her.

"All right, I made a mistake, Peter. Let's just leave it at that. I don't want to talk about it." She knew that this last comment would ensure that she did talk about it, or at least would have to listen to Peter talk about it.

Peter looked after Joe's disappearing car and appeared to come to a decision. "Well, that's what comes from chasing the losers instead of the winners like me," he said.

She had to listen to him, but she didn't have to hear him. He was so intensely interested in what he was saying that he hardly noticed what she was doing, including the call she made to Walter about his whereabouts the night before. Walter was surprised and blurted out an alibi that he probably wouldn't have shared if he had thought about it, but it was an alibi and she could check it out later. Natalie finished her computer inputs and listened to Peter for as long as she could stand it, and then she said she was filing the paperwork and going home. Like most police departments, the "paperwork" was largely "computer work."

She went by the captain's office to tell him as well. "Andy," she said, "I'm going home, or at least I'm not staying here."

"Can't blame you, Nat," he replied. "You really misjudged that guy you know."

"Yeah," she said and left, trying to look chastised as she was sure she was supposed to be. She was sure there was something going on in her department and that both Peter Pierce and Andy Wilson were part of it. She had to find out what it was for her own sake if not that pediatrician's. If she could find out what was happening to him, she would find out what was going on in the department, and maybe she could help him too, but that would be a bonus.

Peter and Andy were watching Natalie as she left and while neither spoke to the other, they both had the same thought: Natalie Moore was one hot woman and they both were thinking they were going to try to take advantage of her recent disappointment with that pediatrician to get her into their beds. Natalie wouldn't have been surprised if she had known what those two lecherous slugs were thinking and would have laughed at them if she did know. She had never been that desperate in her entire life.

Chapter 23

While Natalie was putting up with Peter and Andy, Joe was driving around trying to decide what to do. He was not sure he wasn't being followed, as Natalie had suggested, and took several circles around different blocks to see if any cars behind him looked familiar. There was a black one that he thought he had seen before, but then there was a dark blue one that looked familiar as well. That was the trouble, he thought: too many black and dark blue cars on the city's streets and they all looked the same. He finally decided that if he were being followed, which he probably wasn't, it was being done by someone more experienced than he and that his efforts at detection were useless.

He then decided that he would stop and call Carolyn and make sure she was all right. He also thought he might need a cover story for showing up at the "scene of the crime" as well, so he stopped and went into a liquor store. He bought a bottle of cheap wine and a bottle of ginger ale that was the same size, asking that both be placed in separate brown paper bags. He had acquired a taste for ginger ale lately.

While in the store he called the ED and got Stacy. "Is Carolyn there?" he asked.

"Yeah," said Stacy, "but she's with a guy who's having a heart attack, trying to save his life or something. You want me to run right in there and demand that she come to the phone to talk to you instead?" The sarcasm was so thick it practically dripped out of Joe's cell phone.

"No," he said. "Just wanted to make sure she's all right."

"Oh, you mean about the break-in over at your house?" replied Stacy. "Yeah, she's fine. Just pissed at some cop or something. I got to go Joe, but I'll tell her you called, okay?" Stacy was hanging up as Joe said it was fine. Carolyn had obviously been telling everyone about her adventures and was also obviously perfectly fine.

He went out and got back into his car and drove to the street outside Walter's office. The space where he had parked the night before was available so he took it because he thought maybe the position of his car might be important. Once there, he poured out the wine and then poured the ginger ale into the wine bottle. If he were noticed by anyone, like Peter for instance, he thought he could pretend he was getting drunk.

He sat and thought about it all, trying to make some sense of it. Mostly he tried to figure out why Natalie had told him to meet her there and why she thought they needed to be so secretive about it and whether he was being foolish to follow blindly along. When he looked at his watch, she was ten minutes late and he was wondering if he had been really foolish. He looked at the passenger's floor for the first time and saw the area cleared of carpet and the hole from which a bullet must have been removed. Less than twenty-four hours ago he had almost died on this very spot. Another five minutes later he began to think that she had thought better of it all and had just gone home. In another minute, though, she pulled in behind him and he got out of his car, holding the bottle in the bag.

Natalie got out of her car, a Japanese model like Joe's, only not quite as old as his and lacking a bullet hole in the window of her driver's door. "Is that a bottle in there, Dr. Nelson?" She looked distressed.

"Just a wine bottle with ginger ale in it." He took it out of the bag and held it up for her to see. "Kind of a cover, in case it wasn't you that showed up." He was embarrassed. "You know, 'the poor doc getting drunk at the scene of his crime.' It was as good an explanation as I could think of, quickly." He smiled a little.

Natalie had not expected him to think of any "cover" and she thought this was a pretty good one. "Not too bad," she said, "considering that you didn't have much time to think of a better one. Is this where you were parked last night?" she asked.

"Yes."

She walked around, looking up at the building as she did. "This is where you were when the shot was fired, right?"

"Yes," said Joe, noting mentally that she was assuming that the shot was fired there, not somewhere else to make it look like he had been shot at as her captain had alleged.

She turned to look at Joe and asked, "Those two windows at the end. Are they your lawyer's office windows?"

"Yeah," said Joe. "Why?"

She didn't answer but instead asked, "So did you park here today by chance or by plan?"

"Well," he said, "I sort of thought the position of the car might be important. Maybe that was why you wanted to come back here, you know, with the car and all that." He was feeling a little embarrassed again as he looked at her and as she looked back at him with a very serious face.

"Then you will probably be able to figure out why I think your lawyer's office is up there." She pointed to the windows.

Joe smiled at this and walked over to his car. He looked into the window where the bullet had left its hole and then looked back at Natalie. He moved so that he could look through the hole in the window and see the hole in the floor. He turned to follow the line of sight and was looking directly at Walter's second floor office window. He looked at Natalie and smiled, saying, "You think Walter shot at me?"

"You know anyone else in this building?" she replied. Joe had the feeling she was not telling him everything she knew at this point, but that was okay … for the moment anyway.

108

"I'm not sure Walter is capable of that strong an emotion, but ..." He frowned. "So you think whoever shot at me did so from Walter's office?" He was puzzled and looked at her. "But how did he know I would park here?"

"Just lucky, maybe. Planned to come down if you parked somewhere else or shoot you when you went up to the office, but realized it would be easier to get you in the car?" She shrugged. "Maybe he figured you would try the buzzer and he could let you in and shoot you there, but when you parked so conveniently he decided this was an easier way." Joe was impressed that she guessed he had tried the buzzer and would probably have gone up to Walter's office if he had been buzzed in. He also wondered a little why he hadn't been buzzed in and shot up there.

Natalie looked at the opposite side of the street where several spaces were "saved" with chairs or orange cones placed in them. "Maybe he 'saved' it for you and moved the cone when he saw you coming."

"Well, some people know I'm proud of my ability to parallel park in tight spaces." He smiled at this and shrugged. "But do you really think he could have seen me coming and moved the cone without me seeing him?"

"It was a joke, Dr. Nelson," said Natalie. "And don't assume it was a 'he' either. Never underestimate the women in your life." She smiled at him and said, "You look like you need a cup of coffee. Come on and I'll buy."

Joe looked at her and said, "I usually only have one cup of coffee in the morning, but I guess I can have another one today. I'll follow you, okay?"

She got into her car and said, "Even 'stupid police' know where to get good coffee."

Chapter 24

They arrived at a coffee shop, not one of the chain places, but just a shop selling sandwiches and coffee and some soda. A sign on the counter announced that the grill was closed. They sat at one of the tables with coffee in front of Natalie and ... "What is that you're drinking, Dr. Nelson?"

"Hot chocolate," Joe replied.

Natalie put both hands over her eyes and shook her head, saying, "I can't believe I'm sitting here with a pediatrician who's drinking hot chocolate. We're going to have to do better than this." Joe just shrugged and looked embarrassed.

She put her hands down on the table and said, "So what the hell do you think is going on, Dr. Nelson?"

"Well," said Joe. "I have lived my life by two rules ... always. The second rule is that anyone who swears at me has to use my first name, so please call me Joe. And I have no idea why anyone would shoot at me. I mean, could this have been an accident? Someone in Walter's office cleaning a gun and 'Oops, did that just go off?' I'm a pediatrician, but I don't think I have a single patient who would believe that one."

Natalie had to chuckle at this, "No, I don't see how this is anything but what it looks like." She turned serious and added, "Someone tried to kill you, Joe."

Joe just nodded and took a sip of hot chocolate.

"So who wants to kill you?" she asked. "Pretty simple question, really."

"No one that I know of," Joe said.

After a minute and a sip of coffee, Natalie said, "Well let's eliminate the obvious players, shall we? Your wife, for instance. The gun was in her house. She could've gone home, got the gun, shot at you, and gotten back to the house and faked a break-in. Is this divorce all that 'amicable'?"

Joe must have looked shocked because Natalie added, "Unless you know who it was, we have to consider everyone."

Joe slowly nodded and pulled out his cell phone and dialed a number. In a minute he said, "Hi Stacy. Me again and I got a question for you."

He put the phone on speaker in time for Natalie to hear "... still with that heart attack, Joe. I'll tell her. I promise."

"Different question, Stacy, and I'm serious. Carolyn was working yesterday three to eleven, right? Did she leave the ED at all last night? I mean for even a short time for anything?"

"We were out straight last night, Joe. No one left, even to go to the bathroom. What are you talking about?"

"Not important, Stacy," Joe said. "Yeah, tell her I called, but nothing important." And he hung up.

Natalie shrugged and Joe just shook his head. "Divorce can be messy, but ours isn't. But it's better to make sure, I guess." Natalie had expected him to tell her that she was wrong or to get angry or something, but to just call and check an alibi ... not what she thought he would do.

He looked up at her and said, "You know, Sergeant Moore, it was Walter's office and he knew I would be coming there, so isn't he near the top of the list?"

"I thought so too, so I checked him out, while I was pretending to give a damn what Peter thought my problem was.

"Your attorney said he was in a bar on Somerset Street with a client. It's a place where gentleman can go to find companionship, and I don't think he would have told me that, particularly over the phone and particularly since he is an attorney, if it weren't true and if he weren't scared I was going to arrest him and cut his balls off. I will check it out though."

"No, he wouldn't have admitted anything unless he was scared," said Joe. "I think Walter is fairly fond of his balls."

Natalie smiled again, but she was discouraged by the lack of an easy answer. Usually the suspects were fairly obvious, but she was also impressed with how cool this hot-chocolate-drinking pediatrician was processing all this. "What about the malpractice case?" she asked. "Anyone there who would hope for a 'quick' settlement instead of a courtroom verdict? Are you winning there and someone wants to make you pay?"

"Well, since we are being brutally honest, Sergeant Moore, I am losing there and 'they' have me by the 'balls.' If they've waited this long, why take out the defendant when, in a couple days, he'll be found guilty and hung out to dry."

"Look, Joe," said Natalie. "If I have to call you 'Joe,' you have to call me 'Natalie,' okay? What was that argument about with your attorney that Peter and I interrupted? Anything there that would help point toward someone?"

"I don't see how," Joe said, "Natalie," he added, smiling across the table at her. "It was a crazy thing anyway and I'm not sure what it means, but almost the last thing this witness said was that there was an intercardiac injection, which he didn't think was significant. I was trying to tell Walter that it had to be significant."

"Okay, Joe," said Natalie. "I've got an idea. Why don't you be the 'doctor' and I'll be the 'layperson' for this one, okay? What the hell are you talking about?"

"Oh, sorry," said Joe. "Michaels, the pathologist who was testifying, said that my patient had an intercardiac injection. That never happened. It's an injection right under the ribs," he indicated the spot on himself, "and goes right into the heart. It never happened to my patient so either this pathologist was mistaken or ... well, I don't know what else, but I don't see how it could have been the reason I was shot at. I didn't even know about it until the end of the court session today."

"So maybe the pathologist made a mistake or something?"

"Not this guy. He's good and compulsive too. It's not something that anyone would mistake for something else anyway. It's a needle going right into the heart." Joe shook his head.

"Maybe someone else did it while you weren't there, you know, with your patient, I mean. Possible, don't you think?" Natalie offered.

Joe shook his head again. "The whole cardiac arrest lasted less than an hour and I was there for almost all of it. There wouldn't have been any reason to do it anyway. We had a good line to give meds through and besides, no one even does that kind of injection anymore. Twenty years ago it was common but now … no one does it."

Joe shook his head in puzzlement. "Besides, I have the original autopsy and Dobbs never mentioned it."

Natalie looked puzzled and Joe said, "Michaels was the guy today and he did the second autopsy at the family's request. Dobbs did the first one at our hospital."

"So maybe someone stuck a needle into your patient between the two autopsies?" Natalie asked.

"No," said Joe, shaking his head. "The path guys can tell a postmortem injection: an injection that happened after she was dead. It had to have been there at the time of the first autopsy."

"Yeah," said Natalie. "I've seen that on TV." Joe looked at her and she said, "Well, I watch TV, ya know."

Joe shook his head again. "Anyway, I can't figure how it has anything to do with the shooting. It just happened today, I mean, and I was shot at last night."

Joe was quiet, thinking, and Natalie just waited for him. He finally looked at her and asked, "So you think someone in your department is after me too. Not the shooter, I mean. That would be over the top, but is there anything besides your obnoxious partner that makes you think that?"

"Do you need anything more than Peter to make you think that?" She glared at him. "It's just that feeling that these guys are playing this. I mean, Peter called you a liar that first night for no reason. And then he stays late to get the ballistics report rush, rush. I've only been there six months, but he hasn't done any extra work since I've known him and now all of a sudden he stays late. And the gun, for Christ's sake. He practically asked your wife if she had one, like he knew she did, and for no reason at all, he takes it with him—the only thing he takes, and he gets it fingerprinted before he even gets the ballistics report. And he doesn't get any fingerprints at a break-in. Like he already knew we weren't going to find anything, or he didn't want to find any." Natalie sighed and went on, "This department is dishonest and corrupt and I ... well, I was planning to put in my time and leave, but the whole damned thing is just more than I can stand. Look Joe, I've always been a pain in the butt on this stuff, a 'maverick' I guess they call it. You might be better off not knowing me, so if you want to go it on your own that's cool, but I have to find out what's going on in my department."

"'Something is rotten in the state of Denmark,' right? I'll stay with Natalie for a while longer before I go it alone if that's okay."

Natalie smiled. *Yeah, that would be okay with me,* she thought. "Shakespeare, *Hamlet,* right? Marcellus says it, actually. That thing about something rotten in Denmark? Didn't think a cop would know that one, did you?"

"Most cops, no, but Natalie never ceases to amaze me."

They sat in silent thought for a few minutes and finally Natalie said, "I need another cup of coffee; what about you?"

"Yeah," said Joe. "Maybe I'll try real coffee this time."

Chapter 25

When she returned with the coffee, Joe hadn't moved. "Makes no sense to me," he said. "Thanks for the coffee. I have another hour before I start my office hours. You want something to eat?"

"Yeah, maybe that will help. Shall we get a sandwich here?"

"What's good?" Joe asked.

"Nothing," answered Natalie. She turned to the man seated at the register and said, "Hey, John, what's good tonight?"

"Tuna's fresh," he shrugged.

Natalie looked at Joe, who nodded. "Two, John. With chips, and could you bring them to the table, please?"

John looked as if this was an enormous inconvenience, but he got up to perform the arduous task as Natalie turned back to her companion. "So, I've got another question, Joe. You're pretty cool with all this. I mean, you're getting divorced. You have a malpractice case going on, and someone is shooting at you, and you're still going to run office hours tonight. Doesn't anything upset you? I mean, I was in the army, in Afghanistan, and you make me look like a wussy. What have you been through that's made it impossible to scare you?"

Joe blushed and said, "I don't think I could ever make you look like a wussy, Natalie … or do you prefer 'Nat' or something?"

"Hate being called 'Nat.' But how did you get the 'nerves of steel'? Military?" she persisted.

"They wouldn't let me into that club, Natalie." He smiled, and when she smiled back, he went on, "When I was young, I worked in the coal mines and well … one day there was a roof fall, and they had to cut my leg off to get me out." He reached down and pulled up his pant leg, exposing the prosthesis.

"Shit," said Natalie. "How old were you?"

"Twenty."

"Shit," she said again.

"Not so bad," he said. "I got to go to medical school because the mines wouldn't take me back and the army didn't want me." After a minute he added, "And I learned not to get scared of things that don't matter."

"You don't think getting shot at matters?"

Joe sighed and said, "When I was down there with my leg caught under that rock, my father came down to help. He looked around and knew there was no choice and then he said to me, 'Ya gotta fight back. Better to be shot running than standing still.' So they cut my foot off down there with a little whiff of morphine for the pain, and I've never stopped fighting back, never stopped running since. I'm not about to stop now."

The tuna arrived and they ate. It was fresh but not very good. Joe drank his coffee and liked it, or at least he liked the company. Finally he asked, "So, you were in Afghanistan?"

She shook her head. She never talked to anyone about Afghanistan. People who had not "been there" couldn't understand, but this guy had been trapped in a coal mine and had his foot cut from him and she liked him so ... "At first it was okay. Doing a job that needed to be done and I loved the camaraderie. Then one day ... well, we were driving back to base and got ambushed. One dead and us holed up, waiting for the guys from the base to come chase the bad guys away. Only five or ten minutes away, so we just hunkered down and waited."

She sighed again and finally continued. "Well, when the guys from the base arrived, they mistook us for the enemy since the Taliban had already cut out. We lost two more to the friendly fire. The worst of it was that when I went to see what was going to happen with it, they were still 'investigating.' It was a year and a half before it was finally released at all. Maybe nothing should've been done. It was just a mistake, but ..." She shook her head. "It was like it had never happened at all."

Joe said nothing. There was nothing to be said. Natalie sighed again and shrugged, "One day I *will* get over it, but ... but I don't think it'll be today."

They sat quietly until Joe's cell phone rang, bringing them both back to the moment. "Hello," said Joe. He had not yet learned to look at the phone to tell who was calling.

"Hi, Joe," said Carolyn. "Stacy said you called about something and acted very weird. She thought I should call to make sure you were all right. So ... are you all right?"

"Well, I was just checking to make sure you were all right. With the break-in, I mean," he replied.

"How'd you hear about that so quickly? Did Stacy tell you?"

"No," said Joe. "Two police sergeants told me."

"Oh right," said Carolyn. "I keep forgetting it's your house too. I'm fine. Are the two sergeants Peter the jerk and Natalie? I think Natalie is a good cop and kind of cute too if she would do something about her hair."

Natalie could only hear Joe's side of the conversation. She reached over now and said, "Is that your wife? Let me talk to her. I want to ask her a question."

"Who's that with you, Joe?" asked Carolyn.

"It's Natalie 'the good cop' and she wants to ask you a question."

He handed the phone to Natalie in time for her to hear Carolyn say, "I hope she didn't hear me say she's cute."

"Um ... no, I didn't hear you say that, Dr. Prentiss. I just had a question for you. About the gun," said Natalie.

"I didn't mean anything about your hair, Sergeant Moore. It's just that I think it would look better if you let your bangs grow out. That's all. What about that stupid gun?" asked Carolyn.

Natalie instinctively reached for her bangs and then looked at Joe. She realized that Joe had heard Carolyn's comment about her being "cute," which caused her some embarrassment. "I just wanted to ask you, when was the last time you saw that gun?"

"Oh," said Carolyn, thinking now. "Probably a couple of months ago, maybe. I don't use it at all. Are you and Joe at the station or something?"

"No," said Natalie. "We're at a coffee shop having bad tuna sandwiches. Why do you have it if you don't use it? And why is it registered in Joe's name?" Natalie might have been more discreet about where she and Joe were if she hadn't been worried about the gun that had been used to shoot at Joe—not to mention her hair.

Carolyn was paying attention though. "At a shop having sandwiches? I'm going to have to watch more TV to keep up with the current police procedures. Anyway, there were a couple of break-ins in the parking lot here at the hospital, and I thought I should have some protection. Joe has had permits in the past, hunting or something, so I got him to get the permit. But then when I was telling everyone at work that I would have a gun, the security guys told me I couldn't bring it into the ED. I mean, what good is a gun in your glove compartment when the muggers are chasing you around the parking lot?"

"We're just discussing the case … away from the station," replied Natalie. She wasn't sure why she felt uncomfortable about this. "Who knew you had the gun?"

"Everyone," Carolyn said. "I was so angry at security that I told everyone and even showed people a couple of times when we had a party at the house."

"So everyone knew where it was?"

"Yeah," said Carolyn. "It was no big deal. I mean, it wasn't stolen and nothing else was either as far as I can tell. What's the problem, Sergeant Moore?"

"Well," said Natalie, "it was the gun that was used to shoot at Joe last night."

"What!? What are you talking about?" asked Carolyn. "The gun was in my desk last night. Joe was shot at? What's going on?"

Natalie looked at Joe and, with her hand over the phone, said, "I guess you haven't told her about last night yet." Joe just shrugged and shook his head.

Natalie took her hand off the phone and said, "I thought Joe would've told you, Dr. Prentiss. He was shot at last night outside his attorney's office and the ballistics indicate that it was his ... I mean your gun that was used to fire the shot."

"You're joking!" said Carolyn. "Someone shot at Joe? With my gun? I mean, how could that be? It was in the desk drawer. You took it yourself last night. He's a pediatrician, for crying out loud. No one shoots at pediatricians."

Natalie thought of asking what kind of doctors people did shoot at but instead said, "The shot was probably fired earlier in the evening, before you got home. The way we're figuring it, someone broke in and took your gun, shot at Joe, and was able to get it back into the desk before you got home. Someone who probably didn't have a key to your house since they broke in."

Carolyn was quiet for a minute. "So that's how you and Sergeant Pierce figure it. That someone stole my gun to shoot at Joe and then returned it before I got home?"

Natalie waited and weighed her words. "The 'we' here is Joe and I, not Sergeant Pierce."

"Not Sergeant Pierce? What's going on, Sergeant Moore?"

"I don't know," said Natalie. "I do know that I don't trust Sergeant Pierce though, and I do trust your husband, and I think I trust you. Someone got your gun. I think it may have been last night, but possibly earlier, and then they shot at Joe from his lawyer's office window. Then they got that gun back into your desk drawer before you got home last night at what, one o'clock you said? Is that right?"

"Yeah," said Carolyn. "One o'clock. You don't trust Sergeant Pierce? He's obnoxious, I agree, but he's a police officer. Why don't you trust him, Sergeant Moore?"

"I think I'd like to talk to you in person, Dr. Prentiss. I can tell you more later, when we have more time and fewer people who might overhear," said Natalie, looking around the coffee shop. "I don't think you're in any danger or anything, but … be careful, Dr. Prentiss, okay?"

There was silence until Carolyn answered. "Okay, I think I trust you too. But I would trust you more if you called me Carolyn."

"What time do you get off, Carolyn?"

"Midnight or one o'clock again tonight, Natalie."

"Then why don't we meet you then, and we can talk this out if that's okay with you," said Natalie looking at Joe. Joe nodded.

"Can I speak to Joe for a minute?" Carolyn asked.

Natalie handed him the phone and Carolyn said, "You got shot at last night and you never called me! What were you thinking, Joe?"

Joe thought before he said, "Well, you had a break-in and never called me."

"Big difference, Joe," said Carolyn. "Listen, Joseph Nelson, if you don't start acting more responsibly, I'm going to have to cancel the whole divorce and you know what that will do to my brother, Douglas. Do you want that on your conscience? I'll see you tonight, right? I mean, you are coming with Natalie aren't you?"

"I'll see you tonight." He smiled at the phone.

"Good," said Carolyn. "And for God's sake, be careful, will you?"

"Yes," he said but she had already hung up.

Chapter 26

Joe insisted on paying for the bad tuna as well as the coffee and hot chocolate, pointing out that all his money would belong to the plaintiffs in a few days.

"So you're going to run office hours tonight?" asked Natalie.

"Yeah," he said. "There are a few patients that I want to follow up with and a few that want to follow up with me. It'll take my mind off this stuff."

"Good luck if you can do that. I can't make any sense of it," said Natalie.

"Neither can I," said Joe. "Are we going to meet at the hospital or somewhere else? To meet Carolyn, I mean."

"At the hospital, I guess. What time?"

Joe thought and said, "Carolyn gets relieved at eleven, but it usually takes an hour or so for her to clean up the cases she has and sign them out. Maybe we should be there at eleven anyway, just in case."

"I'm going to check out Walter's story and then … I don't know, whatever else I can think of, and then meet at the hospital ED," said Natalie. "Shall I call you when I get there?"

"Yeah," replied Joe. "That's the best thing to do, I guess. See you then."

"Do you want my cell number, Joe?" He blushed a little and they exchanged numbers.

He walked to his car and looked back before he got in. She was watching him and was still watching as he drove away. She got in her car and drove to a bar on Somerset Street. It was a bit below the "elegant" standard she would have expected a big-time lawyer to frequent, but it was not a "dive" by any means. There were several unattached people, and it was clear that at least some of them were looking for someone to become attached to, for the evening anyway. Several men noticed Natalie as she came in and sat at the bar. One or two looked like they might have been planning to come over to introduce themselves if she hadn't produced her badge when the bartender approached. No one came over after that, but several people watched closely from a distance.

"Sergeant Moore," she said. "I need to talk to someone who was working here last night. Would that be you?"

"Let me get the manager for you," offered the bartender.

There was a man in a suit at her side almost immediately. "Can I help you, Sergeant …?"

"Moore," said Natalie. "Just a question or two. Nothing important and I can be gone in a few minutes."

"Always glad to help the police keep moving," said the manager. He hadn't introduced himself, Natalie noted, but because this was informal at the moment, it didn't matter.

"A witness to a shooting told me he was in here last night and I just need to confirm that. I think he's telling the truth, but you know how the bosses down at the station are." Natalie was trying to be on the manager's side as much as possible—everyone inconvenienced by some "boss" downtown.

"Name's Walter Mosby and he said he came in about six with a friend and was here for two or three hours," Natalie said.

The manager considered his options: Ask for something more official than a cop walking in and asking questions. Pretend he didn't remember, which was his usual out. Or just tell the truth. He hated telling the truth, but that seemed the best option tonight. "Yeah, he was here with someone. I don't know who it was with him. He called him 'Bert,' though, and they left around ten. I think they left alone." At least he had the chance to lie a little on that last part, about Walter and Bert leaving alone. If this sergeant pressed him, his memory could fail him anyway.

Natalie looked at the manager. She wished everyone would just tell the truth, especially the ones who lied so poorly. His story checked with Walter's though, and she thought that if Walter had talked to him about the story, he would have done better with the lie than he had. He probably wouldn't have taken a chance on lying to the police for Walter anyway.

"Thanks," she said. "Just need to put it in my report is all. You have a good night." She smiled at him and he didn't flinch. She thought he would have if he had lied about Walter being there instead of just a little lie about the details, which is what she thought he had done. She left with several eyes following her, but no one got up to follow her with anything except their eyes.

As she left, she thought: *So Walter had probably been there last night at the time of the shooting with someone named "Bert" and probably left with someone that the manager didn't want to identify.* That last part was interesting but not important to her right now. Walter was not the shooter and that was important. It occurred to Natalie that this alibi was awfully convenient for Walter, but she wasn't sure what that meant either.

The fact that Walter hadn't fired the gun begged the next question: did he have anything to do with the person who had fired the gun from his office window? He hadn't reported any break-in there and that was at least noteworthy. How had someone gotten into his office to shoot out the window without Walter knowing about it? If he knew about it, why hadn't he reported it? All of this cast Walter in a very suspicious light, but because this was an "unofficial" investigation, Natalie had to use something other than the "official" means of seeking the truth. A search warrant for Walter's office was not going to be had without alerting Peter and Andy to what she was doing. No, something more imaginative would be necessary.

She drove back to the building that housed Walter's office, which was a mix of offices and residences. There were no lights on in Walter's office. She got out without really knowing what she was there for, but tried Walter's buzzer which gave no answer. She then tried several of the other buzzers in the entry. One used the intercom to ask who it was, and she just shrugged and remained silent. A mistake, she hoped they would assume. Two made no answer and the fourth rang her in without a question. *Probably expecting a pizza,* she smiled.

Once upstairs, she looked at Walter's door. There was no evidence that anyone had broken in last night. Either they hadn't or the repair had been done very quickly and very skillfully. Those two were generally mutually inconsistent. Repairs done skillfully were generally not done with any speed. She tried the knob but found it locked, of course. Should she try her hand at breaking and entering? Not worth the risk, she decided, and besides, what could she find that would clear up anything?

What she did know was that Walter had not been the shooter, but that someone had gotten into his office to shoot at Joe, and they had done that without breaking in. Did that mean that Walter let them in? Not that simple, but she was sure that he was part of this and in pretty deep too, she thought.

She looked around and found the back exit to the building. No alarm, but the door locked when it closed. Someone could have exited this way but not entered the building or re-entered once outside. She opened the door and verified that it let out onto the alley that exited to a side street where a car could have been parked last night. Whoever shot last night could easily have left this way and been on his, or her, way to put the gun back before the police had arrived on the scene.

Chapter ⟍⎌⟋ 27

While Natalie was visiting bars and worrying about Joe, Carolyn was treating patients in the ED and worrying about Joe. Joe was not particularly worried as he entered his office. "Hello Rose," he said to the young lady sitting behind the counter in the waiting room. There were two parents with young children in the waiting area and one teenager. He recognized them all and greeted them by name. He always found the office practice more satisfying than his shifts in the pedi ED where most patients were unknown to him when they arrived and most he would never see again.

"There are several people who have called in to ask to see you tonight, Dr. Nelson. How many can you see?" asked Rose.

"I have to be done by … well, maybe ten o'clock, so the last one in at nine thirty. Is that okay with you?"

"That works for me," said Rose. "I'll call them back and give them times so they don't all bunch in at once."

And so it went. The routine immunizations and physicals were being handled by Joe's partner while the trial was going on, so these evening office hours were for just the people who specifically wanted Joe: a few follow-ups with problems that had improved and a few that were not improved and needed further treatment or a referral. Some asked discreetly about how "things were going" and Joe commented with equal discretion. They all knew the trial was what they were talking about, but by mutual and unspoken agreement it was not mentioned.

One of his last patients was Laura Perkins. At twenty, she was almost an adult and would need to have a new doctor by the time of her next visit. By life experience, she was well along in her adulthood. She had grown up in a terrible home situation with a drinking and drug-using mother and brother. Her father was unknown to her. Her mother's care had eventually become Laura's responsibility when her mother became terminally ill with AIDS. She had died about two months ago. Her brother had been arrested shortly after that in connection with a murder. By all expectations Laura should have been lost to society by now. Instead, she was a triumph of her own will and some good fortune.

Laura's closest friend, Isabella, had been her savior, Joe thought, providing a stable reference and a place to go when things got crazy at her home. Isabella and her father, also a "Joe," had taken Laura in and she had gotten a steady job, stayed clear of drugs, and was now enrolled in the Certified Nursing Assistant program at the community college. Isabella's father was friendly with and—according to the rumors—was about to marry a local doctor, Diana Connors, who practiced at the other end of the county. Consequently, Joe vaguely wondered why Laura was in his office tonight although she was always someone he liked to see and talk to.

"How are you, Laura?" asked Joe. "I was sorry to hear about your mother."

"Yeah. It was kinda bad at the end," said the young woman with red-dyed hair, multiple piercings, and tattoos sitting opposite Joe. "I just need a refill on my prescription, Dr. Nelson, and to discuss a problem."

"Okay," said Joe. "What prescription and what problem?" This was not going to be a chatty visit—that was clear. Laura always thought she was wasting other people's time by talking about herself.

"Well the prescription is for my birth control pills. I don't need an internal exam since I got one from Dr. Connors about six months ago. I can get her to send you the records if you want. I had Chlamydia and she treated it and said everything was all right."

"You had Chlamydia, Laura? Did Dr. Connors talk to you about 'safe sex'? About using condoms, I mean?" asked Joe.

"Oh yeah, of course," Laura shrugged. "I always use condoms. My mom got AIDS from not using them." Laura looked embarrassed now. "This was kind of a 'date rape' thing."

"A 'date rape'?" Joe looked incredulously at his patient with her nonchalant attitude.

"Yeah," said Laura. "A friend of my bastard of a brother slipped something into my drink at a party. 'Roofies' I guess they call it. Isabella's father took care of that though."

"Isabella's father?" Joe asked. "What exactly did he do, Laura?"

"Went to the police, of course. The state police, not the local ones. The local police won't do anything. That's how they found out my brother had killed that guy. When they were checking out the drugs and all that, I mean." Laura said this as if that were the only logical thing a responsible person would do: go to the police. It was also implied that a pediatrician should know that was what a responsible person would have done. "So I'm, like, seeing a counselor and everything, so that's okay, but I got this other problem that I can't discuss with Dr. Connors. She's going to marry Isabella's father, you know."

"I heard that, Laura. That's a good thing, right?" Joe wasn't sure what could be more important than what he had already heard from Laura, but he hoped it wasn't that she didn't want the marriage.

"Oh, Dr. Connors is great and I can't wait 'til she's, like, well, sort of my step-mother since Isabella and I are like, almost sisters, you know? But that's the problem. I can't discuss some things with her. You know, personal things."

Things like Chlamydia and "date rape," which she had already discussed with Diana Connors, thought Joe. He wasn't sure he was ready for the really big problem if the little ones were losing your mother to AIDS and having your brother charged with murder and being an accomplice in your date rape, but … "Well, what can I help with?"

"It's my … well, my acne." Joe must have looked surprised at this revelation because Laura almost immediately said, "Well, I can't discuss zits with her, can I?"

"I guess not," said Joe, regaining some composure. "It doesn't look that bad, and you're probably past the worst of it now at your age, but I could prescribe some erythromycin for you if you want to try that. It's an antibiotic that sometimes helps. There are other medications too, but some have side effects, so I usually save those for people who don't respond to erythromycin."

"Yeah. That'd be okay, but I was wondering if it's true that using the computer too much makes zits worse. I saw that on the Internet and, like, I use the computer, but I'm going into the CNA program, that's certified nursing assistant you know, and have to do a lot of it on the computer."

"Ah … No, I don't think that's really true, about the computer making zits worse, I mean. There's a lot of misinformation on the Internet as well as real information, Laura." As a matter of fact, Joe didn't think Laura should worry about much after he had seen how well she seemed to be handling her other problems. As a matter of fact, her problems kind of made his look pretty insignificant.

A thought came to him and he looked at Laura and asked. "Can I ask you a question, Laura?"

"Sure, Dr. Nelson."

"It's a computer problem and I just wondered if you might be able to help," said Joe. He pushed the button on his intercom and said, "Rose, do I have any more to be seen tonight?"

Rose seemed to hesitate. "Just one and she says it's real important."

"Okay. I'll be a couple of minutes. You can go on if you want, Rose."

"I'll wait, Doctor," Rose replied. Odd, thought Joe, but he let up the button on the intercom and said to Laura, "It's a report from the hospital that I can't make sense of. Come around and have a look."

Joe pulled up the medical records from his hospital and went to the autopsy report for Linda Murphy. The one that Frank Dobbs had done. The one that didn't mention any intercardiac injection.

Laura came around and looked at the screen. "From the hospital. What did you want to know? I don't know anything about this stuff."

"Not the record," said Joe. "How could this get changed once it's in the computer? I have the report of another autopsy done later that shows different results and that one is probably accurate, so I'm thinking that maybe this one showed the same results but was changed somehow. That's the only way I can figure two good pathologists could examine the same person and one finds an intercardiac injection and the other doesn't find it. I was wondering if they both found it, but someone changed this report. The intercardiac injection had to be there when the first autopsy was done too." He was also thinking of Larry, the obsessive-compulsive pharmacist, who said someone had altered the records on the missing adult Lidocaine, but only on the computer.

"Hospital stuff," said Laura. "Can I play with it a little, Dr. Nelson?" Joe moved aside and Laura tapped amazingly quickly on the keys. "All sorts of security on this stuff. It's a medical record, you know. This one was signed three years ago so no one, not even the guy who signed it, can change it. You could add an addendum or something, of course, but the old record would still be there. It can't be changed."

"Yes," said Joe, disappointment in his voice. He knew how to add an addendum and already knew he couldn't alter a signed record. Frank Dobbs had signed this one before he died.

Laura must have heard Joe's disappointment because she immediately said, "Sorry, Dr. Nelson, but you can't change this one. No one could change it once it's signed. Just add an addendum."

"And there's no addendum?" said Joe.

"Someone could have added one, but I can't see it."

The language she used confused him a little. An addendum could have been added but she couldn't see it? In the past, Joe had been struck by the facility with which younger people that had grown up in a world where computers were always present dealt with them so naturally and easily while older people like himself found them difficult, sometimes impossible to understand. He thought of how he had talked to these younger people for several minutes before realizing that neither one really understood what the other was talking about, what the other understood and what they didn't understand. What one took for granted, the other found incomprehensible. He decided that Laura and he better talk clearly or such a thing might pass for a conversation between them as well.

"What do you mean, 'You can't see it,' Laura?" he asked.

"Just that I don't see it on the monitor." She pointed to the screen in front of her.

Joe had the feeling they were still missing each other. "You mean it isn't there, right?"

"Yeah, not on the monitor," said Laura.

Joe took a deep breath. "Not there at all, you mean."

"Not on the monitor," shrugged Laura. "It could be in the computer."

If a lightning bolt had struck him, Joe could not have been more surprised. "What could be in the computer, but not on the screen?"

"Anything could be," replied Laura. "You know, it could just be 'hidden,' 'masked' they call it."

"Hidden?" asked Joe.

"Yeah," said Laura. "Like, if you don't want stuff to show up on your monitor because it's too cluttered or something, or maybe you just don't want everyone to see it, so you like, 'hide' it. You know, with a right mouse click, or sometimes you have to do it from the desktop. It's simple."

"So," said Joe. "What we're seeing on the screen, the monitor, could be an addendum that looks like a complete report, while what used to be the report couldn't have been erased, but could be hidden, could be 'masked,' so we can't see it. We can't, what would you say, 'unhide' it?"

"Display it," corrected Laura. "Only the one who hid it can 'unhide' it. Or the supervisor of the department or something." She smiled at the ignorant pediatrician. "Unless you can print it."

Joe silently gave the curse of all older members of the species who found themselves in this position: *I hope I live long enough to see some twenty-year-old confuse you with her knowledge of something that no one has even dreamed of right now, and I will laugh at you as you laugh now!*

"Print it?" he asked.

"Well, yeah," said Laura. She wasn't really laughing. Probably she would wait until she could tell her friend Isabella. Joe hoped Isabella's father would defend him. "Some programs have a 'hide' that doesn't block the print part. This one is like that."

"How do you know?" he asked.

He was prepared for a lengthy discussion of the different programs and so on, but Laura just said, "It's the same program we use in the CNA courses. Lots of the kids work in the hospital part-time, you know, so they train us on that system."

Joe smiled. Finally a logical bit in this conversation. "So how do we print it?"

"Hit *print*," she said.

Joe did, even knowing it couldn't be this simple. Further humiliation had to be lurking. The monitor showed the print-select screen and he went to hit "OK," but Laura reached over to stop him. "You have to use the advanced menu."

"Why don't I let you do it?" he said, getting out of his seat.

Laura sat and went through the advanced menu. "See, it has a 'print all hidden.' You have to lock that too or it just stays hidden on the monitor but will print okay. You know, if you hit the 'print all hidden,' it will still print. If someone just hits 'print' off the 'print select' menu, it will just print what's on the monitor. Only the guy who hid it in the first place can block it out of the advanced print menu too. Only that person or a supervisor can display it again if they do that." She shrugged, "Lots of ... well, some people don't know to do that."

Lots of older people, thought Joe. "So how can we tell if it will print?"

"Just read it and see." Laura pointed to his printer which sprang to life and spat papers at him. He looked at the printed pages and realized at once that there was more than was on the monitor. He folded the pages and slipped them into his jacket pocket to read later.

Turning to Laura, he said, "Can we tell who did this?" He didn't think it would be that simple.

Laura turned back to the computer and minimized the display and then went to the properties menu. "Lots of people accessed this but only one added anything. It looks like it was the same guy who signed it," she said. "He opened it on April second three years ago and wrote some stuff and hid some stuff and signed what he wrote and that's it."

"That would be Frank Dobbs," said Joe.

"Yeah, if his user is 'FDobby.' Weird guy, I guess."

"Or anyone with 'FDobby's password?" asked Joe.

"Well yeah, but he would've kept that secret," said Laura.

Or written in a dozen places so he wouldn't forget it, thought Joe. Joe had his written in only half a dozen places, but he was younger than Frank had been. Laura stood and was getting ready to leave when Joe asked, "He was weird all right, but why do you think so, Laura?"

"Oh, I guess it's not that weird to be on your computer at two thirty in the morning, but not doing hospital work. I'll never understand grownups."

"Not until you become one, Laura," he said.

"Yeah. Like that's ever going to happen. Thanks for the prescription, Dr. Nelson. I might try it."

"No, Laura. Thank you. You were a big help. A really big help."

Joe followed her out to the waiting area and said to Rose, "No charge for Laura tonight." He smiled after her until his gaze fell on Gloria Murphy, the not-so-patient person who had something important to talk to him about.

Chapter 28

Gloria Murphy looked angry, angrier than she had been in the courtroom. "I have to talk to you, Dr. Nelson," she said as she watched Laura leave.

"I don't think that's a good idea, Miss Murphy. We're involved in a legal case right now," replied Joe.

"I know that, but you and I both know what's going on, and it's time to settle this once and for all. I've been in court and I've heard what was said today, and I was there when Linda died. You know what happened, and after today, I know what happened." She stared at him defiantly.

"Have you spoken to Ronald, your attorney, Miss Murphy?"

"Screw Ronald!" she shouted. "No, that's too good for him. Look, Dr. Nelson, my niece is dead and you and I know who is responsible, and you and I have to settle this before someone else ends up dead—like you, for instance. Do you want to wait for a lawyer to save your life? Billable hours are all they care about."

Joe drew a deep breath. "I'll meet with you with our lawyers present and only with both of them present. I think you should leave now and try to calm down."

Gloria looked at Rose. "Maybe you're right. Maybe we should talk later … in private. I'll leave, but I won't calm down. There's someone else I have to see first anyway, but you meet me at eleven o'clock at my … no, not at my house. Too many people. Too many witnesses, just like here." She looked at Rose and smiled. "Eleven o'clock in Murphy Park. There's a plaque in the middle with a nice, sweet dedication to my mother the bitch. She ought to have a part in this, don't you think, Dr. Nelson? This is her fault too. And no police, and no damned lawyers. None of them can be trusted, especially yours."

"I'm not going to be there, Miss Murphy," said Joe.

"You'll be there all right. I know you will," said Gloria. "And make sure you mail that!" she said to Rose as she turned and walked out the door before another word could be said.

Joe sighed and looked at his assistant. "I'm glad you stayed for that. I'm not sure, but I think Miss Murphy may be going certifiably crazy."

"She's something all right."

"Let me walk you to your car at least," Joe said.

"Right out front, Joe. I got to stop at the store and I got to mail my bills too, so I'm going to run along, okay?"

Joe nodded and Rose left. He watched to make sure she got to the car all right and when she had, he locked the door and opened his cell phone. What he really wanted to do was read the printout, but first he had to talk to Walter about Gloria Murphy. After last night he wondered if Walter would answer, but he did on the first ring. "Walter, this is Joe Nelson."

Before he could say anything else, Walter started to speak in a rush. "That police sergeant has been asking me questions, Joe. I don't know anything about the shooting last night. Bert came by the office and I went out with him. He said it was important and I figured you would catch me in the morning. I don't know anything more."

"That's fine," said Joe, although it wasn't really fine at all. "I have another problem. Gloria Murphy showed up at my office this evening demanding that I meet with her."

There were voices in the background as Walter said, "I don't think ... Wait a minute, Joe. I want to go somewhere a little more private." Joe was put on hold for a minute and then Walter came back on the phone.

"She wants to meet with you? Why?" he asked.

"I'm not sure," replied Joe. "She said something about us both knowing what was going on, and I think she might have been threatening me. I'm not sure why she said that, but I don't think it's a good idea for us to meet with her, do you?"

Joe could hear voices again and Walter said, "Let me shut the damned door." Joe was on hold for another thirty seconds, and when Walter returned, the background was quiet.

"I'm not sure," said Walter. "Maybe she wants to tell you something or even propose a settlement."

Joe was not expecting this response. "You think we should meet with her, Walter?"

"Well, maybe you should," said Walter tentatively. "See what she has to say."

"With you, of course."

"Did she ask for me to be present?" asked Walter.

"Well, no," said Joe. "She actually said you shouldn't be present."

"Well, then maybe I shouldn't be."

Joe was silent. This was not what he had anticipated at all. "You think I actually should meet with her tonight? Without you?"

"I might upset her more, Joe. If she wants to propose a settlement, then I can get involved. If she just wants to talk, it might be better if you were alone."

"You really think that's wise, Walter? Alone, I mean?" Joe asked.

"Well, if that's what she requested. We have nothing to lose after all, the way the case is going right now." After a moment of silence Walter asked, "When does she want to meet?"

"Eleven," said Joe.

"Well, you've got time to think about it," said Walter. "Where are you meeting her?"

Joe realized that Walter was assuming he was going to meet with Gloria, and he was apprehensive about this assumption. "Yes, time to think. I'll talk to you later, Walter," he said and hung up. Only then did he realize that he had planned to call Walter about the intercardiac injection that evening and because he had been so preoccupied with Gloria, neither of them had even mentioned it.

He shook his head. What was Gloria so intense about? Maybe he should meet with her, or at least talk to her. It was only a little after ten—time for a few more phone calls to help sort this out. First to Carolyn. When she got on the phone, quickly this time, Joe asked for Douglas's phone number. "Douglas?" she said. "What on earth do you want my brother for?"

"Legal advice," Joe said.

"He can't represent you in the divorce, Joe," she said but gave him the number. "That's his special number. He gave it to me after last night's adventures. See you at midnight anyway, right?"

"Yes," said Joe and hung up to dial Douglas.

Douglas answered on the second ring. "This is Joe," he said. "Your still brother-in-law. I need some advice."

"If you need a good attorney, Joe, I don't know any," said Douglas with a chuckle. "And I'm not sure I can give you advice without it being a conflict of interest."

"It's not about the divorce, Douglas," said Joe. "Carolyn and I have that all settled anyway."

Douglas must have been in a really good mood, Joe decided, when he didn't begin to berate him about how he should be represented by legal counsel. "You know, Joe, I'm really grateful that you're taking care of my sister in all this. She's my older sister and … well, you know how older sisters can be when you're growing up, so I give her a hard time any chance I get. To get even, I mean, but I love her and you've been great to her. She's special and I'm glad you're the one she married even if you two insist on parting ways. I won't try to talk you out of it, but I hope you stay real good friends. The two of us too, I hope. I'm sorry, Joe. I had a couple drinks tonight, but I mean all that I just said. You're a great guy." Douglas sighed and then asked, "Do you think she'll ever really get to be surgeon general, Joe?"

"I don't know, Douglas. She'd be good at it. But listen, I have a question for you."

Douglas cut him off again, "I think she would too. I don't have her ambition though. I just want to be governor and only of this sorry state. Small goal, if I say so myself. Carolyn got me thinking about that when she made me get on the board at the hospital, what, four years ago now? I like it and so ... ya know, maybe she'd let me run for governor, what ya think?"

Joe sincerely wished this was some other night when he could take time to talk to Douglas. He had always liked him and was glad he was liked in return, but he needed advice. "Douglas," he said. "I need to ask you a question."

"Shouldn't you ask Walter?" Douglas offered.

"The question's about Walter," said Joe, and continued before Douglas could protest any more. "Gloria Murphy came by my office tonight and demanded that I meet with her."

Douglas was immediately alert. "Did you contact Walter?"

"Yes," said Joe and was about to go on, but Douglas spoke first.

"And he said not to, and I concur. Don't meet with plaintiffs during a trial. Let your lawyer handle this, Joe."

"Walter told me to meet with her," said Joe.

"What?" said Douglas. "Are you sure? I mean you didn't misunderstand or something did you?"

"I asked him three times, Douglas, and each time he said I should meet her. And meet her alone. I don't think that's good advice."

Joe waited while Douglas thought. When he spoke, it was a sober voice that said, "I'm not your attorney, Joe. I'm just a friend who happens to be an attorney, but I think it is absolutely crazy to meet with Gloria Murphy or anyone on the plaintiffs' side, particularly alone. Don't go, Joe. That's my advice."

"I hear you, Douglas. One more question: can you think of any reason why Walter would tell me to go? Anything at all?" Joe waited.

Douglas finally said, "No."

"Thanks, Douglas," said Joe.

"Joe," said Douglas. "You're a good friend and still my brother-in-law. Be careful, will you? Be very careful."

"I will," Joe said and hung up. Time for his last call.

Chapter 29

Natalie answered on the second ring. Joe was lucky with calls tonight. "Oh hey, Joe," she said and went on immediately. "I checked out Walter's alibi. He was at that bar with someone named Bert. I checked out his office too and there was no sign of a break-in, so Walter must've been in on the shooting, ya think? What's up with you?" she said. "Time to head to the hospital already?"

"Things are getting a little unraveled here, Natalie," replied Joe. "I've got a problem."

"Yeah, I know. People are shooting at you. Are they still shooting at you or is something else unraveling?" she asked.

"It's something else and it makes getting shot at seem simple," Joe paused and then went on. "Gloria Murphy is the principle plaintiff in the malpractice case I'm on trial for right now and … Well, she showed up at my office and demanded that I meet with her tonight … alone. She said that 'we' knew what was going on and then she said that 'we' needed to do something about it before someone else got killed … like *me*."

"So let me get this straight. She says you know what's going on and that you might get killed and then asks you to meet so she can what … kill you? I'm not sure you should be so accommodating," said Natalie. "She could've been the one who shot at you last night. What does Walter say about this? He's your attorney in this case. Did you talk to him?"

"He says a police sergeant is calling him about the shooting last night and he swears he knows nothing about that, but he also said he thought I should meet Gloria … alone. I thought that was strange advice," said Joe.

"That sounds like *bad* advice to me," said Natalie.

"Well, I called Carolyn's brother, Douglas. He's an attorney and he said it was crazy to meet with her, and he also said that he couldn't understand why Walter would say anything except 'don't go.'"

"So why haven't you told me you're not going?" asked Natalie.

"Well," said Joe. "That's why I'm calling you."

"Ah," replied Natalie. "You must want to tell me where your last will and testament is hidden so when you end up dead … Are you really thinking of meeting with this lady?"

"Well, not alone, but she didn't really threaten to kill me, she just said I might end up dead, and after last night I guess that's true. She also said she knows what's going on and although she thought I did too, I don't. So maybe I can ask her to explain what she *thinks* I know and then maybe I *will* know what's going on."

Natalie was quiet for a minute before she said, "Are you calling me to tell me who's going with you to meet Gloria Murphy, or do I already know?"

"Well, I was hoping that maybe you would," he said. Then remembering what she had said about needing to find out what was going on in her department, he added, "She might know what's going on with the shooting and why Peter Pierce is acting the way he is too."

"You're crazy to meet with her, Joe," said Natalie. After a minute she asked, "Are you going to go if I say I won't go with you?"

"Yes, I probably will," replied Joe. "There are so many loose pieces here and I just have a feeling that Gloria knows how they fit together. I think I want to take a chance on meeting with her."

"Okay," sighed Natalie. "Where and when?"

"Murphy Park in about twenty minutes," replied Joe. "There's a plaque in the middle dedicated to Gloria's mother. I'll meet you at the entrance."

"The park in the dead of night," said Natalie. "Great place for a shooting."

Chapter 30

They arrived at the same time outside the entrance to Murphy Park. It had been bought by the family of that name after Lorraine Murphy, the matriarch, had died. It had then been refurbished from its state of decay, dedicated to the city and its noble residents, and, of course, to Lorraine Murphy. The rumor—there always seemed to be rumors surrounding this family—was that the "gift" had been dictated in her will and had not been anything spontaneous on the part of her loving children.

There were no other cars parked there tonight. Natalie got out and walked over to where Joe was getting out of his car. "We're five minutes early. Should we wait here or in the park?"

"She might be early," said Joe. "Maybe just wait in the park by the plaque?"

Natalie shrugged and they walked down a path between trees and well-trimmed shrubs. The grounds were kept and lit well and Joe wondered if Lorraine had taken the precaution of setting aside money for that purpose, rather than trusting the city with looking after the park that had run down once already under the city's care. They arrived at the plaque in the center of a well-lit area but found no one waiting. Several benches surrounded the plaque and Joe motioned to one of them, asking, "Should we sit while we wait?"

"Not that one," said Natalie. "Too much light. That other will sit us in darkness and we'll be able to see anyone coming down the path before they see us. If we sit still. You *will* sit still, won't you?"

Joe wondered if her insistence was the result of her police or military training. He did not ask but sat next to her on the bench. "I'll sit still," he promised.

They waited and, despite his promise, Joe found it difficult to sit still. Natalie was not having as much difficulty and finally she asked, "Did you bring your gun, Joe?"

If they had not been in the darkness, she might have seen him blush in his embarrassment. "I left it in the car."

"I should have asked you before we came in," she said without much concern. Perhaps this was because she didn't think that he would be that much help anyway, even if he had a gun, Joe thought. He was actually a fairly good shot, learned from years of hunting in the mountains where every boy was a hunter and practiced shooting every chance he had.

Joe finally said, "I've never read that plaque. Can I go over and read it now, do you think?"

"Yeah," she replied. "I'll try to draw their fire while you make a run for it."

He smiled at her, although she couldn't see it, and then got up and walked over to the plaque. It was an excessively flattering account of the woman Joe had never known, of her loving children and friends she left behind and how her only wish was for their happiness. This park would be but a small effort to fulfill her wishes and repay only a small part of … blah, blah, blah. Joe was usually tolerant of this sort of flowery prose, but this piece was way over the top. He wondered if it had been written after her death or dictated by the matriarch herself before that death with instructions as to where it should be placed. He glanced at the time on his watch and returned to sit next to Natalie. "Ten minutes late," he said.

When Gloria was fifteen minutes late, Natalie asked, "You got the time and place right?"

"This is what she said," replied Joe. "She started to suggest her home but said there were too many people, 'witnesses' was her actual word."

"That's a little chilling—to put it that way, I mean," said Natalie.

When Gloria was twenty minutes late, they were startled by Joe's cell phone. He had it open after only one ring. "Hello," he said as softly as he could.

"Joe, this is Carolyn."

"Oh," said Joe. "Are you ready now?"

"No," said Carolyn. After a brief pause she said, "Gloria Murphy, the plaintiff in your trial? They brought her into the ED. She's been shot. I think she's dead, but they have a code going on. Two or three bullets in the chest."

Chapter 31

Joe turned to Natalie and said, "Gloria Murphy is probably dead in the ED right now. She was shot two or three times in the chest."

"I hope it's not with your gun," said Natalie, shaking her head. They both started running down the path. Although both of their cars were parked on the street, they ran to Joe's car. The street was as deserted when they reached it as it had been when they arrived. Only one other car was parked there—a black, nondescript one, Joe noticed. No wonder he had had so much trouble trying to determine if someone was following him. This town was full of nondescript black cars.

"Let me see your gun, Joe."

Joe reached over to his glove compartment and looked in. It was still there, and he handed it to Natalie who pulled out the magazine of the automatic and looked at the bullets. "Only one missing. You didn't reload it, did you?"

"No," said Joe. "I don't have any bullets except at the house. How did the police do the ballistics tests?"

"They use their own bullets and their own magazine if they can. Standardizes the results better," she replied.

She smelled the barrel and added, "Doesn't smell like it was fired either. Not tonight anyway." She looked a little puzzled now.

"I want to drive to the hospital and see what happened. Carolyn might be able to give us an idea how Gloria got shot or something," said Joe. Natalie nodded, saying she wanted to know too.

They drove separately and Joe called Natalie as they approached, telling her to follow him into the doctors' parking lot. He pulled through the gate, using the electronic bar code on his ID badge to open it, and then pulled over and got out to swipe it again and let Natalie in.

"Park up near the entrance and I'll be right behind you," he said. "And better leave your gun in the car, too." They parked and went up to the ED using the staff elevator and Joe's ID again.

Once inside, he pointed her to the staff lounge and said, "Wait in there and I'll see if I can find out what's up." He came back only a minute later with Carolyn, whose gown and gloves were smeared with blood.

She pulled those off and said, "Hi, Natalie," as if they were the best of friends even though they had met only once and that less than a day ago. Natalie found herself liking this woman.

"It doesn't look good," Carolyn went on. "Shot three times in the chest, at least two could've hit the heart, and she was pulseless, asystolic, when she arrived. John ran the code, thank God. I put in a chest tube on the right and got back blood. They opened her chest and are still trying to sew the wounds. I don't think there's anything they can do, really."

An older, uniformed police officer came in. "Hey, Natalie, are you …?"

"No," said Natalie quickly. "Just a visitor tonight."

"I saw Peter around and the captain too." He turned to Carolyn and asked, "What can you tell me, Carolyn?"

"Just that it will be over soon, Wayne. One bullet is still in her." Carolyn went to the computer screen where the X-rays could be viewed. There were no "X-ray films" anymore, only digitalized images. An image of a chest appeared and on it was a small, white object. Carolyn pointed at it and said, "There's the bullet right up against her spine. Twenty-two, you think, Wayne?"

Natalie knew Wayne. He was a long-time officer who was as good as many of the men and women who outranked him. He had never progressed above patrol status partly because he refused every opportunity for advancement. When asked he simply said, "I hate paperwork," although he also would say more privately that it was too difficult to stay honest with increasing rank. In spite of this, he was good at the crime scene investigation procedures and wasn't reluctant to do the work when he had a chance or when he thought it was being done poorly. He apparently thought so tonight.

"Looks like a twenty-two," he said.

"Were you there, Wayne?" asked Natalie.

"Yes," he said. "But you don't want me to tell you about it, do you? I mean, I'm not supposed to discuss it with anyone except the investigating officers." He smiled and went on immediately. "Neighbor called to say she heard a shot. Are the times important to you?"

Natalie nodded.

"Well, it was at ten forty-two the call came in. Two of our guys were there in about three minutes but couldn't see anything in the house and no one answered. They might've just left, but the neighbor came over and told them that the sound came from the garage. She also said she thought there was a black, or maybe it was dark blue, car in the driveway when she went to make the call but it was gone when she got back." Wayne winced as he said that.

"Well, anyway, they looked in the garage window and thought they saw someone on the floor and called for backup. That was me and when I saw what they saw, we broke in. She was dead then, but we started CPR. Three shots close up with burns on the clothing and two went through her and the windows of her car and out the other side and into the wall of her garage." He frowned again. "Looks to me like she knew the person who shot her, to let them get that close, you think? No struggle that I could see."

Peter came in and looked at Joe and Natalie and said, "What, may I ask, are you two doing here?"

"Visiting my wife," replied Joe.

"There's been a murder tonight, and you are likely to be one of the suspects, Mr. Nelson. Considering that she was suing you and winning, I hear."

The captain had followed Peter into the room. He scowled and said, "What the hell are you two doing here? I told you to stay out of my way or you'd be in trouble and now you'll find out I meant it. I think we need to take you down to the station for questioning, Doctor, and you, Sergeant Moore, may consider yourself officially relieved of your duties. 'Suspended,' I think they call it, without pay in this case. Neither of you can expect to be clear of this any time soon if you are ever clear of it at all."

"Andy," said Natalie. "Joe works here. He ..."

The captain was beginning to speak again as another man entered the room. He was wearing some sort of uniform, a chauffeur perhaps, and he held the door open for yet another man to enter. The second to enter was short, only two or three inches above five feet, with well-cut dark hair and a scrupulously trimmed mustache, dressed immaculately in a very expensive suit. He said nothing but just stood quietly and waited. His short stature did not seem to diminish his commanding presence.

"You two are in big trouble now!" yelled the captain. "I told you I wasn't going to waste time on you, but this will be my pleasure!" He continued yelling but no one was looking at him. Instead, they were looking at the figure that had just entered. Slowly everyone's eyes settled on him until finally even the captain realized there was someone behind him. He turned to face the man and stopped speaking as abruptly as he had turned.

"Forgive me for interrupting," the man said. "If it is not too much trouble, I was hoping to speak with these people, Captain."

"Oh, of course," stammered the captain.

Joe looked at Carolyn and then at Natalie, who showed no evidence of recognition on their faces. He turned back to look at the man, but still could not see anything familiar about him at all.

"Thank you," the man said. "If you would not mind waiting outside for a moment, I'm sure we can have you back in shortly." It was not at all clear to whom he was speaking, but everyone seemed to know who was to leave and who was to stay. Three police officers left.

Chapter 32

There was a brief period of silence while the remaining people assessed each other. The chauffer had stayed behind as well and was the only one in the room who appeared totally at ease.

"Charles, perhaps you should wait outside the door as well. To ensure our privacy," said the man who was obviously in command.

The chauffer turned immediately, saying, "Of course, Sir," and was outside the door in seconds.

The man then turned to the three remaining and said, "I am Reginald Murphy and while I recognize two of you, Dr. Nelson and Dr. Prentiss, I have not had the pleasure of meeting you, Miss." He looked at Natalie.

For the first time in their brief acquaintance, Joe saw Natalie unable to speak. After a few seconds he said, "This is Sergeant Natalie Moore, Mr. Murphy. She's with the police department."

Reginald Murphy frowned at this a moment and then said, "Yes, of course. I know of you, Sergeant, but did not recognize you."

There was another silence until Joe spoke again. "We're all very sorry about your sister, Mr. Murphy. Deeply sorry."

This seemed to break an impasse and both Carolyn and Natalie began speaking at once.

"Yes, I am ..." began Natalie.

At the same time Carolyn said, "She did not ..."

They looked at each other and somehow communicated that Carolyn would go first. "She did not suffer at all, Mr. Murphy.

She died instantly and probably felt no pain. We did ... are doing everything, but ..."

Reginald looked at her and replied, "I know you are doing what you can, but it will make no difference, I'm afraid. There has been ample suffering without the need of anymore," he said cryptically and shook his head. No one asked him to explain.

He returned from his thoughts and asked, "Were any of those police actually present where my sister was shot?"

Natalie spoke, "Wayne was there. He was second on the scene. The backup, I mean." She appeared a little nervous, but Reginald didn't seem to notice. Perhaps he was preoccupied or perhaps he was just used to people being nervous when they were around him.

Reginald nodded and went to the door. Everyone was still standing, and as he opened the door, he motioned toward the chairs. "Please sit down. This may take a few minutes."

"Charles," he said as he opened the door.

There was a whispered conversation between them. At one point, Reginald turned back and asked, "Wayne, you said?" Natalie nodded.

He closed the door and looked at the people still standing within the room. "Please," he said, motioning toward the chairs. "It may take Charles a few minutes to locate that officer."

Charles was obviously looking for Wayne and not guarding the door because before anyone could seat themselves, another doctor wearing scrubs came in. Joe recognized John Larson, one of Carolyn's coworkers. "That was a mess all right. We never ... Oh, I'm sorry for interrupting," he said looking at Reginald.

"This is Reginald Murphy, Gloria's brother," said Joe.

There was a brief moment of silence while John connected the "brother" with the patient he had just unsuccessfully tried to resuscitate. John might never have even heard her name. "Oh, Mr. Murphy. I'm so sorry about your sister. We did everything we could, but ... She was too badly injured and ..."

"Yes, I know," said Reginald.

An awkward silence followed and finally John said, "I'll talk to you later Carolyn, okay?"

Carolyn looked at him and seemed to realize what he was saying. "Oh, I don't really have any signouts. The lady in twenty-three is admitted and waiting to go upstairs, and the only other two are waiting to be discharged."

"Already gone," replied John. "I truly am sorry about your sister, Mr. Murphy." He left, nodding to Carolyn and Joe as well.

There would probably have been another awkward silence if Charles and Wayne had not come in as John was leaving.

Chapter 33

No one had yet had a chance to sit when Wayne entered, the door held open by Charles with the same deference he had displayed to Reginald Murphy earlier. Perhaps this was simply his character or perhaps he saw Wayne as an associate of his employer, an extension, therefore, of Reginald. Whatever the case, Wayne entered and Reginald greeted him as he would a long-lost friend.

"Wayne," he said, "I believe you have helped with security at the estate several times in the past and done an admirable job, I might add." After a pause to allow Wayne to reflect on this compliment he continued, "It was a sadder mission that you had this evening."

Joe vaguely wondered if Wayne was at all fooled by this display. He strongly suspected that Charles was, in fact, the one who remembered Wayne and had given his boss the information necessary to "recall" their past association. He was also sure that if there was any grief over the death of his sister, the display they were seeing was more a performance than evidence of it.

Reginald continued in his artificially friendly manner. "My sister was killed this evening, and I am hoping that you can help us discover what really happened." Reginald put on a serious face and continued. "I trust you and believe that you may have observed things that others might not have observed. I trust these people as well," he said indicting the other three. After a pause to allow this to have its effect he added, "I do not trust the police force to adequately put this to rest."

A remarkable statement, Joe thought. Reginald had managed to say, in a short time, all that he needed or wished to say. For whatever reason, and Joe could not see any reason at all, he had said that he trusted them and that he questioned the "adequacy" of the police. Reginald must know more than Joe knew, but he had said no more than was necessary.

Wayne looked at Natalie who nodded slightly. He seemed to be thinking and everyone waited while he did. Finally he spoke, "I share your trust of these people, and I'm afraid I also share your distrust of the department. I'm not allowed to tell you anything about the case, Mr. Murphy, so the conversation we're having will never have taken place. What is it you would want me to say if I could talk to you about this evening's events?" Wayne asked with more eloquence than Joe had ever heard him use before. Two were playing this game and Wayne was clearly a match for his counterpart.

Reginald smiled and said, "My sister was killed. Do you know by whom?"

"No," Wayne replied simply. After a moment he went on. "I can tell you something about him. I say he, of course, but it may have been a she. He probably drives a black or dark blue car and is of average height." Reginald looked at him quizzically and Wayne cleared his throat and continued. "A car was in the driveway when the neighbor called and gone when the police arrived. As for the height, the bullets went in at the level of the heart and went straight in and out her back at about the same level. They were fired at very close range. Therefore someone who was shorter, say yourself, Sir, would've shot upward to hit the heart, or if firing straight and level, lower, into your sister's abdomen. Likewise, someone significantly taller would have fired down or higher. The shots were fired from inches away. There were flash burns, powder burns they're sometimes called, not only on her outer garments but her inner ones and her skin as well. Two of the bullets passed straight through her and the windows of her car and are buried in the wall behind her car.

"They were fired level, not upward or downward." He held his hand out to show where the murderer would have held his hand and his gun. "It was a small-caliber gun, a twenty-two, and probably a small gun since one of the bullets lodged against her spine but broke no bone." He looked at Carolyn, who nodded. "A low velocity projectile, I think. There was blood on the outside of the car; therefore I think she was against the car when she was shot. The door was closed though, and there was no significant blood inside and no real evidence of a struggle either. She knew the person who shot her well enough to let him get very close."

Reginald did not seem upset at all by this detailed discussion of his sister's death. "And when was she shot, Wayne?"

"Her neighbor heard two or three shots at about ten forty. Her call was at ten forty-two." Wayne waited before continuing, "I arrived at ten fifty-five and your sister was dead when I found her. We attempted CPR but …"

"Yes," Reginald said. "Is there anything else you can tell us?"

Wayne shrugged and Joe asked, "Is it a two-car garage, Wayne?"

"Yeah."

"Did Gloria have only the one car?" Joe asked, looking at Reginald.

"Yes," said Reginald, a little puzzled too.

"Was the second space clear? I mean, could you park a car in it or was it full of storage stuff?" Joe asked, looking at Wayne.

"No," said Wayne, smiling. "Empty. Clear enough for … for an SUV or a pickup."

Reginald was still puzzled. "I don't follow exactly …?"

Joe looked at him and said, "Someone was probably using that space in Gloria's garage, probably to park an SUV or pickup and probably very recently or it would have had things accumulating in it. Empty spaces in garages usually fill up pretty quickly. My space at the house is already full, isn't it?" He looked at Carolyn. "And I've only been gone six weeks."

Reginald smiled himself and said, "Thank you, Wayne."

Chapter 34

Wayne turned to leave as Peter and his captain came into the room. Charles had obviously been trying to delay them without success and looked toward his boss with an apology written on his face. Peter stood aside to let his captain speak.

"I'm sorry to tell you this, Mr. Murphy, but your sister is dead, and I think we have the prime suspect right here." He looked at Joe. "Can you tell me where you were this evening, Doctor?"

"At my office and then on my cell phone," he replied, holding up his phone. He knew the time in question and saw no reason to say he met Natalie as their meeting occurred after Gloria had been shot.

The captain snatched the phone from him and said, "We will check that out if you don't mind, but I think you could have found time between calls to have shot someone. I'm prepared to book you right now if this is the best you can do. Your motive in this case is pretty strong and you're pretty clever, but you're going to spend the rest of this evening in my jail."

Before anything else happened, however, Reginald spoke. "That would be rather inconvenient for me, Captain. I really would like to continue my conversation with Dr. Nelson, and I was hoping you could simply take a preliminary statement here in order that he could accompany me now." Reginald was smiling but there was an assured firmness about him. Joe was always amazed at how powerful money could be.

The captain retreated immediately. "Oh yes, Mr. Murphy. We can just get a quick statement and he'll be free to go with you."

"And Dr. Prentiss and Sergeant ..." Reginald looked at Natalie.

"Moore," she offered.

"Yes," said Reginald. "And Sergeant Moore."

Within minutes, the captain had taken statements from Joe and Natalie; told them he would talk to them later, and smiled at Reginald, saying, "That's all we need tonight, Mr. Murphy."

"Thank you, Captain." He turned toward those who would be accompanying him and added, "I am hungry. Perhaps we could continue this where I can get a bite to eat." He motioned toward the exit and Charles held the door open. He continued to hold it open for the other three as well.

Once outside, Reginald walked toward the limousine waiting by the emergency department and Charles indicated they should follow. He then hurried to catch up in time to open the door of the limo for his boss. Natalie pulled Joe back to walk more slowly and said, "Do you think it's such a great idea to be riding in this guy's limo after his sister just got shot and you're the 'prime' suspect?"

All three stopped while Joe thought and then he said, "I think I'd rather take a chance with Reginald than with your 'Captain Andy.' If I leave in my own car, I may spend the rest of the evening in his jail and be found dead in the morning. This is getting pretty crazy. Besides, I want to hear what Murphy has to say. If I had listened to Gloria in my office, I might know what's going on now and she might not be dead."

"So do we take the dinner invitation or not?" asked Carolyn.

Natalie shook her head. "If he kills me instead of you, I'm going to be really pissed, Joe."

"I'll make it up to you if he does," said Joe and walked over to the waiting limo, followed by the two ladies.

"We have our cars here, Mr. Murphy," said Carolyn when they were seated in the limo.

"Yes, of course you do," replied Reginald Murphy. "I will have Charles return you here after we are done." He said no more and just looked out the tinted window as they rode silently along.

They finally arrived outside Bruno's at one o'clock in the morning, at least two hours after closing time, and Joe expected something to happen other than what *did* happen. Bruno himself opened the front door of the restaurant, and Charles opened the limo door, and they all went in as Reginald thanked Bruno for staying open late and Bruno said how glad he was to accommodate Mr. Murphy. The restaurant was empty so they had no trouble finding a seat.

They were not alone for long. As the server came over to their table, another man entered wearing a leather jacket and hat. He sat at a table nearby but not too close. When he took off his hat, there was a head of curly black hair and a black mustache. He nodded toward Reginald but said nothing.

"May I get you something to drink?" asked the server as if this were just another boring night on the job. "Coffee for you Mr. Murphy, or would you prefer scotch tonight?"

"Scotch," replied Reginald. The others asked for coffee. "And could you find out what Luis would like and ask him to move to a table farther away to drink it, Jacob."

Jacob was the server Joe remembered from two nights ago, but he hadn't introduced himself tonight. Reginald must have known his name already.

Scotch and coffee were served, and the man in the leather jacket named Luis took his drink a few tables farther away. "I am expecting one other in a moment but wish to speak privately first," said Reginald. He took a drink and sighed, looking around the table. "I have a confession to make. It is I who killed my sister."

Chapter 35

There should have been more surprise, but this evening had been so full of surprises that no one even flinched. Reginald sighed and continued, "As surely as if I had pulled the trigger myself, I am the one who killed her."

There was silence while the other three watched Reginald Murphy as he took another drink and weighed his words. "I must apologize to you, Dr. Nelson." He nodded to Joe. "This trial you are going through was largely at my instigation. My apologies to you too, Sergeant Moore, but the police in this city are corrupt and they cannot be trusted at all."

He turned back to look at Joe. "I must say that I never did think you could have done anything to cause my niece's death, but I was equally certain that it was not a natural event. I would have offered you money to investigate it; I actually inquired as to how you would respond to such an offer but was told you could not be enlisted for money alone. You don't care much about money, do you, Dr. Nelson? Maybe that's why I became convinced it was you who could unravel this problem." He shrugged and went on. "I admire you for that but felt I needed to give you another reason to investigate it and so ... Well, for once my sister Gloria and I agreed, and so we proceeded to bring the suit against you. Again, my apologies."

Joe was too astounded to even respond, but Reginald didn't seem to notice. He took another drink and continued. "I feel my sister was caught in this whole thing and that she probably realized somehow what had happened and ... well ... she died as a result. I am hoping you will help find out what happened to her, Dr. Nelson; but as I said, I was the cause, and I know what the reason for her death was as well."

Was Reginald getting drunk or going crazy or purposely talking in cryptic circles to the bafflement of his audience? Joe could not decide. Jacob replaced his drink with fresh scotch.

"Do you know why she died? Why my niece died?" asked Reginald, looking at no one. "It is money. This family is drowning in money. It is the devil's excrement—that is what money is. This family is drowning in the devil's excrement and it will kill all of us. It killed Gloria, I am sure, and killed my niece. Whatever was the final reason and whoever was the final assassin, the real cause was money. My sister and her husband, Linda's parents, are hiding in its darkest cave, afraid to venture out from behind their money to see the world at all. And I … yes, it is killing me too." He raised his glass in a toast, or perhaps as an example; it was not clear. He then finished his drink and sagged in despair. If it was killing him, he was not prepared to give it up.

When he looked up a moment later, it was to greet a new arrival. "Ah Ronald, so sorry to have awakened you at this hour." Reginald did not look that sorry as the attorney for the plaintiff, Ronald Craft, took a seat at the table. He was in a suit and tie and did not look like this was so inconvenient that he hadn't been able to dress properly. Jacob was there at once to ask if the new arrival wished for a beverage. Ronald did: scotch like his boss.

"I have some things we need to get moving tonight, and that is what required me to awaken you at this early hour," said Reginald. A scotch appeared before Ronald and a fresh drink before Reginald.

"First," said Reginald, "you should meet your new clients. You know Joe Nelson, and this is his wife, Carolyn Prentiss-Nelson, and this young lady is Police Sergeant Natalie Moore. They are implicated more or less in the death of my sister, Gloria. I wish that they be protected from any interference that the police might offer."

Ronald appeared ready to protest, but Reginald waved him away. "Although it doesn't seem to matter to the legal system, you may wish to know why I believe they had nothing to do with Gloria's murder."

He motioned to the leather-coated Luis who jumped up and proceeded to the table. "This is Luis Perez. Señor Perez is a private investigator." All eyes shifted to Luis. "I asked him to keep an eye on Dr. Nelson after I heard he had been shot at last night. He has been following Dr. Nelson and can verify his whereabouts at all times since he left the police department last evening, now almost ten hours ago, is that not correct, Luis?"

Luis might have been a "Señor," but his accent was as American as anyone else's in the room. "Yes, Sir, I can."

"My sister was shot at ten forty, and where was Dr. Nelson at that time, Luis?" asked Reginald.

Luis opened a notebook and said, "Driving to Murphy Park, Sir."

Reginald smiled with triumph, and Ronald took a drink of scotch while Natalie and Carolyn looked on in bewilderment, but it was Joe who next spoke. "You were driving a black car, weren't you, Luis?"

Luis looked over at Joe. After a moment he nodded.

"That was the one I noticed following me," said Joe.

Reginald now looked at Joe, but spoke to Luis, "You may have to buy a less conspicuous vehicle, Mr. Perez."

"It's probably a rental, Mr. Murphy," said Joe.

The flush on Luis' face said that this was true. Reginald's face showed amazement which turned to amusement as he said, "Nonetheless Ronald, as you can see, you have three innocent clients."

"And Sergeant Moore? Were you following her as well?" asked Joe.

Luis was still recovering but managed to say, "No. She was with you earlier this evening as I told you Mr. Murphy," he said, looking toward Reginald. "And then she joined you again at seven minutes before ten this evening."

"That would seem to make it impossible for her to have shot Gloria as well, and of course, Carolyn was in the ED all night," Joe concluded. He did not need to draw the conclusion apparent from this information.

Ronald cleared his throat and said, "Well, I must remind you that I am engaged in a civil suit against Dr. Nelson at the present time and therefore cannot ethically represent him."

Reginald was not to be put off by the legal technicalities. "That is the second issue I wish to discuss. That civil suit should be dropped immediately. Please do what you must do to facilitate that, and I will speak to my sister, Lucinda, and her husband and have them sign whatever is necessary. Do you understand? It is no longer necessary to pursue that case and I very much do not want it to interfere." The finality in his voice made it very clear. He did not wait for discussion.

"Lastly, I think it would be helpful to know what Gloria's will contained."

Ronald must have resigned himself to the irregularities of the evening because he offered no resistance to this suggestion at all. "Everything will go to your sister Lucinda's two children, to be managed by myself until they reach age and under no circumstances is anything to be given to either of the parents—or to you, I might add, Mr. Murphy. She was particularly opposed to Lucinda and Peter ever having any of her money as I recall. I believe she told them as much."

Reginald mused for a moment. "So except for the children and you, her executor, who will collect a fee of course, no one benefits from Gloria's death. Financially, I mean."

"I have an alibi," said Ronald, smiling, and finished his drink.

"Of course you do," said Reginald. "Thank you for coming, Ronald, and you too, Luis. That will be all tonight."

Chapter 36

Ronald and Luis rose to leave and Ronald handed out three of his cards. He pointed to one of the numbers on it and said, "That's my personal number. If for any reason you need me and can't get me through the others, that one always reaches me." Joe took the card but wondered who Ronald Craft would be representing tomorrow. Possibly not Joseph Nelson. Joe would keep his card but wasn't sure he would be calling him.

When Ronald and Luis had left, Reginald turned to Joe and said, "That was quite amazing, with Luis, I mean. How did you know the color of his car, and how on earth did you know it was a rental?"

Joe smiled. "Well, not that difficult really, Mr. Murphy."

Mr. Murphy raised his hand, "Please call me Reggie. All of you, please. Don't ever call me Reginald though. Disgusting name, Reginald." He practically spat it out. "My bitch of a mother did that on purpose, I think, saddled me with that name for my whole life. There are William Murphys and Johns or James or even, true to our heritage, Seans and Ians and ..." He shook his head. "But never a Reginald." The scotch was taking effect, Joe thought. If he was going to get any information from "Reggie," he had better ask the questions fast. "And she made me short in the bargain. Do you know we never had enough to eat? She said it built character to be hungry. Made you 'strive' for the better things in life." Reggie shook his head and then looked up, saying, "So sorry for interrupting, Joe. How did you know about Luis' car?"

Joe paused for a moment and began again. "Well, I was looking for someone following me after leaving the police station earlier. Natalie suggested I might be followed, but all I saw were the black and dark blue cars so common on our streets. When you said that Luis was following me … what else could he have been driving? There was only one other car outside the park this evening, a black one." Joe nodded toward Natalie who nodded back.

"As for the rental part: it was a lucky guess. One look at Luis told me he would never own a nondescript, black car. Not nearly flashy enough for the 'leathered and mustached look' he likes. Besides," Joe continued, "I saw that on TV one time. The PI had to tail someone, so he rented a nondescript car to blend in with the traffic."

Reggie smiled for a moment and then said, "Truly amazing, Joe. I have picked a good man to pursue this, don't you think, ladies? Well, I am going to leave and let you three pursue it then." He rose and Charles was at his side immediately to steady him. "I will have Charles take me home and then return for you people. Please have dinner here while you wait and discuss the situation."

He turned to Bruno, who was standing nearby. "Whatever they want, and of course, add the rest of the night's expense to my account. Thank you again for staying."

"One question, Reggie," said Joe. "I know that your niece Linda's money went to charity. That was well known even before she was born. It was part of your mother's will. But what charities were they exactly?"

"Oh," said Reggie. His speech was beginning to slur. "Some organization for the care of stray cats. Mama loved cats." He shook his head in disgust. "And a homeless shelter for women and then you two, of course." He motioned toward Joe and Carolyn and smiled. "Your hospital got most of it." With that he turned and left with Charles helping him. He must have been drinking earlier tonight, Joe thought, to have become that drunk on the three he had at Bruno's.

After a moment's silence, Carolyn said, "Well, if Linda was really killed for the money, I'm betting it was one of the cats. They are such devious creatures. What are we supposed to do until Charles returns to chauffer us to our cars?"

Natalie looked at her and said, "Maybe we should practice dodging bullets. Someone's out there trying to kill people and we were pretty conspicuous, leaving the ED in a limo like that. I'm locking all my doors and windows tonight for sure."

Carolyn shivered and said, "I hadn't thought of that. I don't think I want to sleep in that house alone tonight. You don't suppose … I mean would you …? Natalie?"

Natalie looked over at Carolyn with surprise and then looked at Joe. "Well, I guess. My place is small, but …"

"No," said Carolyn. "Stay at the house, please. I have plenty of beds and bedding, and I would feel much safer with someone there. I don't want to impose on you. You look nervous about it, but I … This is all so bizarre, and I just want someone there tonight."

"Yeah, that's okay," said Natalie. She looked a little embarrassed and added, "I thought you were going to ask Joe to stay over, that's all."

"Joe?" said Carolyn. "Oh, he's welcome too. He's a pretty good shot and all that but … It's just that I would feel more comfortable with the police there."

Joe just smiled. If this was going to be a "girls' sleepover," maybe he would be better off in his own apartment.

"Then it's settled," said Carolyn. "All three of us will spend the night at the house."

Too late, thought Joe. "So we still have to decide what to do until Charles returns. Reggie brought us here because he was hungry, although he didn't eat anything, I notice, but now I'm hungry. Do you suppose there's anything to eat in a restaurant that's been closed for two hours?" he said.

Jacob, the ubiquitous server, was at his side as if he had been waiting for this very question. "We have the full menu available, Sir."

"Oh, that's not necessary, Jacob," said Joe. "Just something to munch on will be fine."

Jacob leaned over as if to point out something on the menu and said, "Joe. I'm getting paid triple time to stand around and chat with the bar maid who is getting triple time to chat with me. The same with the chef and his helper in the kitchen, for as long as you stay. Stay for a week for Christ's sake. I'll get you beds if you want to sleep here."

"Oh," said Joe. "Won't Bruno mind?"

"Maybe," said Jacob, smiling slightly. "But he doesn't own this place. Reginald Murphy does, so …" Jacob stood now and said more audibly, "And what would you like us to prepare for you this morning?"

The silence that followed was finally broken by Carolyn. "Why don't I order for us all? Have you been here before Natalie?"

"Well, no," answered Natalie.

"The steaks are excellent and the seafood is good too. First, we'll need some appetizers though. Bruschetta and stuffed mushrooms maybe and some wine, I think." Jacob motioned to the bar maid, a red-haired, smart-looking young lady of twenty-five or so who immediately came over to the table to earn her triple time.

"Yes?" she said with a slight accent, maybe French or maybe just an affectation.

"Dom Perignon," said Carolyn. "I've never even tasted any, have you?" she said to her companions.

"We have a '99 that has a well-rounded character and is quite powerful. We also have some others which are as good and may complement your meal better," said the bar maid.

"Yes," said Carolyn. "But I've never tasted Dom Perignon, and when I tell my friends about this evening, I want to say a name that will impress them. Maybe we could have both, do you think?"

"Yes, of course."

"So now we need to pick out the food so you can tell us what wine will go with it. What would you like, Natalie?" asked Carolyn.

"Oh, steak would be fine," Natalie answered uncertainly.

"Excellent," said Carolyn. "The filet mignon, of course."

"And how would you like that cooked?" asked Jacob.

"Medium well," replied Natalie. "I don't like the meat red. And a baked potato too, I guess."

"And I will have the lobster and scallop casserole over rice, I think. And you, Joe?" said Carolyn.

"Oh," said Joe. He had not been paying attention, it was clear. "The chicken piccata, I guess."

"That's what you had two nights ago, Joe. You're getting boring," said Carolyn. "But now you can find us a wine to match our meal, at least," she said, looking at the bar maid.

"Steak, chicken, and fish. I'll come up with something," she replied and left to prove she was worth the triple time.

Then Carolyn turned to Jacob and added, "And a plate of some vegetables and maybe some extra plates so we can share." When Carolyn told her friends about this evening, no one was going to believe a word of it, Joe decided.

Chapter 37

"So I guess we should figure out what happened with Gloria," said Natalie. "Do you have any ideas?" She looked from Carolyn to Joe and back.

Carolyn shivered again and Joe looked pensive for a moment before saying, "I can't help but believe it was about the malpractice trial and the death of Linda Murphy." He pulled out the folded report Laura Perkins had discovered earlier that evening. "I think this is the original autopsy report by Frank Dobbs."

"Don't you already have the original?" asked Carolyn.

Things had been moving so quickly that Joe had forgotten that Carolyn wouldn't know about the autopsy discrepancies. "A pathologist who testified today at the trial found an intercardiac injection, but the report I have from Frank Dobbs didn't find any."

"But you didn't do any intercardiac stuff, did you, Joe?" Carolyn asked. "Nobody has done that for years."

"No, I didn't, and Frank didn't mention any on the report I had, but this guy who did the second autopsy did find it. It had to be there for the first autopsy too, so I thought maybe someone altered Frank's report. I had one of my patients look at the computer and she found the old report 'hidden.' 'Masked,' I think she called it," he said.

"One of your patients?" asked Natalie. "Like a five-year-old or something?"

"Pediatrics covers neonates to twenty-one-year-olds and sometimes older. Laura Perkins is twenty," said Joe, smiling at her.

"Laura Perkins?" asked Natalie. "Not the same one whose brother was charged with murder back, like, a month or two ago? His sister's name was Laura, I think."

"Yes. The same." Joe shrugged. "Amazingly put together, all things considered. You know how they say everyone is connected by six degrees or something? Well, here in the mountains it's more like two degrees. Everyone is related to someone else, everyone is a cousin to someone. It gets so you don't even think about who's related because everyone's related. Anyway, it was she who found this report." He began reading now and handing the sheets to Carolyn.

"Frank found the intercardiac injection too. It's here in his original report," Joe said. He handed Carolyn the next sheet and motioned that she should hand the sheets to Natalie.

Natalie read them but couldn't really make any sense of the medical terminology until it came to the part where it started to repeat. "He already said this part earlier." She looked up.

"Exactly," said Joe. "Someone put in an addendum that looked like the real report, only without any mention of the intercardiac injection and then 'hid' the old report."

"Why?" asked Natalie.

"My guess is that someone gave an intercardiac injection of Lidocaine to Linda Murphy and that's what killed her. That person then altered the report so no one, maybe most particularly me, would realize it had been given since that made it obvious someone had ... well, murdered her." Joe replied. After a moment he added, "My guess is also that Gloria saw that happen and didn't realize what she saw until she overheard me talking to Walter after the testimony today. Well, yesterday now; it's Friday, isn't it?"

"You were yelling at Walter, Joe," said Natalie. "She couldn't have helped but hear you and realize that you thought it was important."

The wine and appetizers arrived, interrupting their conversation. The Dom Perignon was opened to breathe and the bruschetta and mushrooms were eaten. The wine was finally tasted, sooner than it should have been probably, and later this would be blamed for the fact that no one was impressed. In the end they liked the second wine better, the one the red-headed bar maid had suggested, and in a flash of inspiration they sent the "Dom" to be shared by the triple-time staff. They were pleased to have it.

Chapter 38

"So who killed Linda Murphy?" asked Natalie finally.

"I don't know," said Joe. "I'm still trying to get used to the idea that someone did kill her. It all seems so bizarre, even on this evening of the most bizarre events I can remember. But if it was murder, and if it was by an intercardiac injection of Lidocaine, then it could have been almost anyone in the department. It takes only a few seconds to do that. If they had given it through the interosseous line, it would have taken minutes to give and someone would have noticed, but intercardiac is quick. It could've been done without anyone noticing if they were lucky.

"Linda had all sorts of monitoring stuff that could have been moved to cover the injection site. Anyone could have come in, and if no one was watching closely, just given the injection. It would've been right before the second arrest, I'm guessing, and Francine the nurse, Gloria, and Lawrence were there, but Lawrence said there were several people coming in and out and they weren't really paying attention. Anyone in the department could have come in. Gloria could have given it for all we know."

"But why?" asked Carolyn.

"That part makes no sense at all," replied Joe. "Nobody is the enemy of a four-year-old and nobody got her money. It was common knowledge that her money would go to charity if she died before she reached twenty-one. I can't see why anyone would have wanted her dead, much less wanted to kill her."

"So who had the opportunity? Who was in the ED, I mean?" asked Natalie.

"Well, I was there," said Carolyn.

"I didn't know you were there, Carolyn," said Joe.

"Not in the department, but in the hospital. We had one of those never-ending meetings about the new building. That's how Bert happened to be there. He and Walter were at the meeting. I remember I left without going to the ED because I was so annoyed and I knew Bert would be there. Then, when I heard about you and Linda, I felt guilty that I hadn't gone down." She frowned now.

"Walter too?" asked Joe. "Everyone was there. It could even have been Francine or one of the other nurses, but why? No one could have known Linda would be there."

"I don't think Francine ..." began Carolyn.

"I don't think so either, but anyone who was there could have killed her," said Joe.

"I was in Afghanistan three years ago," said Natalie. "I have several people who can verify that. Probably some Afghans too if that's necessary." After a pause she continued, "So someone killed Linda Murphy and then tried to cover it up and, I hate to admit it, Reggie was right. He got you sued, Joe, and that uncovered the murder. So then someone kills Gloria because she realizes what happened, and they tried to kill you for the same reason, except you don't know what's going on. Is that pretty much where we are?"

"Except," said Carolyn, "the 'shooting at Joe' part doesn't make sense to me. I mean, why go to all the trouble to steal my gun and shoot at Joe and then put it back?"

"That puzzled me too," said Joe. "And why shoot at me in the car instead of just out on the street or at my apartment? I think maybe they weren't trying to kill me but to discredit me. Make me look like I was crazy or appeared to be lying so when I realized what was going on, no one would believe me. Maybe all they wanted was to hold up the trial even."

"Yeah, that's strange," said Natalie. "I mean, it would take a pretty good shot to hit the window in your car from that second story; trying to hit you would be even more difficult, so maybe it didn't matter if he hit you. What was needed was to hit the car so we could find the bullet from your gun in your car and then have the trial held up or have you lose your credibility?"

"Yeah. That way the bullet could be recovered and the ballistics checked," said Joe. "Of course, he didn't mind taking a chance that he might hit me by mistake either. Did you ever see the ballistics report, Natalie?"

"No. Peter just told me." She thought for a moment. "It came through awfully quick and the fingerprints too. Your gun didn't smell as if it had been fired either. Maybe there wasn't any report at all. Just ... this is too bizarre," she finished. After another minute she asked, "So I hate to keep repeating myself, but ... why?"

"I hate to keep repeating myself too," said Joe. "But I don't know."

"Well," said Carolyn. "If you had been killed, someone, like me or maybe Natalie, or maybe even Reggie, would start asking why you were killed and then might have discovered that Linda had been murdered and ... But if you just looked like a fool or worse, a doctor trying to convince everyone that he was the real victim in his own malpractice case, then no one would believe you enough to look into the death of Linda Murphy." She shrugged and looked at the others at the table.

"At least not right away," said Joe. "Am I the only one who feels there's some time urgency here? That things only need to be postponed, not permanently covered up? I mean, I'm shot at before I even suspected there was a murder. Whoever shot at me couldn't have expected to keep this covered up forever. It would work for a while, but when the intercardiac injection came out, someone would look into it, wouldn't they?"

Neither Carolyn nor Natalie seemed as convinced as Joe was. "Maybe," offered Carolyn. "If everyone thought you were crazy though ..."

There was silence for a moment until Natalie said, "Another thing that I personally don't understand is why Peter knew enough to say you had shot at your car yourself and kept Carolyn's gun and rushed the ballistics report, or at least said he did. For what? How did he know, and why was it so important?"

Joe frowned. "Was it that important that I be discredited as soon as possible? Before the pathologist testified? Before I realized that there was an intercardiac injection?" He looked around the table and asked, "Is this the mother of all coincidences or the mother of all conspiracies?"

They were quiet for a moment until Natalie asked, "So if we can't get anywhere with Linda or Joe, what about Gloria? Who killed her?"

"Bert?" offered Carolyn. "Her lover?"

"Bert?" asked Natalie. "The Bert that went to the bar on Somerset with Walter? Gloria's lover? Are these people all in bed together?"

"Yeah, that's the one, but I don't think he killed Gloria," Joe said. Both ladies looked at him and he went on, "The empty space in the garage was probably Bert's, for his pickup, and so if he was the one, he wouldn't have parked outside."

"Unless he drove some other car," replied Carolyn. "Without a remote for the garage door."

"Or maybe there were more people than Gloria and Bert there tonight," replied Natalie.

At that point the food arrived and almost immediately after that Charles returned, carrying a plastic cup and brown paper bag. He settled at a table some distance away and nodded to them. When Jacob came over to him, he waved at his bag and produced two fast food burgers and some fries.

Chapter 39

They ate little of the food and drank even less of the wine. The meal was good, but the hour was late and the stress was taking its toll. Each in turn cast a longing glance at Charles who seemed to enjoy his meal and to be as relaxed as could be in spite of the hour. If they did not long for his meal, they each longed for his peace of mind.

"So who are we looking for again?" asked Carolyn when the efforts at eating had ceased. "Someone who had reason to kill a four-year-old and her aunt—but not for money—and someone who could have tried to kill Joe. Even if he didn't try to kill you, Joe, he had to be able to shoot at you." She paused, looking at her half-full wine glass, "Oh, and he or she had to be able to get the police in on all this and work the computer well enough to alter the record, which I couldn't do. Does that narrow it down at all?"

Joe shook his head. "Gloria is out of the running, but everyone else is still a suspect. Maybe Francine can tell us who came into the room. She didn't leave until the second cardiac arrest, so the Lidocaine had to have been given while she was in the room, right?"

"It makes sense," answered Carolyn. "But I don't know. What really happened? We don't even have intercardiac needles in the department, do we?"

Joe was quiet for a moment. "There were needles missing from the lumbar puncture tray. The spinal needle is three inches long and would easily have reached Linda's heart. Whoever did this acted impulsively and is likely to act impulsively again."

"Let's get some sleep tonight," said Natalie, "and I'll get you my alibi statements in the morning if it can wait 'til then."

"Only 'cause I like you," replied Carolyn.

"So should we leave a tip?" asked Joe as they started to leave.

"No," said Carolyn. "Triple time is enough. They should be tipping us."

Charles stood to greet them. "Mr. Murphy asked that I give this to you. It is his personal cell phone number. Only a dozen or so people have it, and he changes it frequently. Shall I drive you back to the hospital for your cars now?"

"No," said Joe and the others looked at him. "To my apartment first. I'll meet you in the limo. I have to take a leak. Give me your cell phone, Carolyn, and I'll enter Reggie's number in it. The police have my cell."

Carolyn handed him her phone, and when she and Natalie were in the back of the limo and out of Charles' hearing, she said, "Joe's got something going on. I've never heard him say that: 'taking a leak.'"

When Joe joined them, he asked, "Did you see any cars on the street out there? I didn't."

"Do you think we're being followed? By Luis?" asked Natalie.

He picked up the intercom and said to Charles, "We're going to sleep over at my place tonight, so just drop us there."

He turned off the intercom and said, "Maybe Luis. The strong arm of Reginald Murphy may shield us when he is close at hand and maybe from the 'official' police, but if we're caught alone, we're on our own."

Charles drove to the apartment where he dropped them off and left. Joe started up the stairs but turned back in time to see the limo disappear and a cab pull up. He motioned for them all to climb in and then gave the address of Carolyn's house. "I called for the cab while I was in the men's room. Just playing it safe. We can see out this vehicle's back window too." There were several vehicles on the street, black and dark blue mostly, but none moved as they pulled away.

They arrived at the house without any evidence that they were followed, and Joe paid the cab. "Sleep in the back rooms tonight, okay?"

"A little paranoid are we, Joe?" asked Carolyn. "You think Charles is the killer?"

Joe shrugged. "The limo's a little obvious to be riding around in, and Gloria was killed tonight; oh, and I'm the only one who has actually been shot at so, yes, I'm paranoid, but they *are* out to get me."

"Touché," said Natalie, poking Carolyn in the ribs.

"Room in back it is then," said Carolyn. "Only one room back there so where are you sleeping, Joseph?"

"I get the couch in the living room. I'm going to make sure we're all locked up. Maybe throw some bedding down for me, okay?"

"Bedding coming down the stairs, and remember that the back door is already broken, so let us know if you need help rolling the piano against it," Carolyn said.

"Do you have a piano now?" asked Joe.

"No," replied Carolyn. To Natalie she said, "It's a queen-size bed in the back room. Is that okay to share?"

"Yeah," said Natalie. "Do you have an …"

"Extra nightgown? Yes, I do, but only flannel ones," she replied. "Sorry, Joe."

The doors and windows were all locked except the back door. Joe wedged the table against it and then rigged up what he thought was a truly ingenious pile of pans attached to the door by a string so that if it were opened, the clatter would awaken him and hopefully the ladies. The bedding and a pair of his pajamas were on the floor at the bottom of the stairs when he got back, and a few moments later he was curled up on the coach, trying to think instead of sleep. He lost that battle very quickly.

Chapter 40

While Joe went quickly to sleep, Carolyn and Natalie were preparing for bed as well. They each glanced at the other, admiring how well they looked for their age although neither really knew the other's age. Carolyn looked with a little envy, while Natalie found herself looking as she would at the competition.

"You don't mind sharing a bed, do you, Natalie?" Carolyn finally asked.

"No," replied Natalie. "I thought you might want to share it with Joe. I could sleep downstairs if—"

"Don't be silly," Carolyn cut her off. "I like Joe ... well, I love him is what it really is, but ..."

Natalie cut her off this time saying, "But you're going to divorce him, and you slept with him two nights ago, and I'm a little confused. It's none of my business, of course," she added.

"It might be your business, Natalie," replied Carolyn. "He likes you, you know. And you like him too. Otherwise, you wouldn't be here at all."

Natalie blushed and said, "I don't think he ..."

"Yes he does," said Carolyn. "Remember how quickly he jumped in to make sure your alibi for the time of Gloria's death was solid? That was the first thing I noticed, when he did that for me. Not a murder, but I was getting chewed out by a staff guy and Joe just shut him down. He was still in training at the time too. He definitely likes you; he just doesn't know it yet. If he takes too long figuring it out, I'll tell him though, so don't worry." She smiled at her roommate for the night.

"But you're going to …"

"Divorce him? Yeah, I have to," Carolyn sighed. "He's the best friend I have, and I want it to stay that way."

Natalie just looked at her and she went on, "If we stayed married, I would have to stay here, or he would have to go with me and neither of us would be happy doing that. He loves it here where his family grew up and I … well, I want to try to make a difference in the big world, not the small one."

"Well, yes," said Natalie. "But do you have to give him up to do that?"

"I'm not giving him up, Natalie. Even if he marries you, he'll still be my friend. Not my lover, but definitely my friend." There was silence for a moment and then Carolyn asked, "You were in the army you said? In Afghanistan, right?"

Natalie nodded.

"Why did you join the army?"

"I … well, I thought it was important to protect this country, and I enjoyed it and …"

"That's the same with me," said Carolyn. "I'm not going to join the army, but I think that I have to protect this country from the decaying health care that the government can't seem to fix. It seems so obvious to me what needs to be done, and I can't just stand by and watch while no one does anything. Joe understands that and … well, I want him to be happy, and he won't be happy in Washington, DC. And I won't be happy here."

"I guess you're right."

Carolyn was quiet for another moment, "Did you have a husband or boyfriend when you went into the service?"

"Yes, a husband, but he didn't like what had happened to me when I came back. I was the second happiest person when he said he didn't think it was going to work out. He was the first happiest."

"I'm sorry, Natalie. That was none of my business."

"Thanks for being sorry," said Natalie.

After a few minutes Carolyn said, "So do you think you can shoot this guy if he breaks in here tonight?"

"I think so," said Natalie. "A guy who'd kill a four-year-old? Yes, I think I could shoot him without too much regret. My counselor at the VA will have a field day with it, but if he comes after you, Carolyn, I'll blow his ass off. You can count on it."

"Thanks," said Carolyn. "I'll sleep well just knowing that."

Natalie smiled to herself and thought, *You'd sleep even better if I had my gun with me instead of locked in my car.*

Chapter 41

It was late in the morning, almost ten o'clock, when the ladies were awakened by the clatter of pans from the kitchen below them. They sat up in bed instantly, in time to hear Joe yell, "Just me. Nothing to worry about."

"Is that an oxymoron or what?" said Carolyn to Natalie. "Who else would we worry about if not you, Joe?" she yelled back to him.

Both ladies came downstairs in nightgowns and bathrobes to find Joe dressed and cooking. "Not enough eggs for anything except pancakes," he said. "But they're about ready if you are. Coffee's fresh too."

"No hot chocolate, Joe?" asked Natalie.

He smiled back at her and replied, "Not first thing in the morning. Do you want the syrup heated or is cold okay?"

"No matter," Natalie said. "Coffee's the only thing that matters to me." She helped herself to pancakes anyway. "These are good," she said after a bite.

Carolyn was eating a stack as well and nodded, mumbling something that seemed to agree. She swallowed and said more clearly, "So did the abbreviated night's sleep clear up all the unanswered questions from last night, or are we still in darkness even in the daylight?"

"Have some more coffee, Carolyn, or I'll refuse to understand a word you say," said Natalie.

Carolyn took a sip of coffee and said, "Neither sleep nor light of day has made anything any clearer to me."

"More clear," said Joe. "has made anything *more clear* to me."

"No clearer to you too, Joe?" replied Carolyn.

"Do you two talk this way all the time? I've only had five hours of sleep and I'm stressed to the max and ...," said Natalie. She calmed a little and added, "It's a good thing the coffee and pancakes are good or I would never sleep over here again."

"I bet your roommate snored too," said Joe.

"Not as bad as mine did," said Carolyn.

"I did not," objected Natalie.

"How would you know? You were asleep," said Carolyn. "Pass the pancakes will you?"

Natalie held up the plate of pancakes and said, "Pancakes for coffee. An even swap."

The deal was done, and Joe sat opposite them at the counter and drank his coffee. "Do you think we can get back to the mundane topic of murder, or will that affect your digestion too much?"

"Okay. So what's the answer, or do you just want to rehash the failed answers from last night?" Natalie looked at him and then took another bite of breakfast.

"Well," said Joe, "I don't have any answers, I guess. I just thought if we went over it maybe ..."

"Or," said Carolyn, "we can eat pancakes and wait for someone to call us up and tell us what the answer is. I do remember that your malpractice thing should be dropped today. You didn't have to show up, did you?"

"No," said Joe. "Walter got it postponed until Monday anyway. I forgot to tell you. Maybe I should call him." He reached for his cell phone and came up with Carolyn's. "The police still have mine. Why did they take it, I wonder?"

"Not to check your alibi," said Natalie. "They just need your number and an order from the court to access your account."

"And not to keep you from making calls since you can use mine or any number of other phones," said Carolyn.

"Then," said Joe, "it must be to get my calls."

"Did you tell Reggie you didn't have your phone, Joe?" asked Carolyn. "Or Walter or anyone?"

"No," said Joe. "Maybe I should call him."

"You know who I think you should call is that pathologist, Frank whatever-his-name-is," said Natalie. "The one who did the first autopsy. Ask him what he found and why the report got changed."

"Ah," replied Joe, "I can't. He's dead."

"Not another murder?" asked Natalie.

"No," said Carolyn. "A mundane heart attack. On the evening of his retirement too. I remember that party and how drunk he got. It was April Fool's Day. He thought that was so ironic that he was 'fooling' everyone by retiring and leaving us to suffer without him. In the end, he got drunk and went home and got 'fooled' himself, when he woke up dead the next morning."

Joe looked at her and said, "Or murdered the next morning. April second was when he, or someone, altered the report, according to the computer record. It was at two thirty in the morning. Frank Dobbs was in no shape to do it, and no one would have taken a chance on altering it unless they knew Frank wouldn't notice it. Unless they knew he was dead … or going to be dead."

"This is getting too crazy, Joe," said Carolyn. "Does everyone get murdered in this thing?"

"The pieces are all here," said Joe. "We just have to fit them together."

"Before someone murders us," said Natalie.

"I'm not sure we—" Carolyn began, but her phone rang, interrupting her. She looked at the caller ID and said, "It's the hospital."

"You're not working today, are you?" asked Joe.

"No," she said. "I'm actually supposed to be leaving to go interview in Las Vegas today."

She shrugged and opened her phone. "Hello," she said.

She looked at Joe and Natalie and said, "Oh, hi Lawrence. I thought you were on your way to that conference or something."

After a pause she said, "Joe?" Both Natalie and Joe signaled that she should not say Joe was with her. She frowned at them as if to reply she knew better. "No, I have no idea where he is. Haven't seen him since he left with Reginald Murphy last night. Lawrence, my hands are all wet from washing dishes, so I'm putting you on speaker while I dry them." She put down the phone and turned on water in the sink.

Lawrence was saying, "Carolyn, I'm really concerned about Joe. There was a fire at his apartment complex last night and the police are looking for him. He's been under a lot of stress and apparently has been arguing with Walter. I think he may be … well, losing it."

"A fire?" said Carolyn. "When was that?"

"Early this morning. Maybe three or four o'clock. I guess it started in Joe's apartment, and it's pretty well gutted. Are you sure you don't know where he is?" Lawrence asked again.

Joe waved his hand, but Carolyn just frowned again. "Maybe you should talk to Reginald Murphy. He might know."

"I can't get through to him, Carolyn. But Charles, his chauffer, said he dropped all three of you at Joe's apartment early this morning." After a pause Lawrence asked, "Where are you now, Carolyn?"

"Oh. I'm in the airport leaving for my interview in Vegas. They're calling my flight now. Got to go, Lawrence." She closed the phone.

Natalie looked at her. "You're washing dishes in the airport?"

"He had me a little flustered, okay?" Carolyn said.

"And Lawrence can't reach Reggie but can reach Charles who's telling him everything about us." Joe started to move. "Look, I think it's a bad idea to be here when the police or whoever gets here. You two get dressed while I call for a cab. Maybe call Charles first though."

"Charles?" asked Natalie.

"Just hurry, okay?" said Joe. "No makeup this morning."

184

Chapter 42

They both thought they dressed in record time, but Joe was impatiently waiting, holding the cab door open when they came out the front door. "Get in," he said.

As they pulled away from the house, they saw a limo coming down the street. Joe smiled and said. "I hope Charles gets the note I left him."

"The note?" asked Natalie.

"Tacked to the front door," replied Joe. "It says we'll be back in thirty minutes and asks him to wait. Just in case anyone asks Charles where we are."

Joe then leaned forward to talk to the driver. "How much would it cost to have you call your dispatcher and say you dropped us at that restaurant back there and that you're going to grab a cup of coffee before you go back on duty? My wife knows I'm screwing around, and I think she knows someone in your office because the last time she knew where I'd been before I got home." Joe pulled out two twenties and offered them to the driver.

The driver looked at Joe and then at the ladies and said, "Three of those would look better."

Joe pulled out another twenty and said, "Thanks, guy."

"Ya know, I figured that was what was going on. Know how I figured it out? You two don't have no makeup." He chuckled and picked up his radio and made the call. Joe might have had some troublesome ladies to deal with, makeup or none, but just then a police car sped by them going toward the house with the flashers on.

"Where to?" asked the driver as he turned off the meter.

"To the city, man," said Joe and put an arm around both Carolyn and Natalie. When they had gone about two miles and Carolyn was beginning to squirm, Joe said, "Hey, stop at that coffee shop. The one with the ATM next to it. I need some cash for the ladies."

The driver nodded and parked outside the shop.

"Come on, girls. Let me show you the size of my bank account before I show you the rest of my stuff," Joe said. He realized he was pushing his luck, even in this most desperate of situations. He handed the driver a twenty dollar bill and said, "Grab yourself a coffee and three more for us too and wait inside while I get the money, okay?"

They walked over to the ATM, and Carolyn started to go in, but Joe pulled her around to the other side, away from the coffee shop. He looked around the corner to see the driver going in. "Good," he said. "Let's cut through the back here to the main street and pick up another cab."

Natalie had a frown on her face, but it was Carolyn who said, "If no one else kills you, I get to do it, okay? What are we doing Joe?"

"Things are moving way too fast and everyone seems to be after us ... or me anyway," replied Joe. "The police are after me, my apartment has been burned out, and Charles is telling everyone where to look for me. They need to have me out of the way in a hurry or they wouldn't be going to all this trouble. Whatever it is, it has to be happening right now."

"What's happening?" asked Carolyn.

"I don't have any idea," replied Joe.

Natalie pulled them to a stop. There was a police car parked at the corner they were about to enter. Two uniformed officers were standing on the sidewalk scanning the passersby. "Might be looking for you, Joe. I don't know what's going on either, but we'd better be real careful around police right now." There were cabs parked beyond the police but no way to get to them.

Chapter 43

As they were trying to figure out what to do next, Carolyn's phone rang again, and Joe handed it to her. She looked at it and said, "Walter?" She showed the caller ID to Natalie and Joe. "Should I answer it?"

Joe looked puzzled for a moment. "Maybe see what he wants with you?" he shrugged. Natalie shrugged too and Carolyn answered her phone.

"Hello," said Carolyn in the calmest voice she could manage.

"Ah," said a slurred voice on the other end. "Is this Carolyn? This is Walter Mosby and I'm so sorry to bother you, but I need to talk to your husband and well … Lawrence said you might know where I can reach him."

Carolyn covered the phone and said, "Oh great. Walter's drunk and wants to talk to you, Joe."

Joe thought for a moment and then said, "Maybe he has a reason to be drunk and maybe that reason will help us figure this out. Worth a try, I guess." He held out his hand and Carolyn handed him the phone.

"Walter," Joe said, "I know that the malpractice suit has been dropped. Is there anything else?"

A slurred voice replied, "Oh yes. The trial's being canceled. The reason I called, however, is to apologize." Joe looked surprised and then put the phone on speaker. He didn't think Walter would notice.

"Apologize for what, Walter?" he asked.

"There's been all sorts of trouble, and I'm afraid I was part of that trouble. I'm sorry, Joe, and I hope you accept my apology. I never intended for it to get so out of hand, but now it's over."

"Have you been drinking, Walter?" asked Joe.

"Only a little," the slurred voice said. "To fortify me for this. I'll never take another drink as long as I live." He laughed now as if this were the funniest thing he had ever said.

"Where are you, Walter?" asked Joe.

"Can't say," Walter replied.

Carolyn covered the phone and whispered, "The caller ID said it was 'Attorney Walter Mosby.' That must be his office?"

Joe paused and then went on casually, "Well, I accept your apology, Walter. I know you wouldn't have let anything happen. I was scared there for a while though. Can you see the street where I was shot at from there?"

"I could if I could get up and go to the window," said Walter. "I just wanted to say I'm sorry. Goodbye, Joe," and the phone went dead.

"Shit," said Joe. "Now *he's* got me worried too."

"You think Walter's the killer?" asked Carolyn.

"He couldn't get the police involved," said Natalie. "Who is it that could get the police involved except maybe Reggie or Andy? Neither of them is the killer, are they?"

"And neither has access to the computer system at the hospital," said Joe.

"Andy might be able to, through the police department?" said Natalie.

"And Reggie is on the board although he never comes to meetings," added Carolyn.

"Not making sense again," said Joe. He took the phone from Carolyn and dialed the hospital ED. "Hello, Stacy. Don't say my name, okay?"

"I know who you are, stranger," said Stacy.

"Is Francine on today, and can I talk to her, and don't tell anyone it's me," said Joe.

"Strangers in my bed," said Stacy.

In a minute Francine's voice said, "This is Francine Hayes. May I help you?"

"Don't say my name, Francine, but this is Joe Nelson."

"Oh," said a surprised nurse. "Can I help you?"

Joe put the phone on speaker. "That day when Linda Murphy died. Who came into the room before the second cardiac arrest?" asked Joe.

"Well, Mr. Marshall and Miss Murphy, Gloria, I mean, were there already, and Larry the pharmacist was restocking or trying to, but I told him we didn't need anything, and I think Bert came in too and maybe that lawyer that was defending you. He was in the department but maybe not in the room. Some of the other board members were walking around and, of course, there were some other docs and nurses in and out too. Why are you asking?" She was getting upset and Joe wanted desperately to avoid that.

She continued immediately without his saying anything. "And then Mr. Marshall noticed Linda had arrested again. It was just me and Miss Murphy and Mr. Marshall then. I thought it was just artifact on the monitor. One of them was moving the monitor leads, but he was right. He made me go get you. That was a good thing he did," she said.

"Thanks," said Joe. No sense upsetting her more, especially because he was trying not to let anyone there know it was he on the phone. "Can you give me Stacy again?"

Stacy was on the phone in another few seconds. "May I help you?"

"Who's on administrative backup today, Stacy?"

"Carl Summers," she replied. "Mr. Marshall's leaving now," she said as if she was trying to tell Joe who was watching her.

"Thanks," said Joe. "I owe you. Anything you ever want, Stacy."

"You can warm my bed and bring me flowers in the morning," Stacy said, but the phone had already been hung up.

Stacy looked up at Lawrence Marshall, who was staring at her. "Your sex life is not to be discussed on hospital time."

"Well, what my gardener does in my flower beds, and whether I get flowers from his efforts is not exactly what I call a 'sex life.' Mine's more interesting than that."

Lawrence Marshall scowled at her and walked away as Stacy continued, "I hope it's more interesting than that for you too, Mr. Marshall." When he disappeared around the corner she added, "Prick."

Chapter 44

"So what was that about?" asked Natalie.

"Just who was there when Linda died and what Francine saw and what Gloria might have seen," said Joe. "We'd better get going and maybe in separate directions. An unattractive man with two beautiful women is bound to draw attention."

The two beautiful women scowled at him but didn't argue that point. "Split up?" asked Carolyn.

"Yeah," said Joe. "Look, Douglas is on the board at the hospital too, isn't he?"

"You think Douglas is the murderer, Joe?" asked Carolyn.

Joe stared at her a moment. "No, of course not," he said. "I need some information from him. But maybe I'd better talk to him in person."

"Well, okay, if you think so. Let me call and find out if he's around." Carolyn dialed and got her brother. When she hung up, she said, "He's in his office and can talk to you now if you want. There's a client waiting but I told him I'd cancel the divorce if he didn't see you for a few minutes. We'll go with you."

"No," said Joe. "You've got to go over to Walter's office and rescue him. I think he may have overdosed. That might take a doctor and a police sergeant, since I think that whoever has my cell phone probably got a call from Walter before we did. The only good thing is that they may not know where he is. I don't think we should call 911 either. There may be people who wouldn't want Walter to recover and some of them answer the 911 calls."

"Shit," said Carolyn. "You could be right. So how do we get there without attracting attention? Alter our DNA so we look ugly?"

"I don't think that would be possible for either of you," said Joe, smiling at them. "They're looking for me, and they might recognize Natalie, so maybe you could go over and get a cab and pick us up on the corner," he said to Carolyn. "A beautiful woman out shopping."

Carolyn looked into the trash container next to them. She pulled out a plastic bag from one of the local "high-end" store chains and stuffed a couple of newspapers into it. She then put on a nonchalant look and walked over and got into a cab. Neither officer paid her any attention, and when she was out of sight of the police, she had the cabbie pick up Joe and Natalie.

Joe gave the address of Douglas' office. "I'll keep your cell phone, okay? Drop me at Douglas' and then head for Walter," he said to Carolyn.

Ten minutes later Joe was in Douglas' office, facing an attorney with a frown on his face. "This better be—" said Douglas before Joe interrupted him.

"I only have a few minutes, Douglas, and I want to make a substantial contribution to your run for the governorship, so let's get it going," said Joe. Either the attitude or the substance of what Joe said put Douglas in a receptive mood.

"Okay," he said tentatively.

"First, I need to make a call," said Joe, and without waiting, picked up Douglas' phone and dialed the main hospital number. "Mr. Carl Summers please," he said when the operator picked up.

To Douglas he said, "Question for you while I'm waiting: Did the hospital investigate the ED contracts at all, Douglas? Any question about work quality or costs?"

Douglas shrugged. "Well, yes, there were. But then the hospital got all that money when ..." He cleared his throat and continued, "when Linda Murphy died and ... well, that made such a difference in the finances, it all just got dropped.

"Especially since we were investigating Bert." He shrugged and cleared his throat again. "Gloria's friend, you know?"

After he cleared his bothersome throat again, he added, "I was not at all sure that was the right decision, but ..."

Joe held up his hand and spoke into the phone. "Hello, Carl. This is Joe Nelson. Douglas Prentiss and I have a question: Did the hospital hold back final payment to Bert for the new ED?"

"Oh, hi Joe. Well, I'm not sure that I should say, but yes, as a matter of fact," said Carl.

"I'll put you on speaker so Douglas can hear as well," said Joe.

"Hi, Carl," said Douglas, looking annoyed.

Joe continued, "And was that payment finally made? Recently? Like today maybe?"

Carl was obviously surprised. "Well, yes, today. Lawrence got Bert to accept an eighty percent payment if we signed off today. Saved the hospital almost a million. I shouldn't be telling you this really, so don't say anything, please."

How could Carolyn be dating this guy? thought Joe. "And did Bert get the check?"

"Oh yes. Lawrence wanted it all done before he left for Aruba. Conference he said, but I never saw a brochure. Ah, but he deserves it after the money—" Joe hung up.

Douglas was not looking annoyed any longer, but puzzled. "I'm not sure—"

"Gloria's dead," said Joe.

"Yes, I know," replied Douglas. "But what—"

"And Bert, her *friend*, just got paid for work he probably shouldn't have been paid for, am I right, Douglas?"

"Well—" Douglas was not going to get a chance to finish any sentences today if Joe could help it.

"I'm going to give you a number, Douglas. It's the exclusive direct line to Reginald Murphy. When you get him on the line, the first thing you are to say is that I told you to call. Understand, Douglas? The very first thing you say."

Douglas nodded.

"And then tell him you need a court order—state, not local. State, Douglas. It has to be state. Bypass the local judges, understand? Reginald can do that sort of thing easily."

Douglas looked more shocked the longer Joe talked.

"You have to impound all of Bert's records. All of them, do you understand? His business and personal and throw in Gloria's stuff and the stuff at the hospital too. Everything. Reggie can do that, so just tell him I told you to do it, okay?"

Douglas looked at Joe and began, "But—"

"Bert's either shredding everything right now, or running for the border, or whatever people do when they have embezzled and murdered people and have to run for it." Joe frowned again. "And Douglas, when you get off the phone with Reginald, call the police station and ask to talk to an officer named Wayne. Tell him Carolyn or I told you to call him and if you get him, get him to go to Bert's office with you and stop them from destroying all the evidence. Do you understand, Douglas?"

"Are you—"

"I'm sure, Douglas. You can trust me on this one and if you do, you will be so famous you'll be able to run for president, except that Carolyn won't let you." Joe smiled at him and he smiled back.

"Okay, Joe. I'm with you. But why can't you do this?"

"I need a lawyer to do this, of course, and besides, I have to get to the airport," said Joe. "How much cash do you have on you?"

"Oh, maybe a hundred or so."

"Give me all of it," Joe said. "I have to get a cab to the airport."

"That's fifty miles! It'll cost two hundred by cab. Let me loan you my car."

"You'll need it, and I can get the rest from the ATM downstairs. Give me the money, Douglas. I can't wait."

Douglas gave him all his money, almost a hundred and fifty, Joe noted.

As Joe left, Douglas told his clients he would be tied up and asked his associate to see to them. He then dialed the number Joe had given him.

"Mr. Murphy," Douglas said, "Joseph Nelson told me to call you, and this is what he said we have to do."

Chapter 45

The cab driver balked at the request, but when Joe gave him two hundred and fifty for the trip, he shrugged and said okay. Joe knew this would be the last thing anyone would expect him to be doing right now. He hoped the cab drivers had not been alerted to look for him, but he had to take a chance. The local police wouldn't want to ask the state police for help, he hoped. A car they would be looking for, maybe even Douglas' car, but not a cab on its way to the airport.

"What about some music?" asked Joe, and the cabbie turned on the radio loud enough to allow Joe to talk on the cell phone without being overheard.

"Joe," said Natalie when she answered, "we're in the ED with Walter. You were right. He had overdosed. We beat the police to his office by only five minutes, but by then the ambulance was already coming too. Wait a minute, Carolyn wants to talk to you."

"Hi, Joe," Carolyn said. "Walter had overdosed all right. Benzos or something, they're not sure, and alcohol too, of course. He's intubated though and it looks like he'll be all right. Good call, doc."

"Thanks," said Joe. "Look, Carolyn. I'm on my way to the airport, and your brother is impounding all of Bert's records. The airport might be safer than being up there with the police scrambling to get us, if you know what I mean, and I may need some backup too." He paused and then said, "And Carolyn, take your car, not Natalie's. They're less likely to be looking for it. It's new and they may not even know what you're driving right now, but they'll know Natalie's car for sure."

Natalie tapped Carolyn's shoulder and pointed to someone coming into the emergency department. It was Sergeant Peter Pierce. Carolyn turned away and said, "Right, Joe," and hung up.

"Is that doctor the one named John?" asked Natalie, pointing to a man in scrubs nearby.

"Yes," said Carolyn.

"Will he get the state police here to protect Walter from Peter and Andy if you ask him to?"

Carolyn didn't answer but walked over to John Lawson. "Hey, John," she said. "The overdose in there." She nodded toward the room where Walter lay unconscious and intubated. "Can you get the state police to watch him? I think he might be involved with the drug trafficking up county, and I don't want the local guys to steal the credit, or to let him get away with it."

"Drug trafficking! He's a lawyer!" John Lawson said, shaking his head. "Lawyers! I should've guessed. The local police are as corrupt as they come. I'll make sure the state guys take over."

"Thanks," said Carolyn.

Natalie looked at her as they walked away. "We all hate the drug dealers, but John particularly does," said Carolyn. Natalie nodded and Carolyn added, "John's brother overdosed and died about five years ago." Carolyn shook her head and said, "He'll forgive me if I'm wrong about Walter and the drug trafficking."

Natalie and Carolyn walked out of the ED through the staff entrance and were directly in front of Carolyn's car. They climbed into it and headed for the airport. There was a uniformed police officer standing next to Joe's car, which was next to Natalie's car, but he hadn't looked at them.

"My gun's in my car," said Natalie.

Carolyn looked over at her. "You won't need it, will you?" she said and looked back at the road.

While Joe was riding to the airport, he familiarized himself with Carolyn's phone. It was much newer than his, complete with

Internet access, and he spent his time looking up flights out of the country. When he got to the airport, he jumped out and ran for the lobby. He knew what flight and gate he was looking for, and he saw who he was looking for immediately—he was walking briskly toward that gate. It had been a lucky guess that this would be the flight he would take, but it was the only one leaving for a South American city that matched the timing.

Here he was and Joe was still alone; no police, no Natalie or Carolyn, and no one who could help a pediatrician in distress. If he did nothing, that man would get away with it all. Once he was inside the security check point, Joe couldn't follow because he had no ticket. The murderer of Linda and Gloria Murphy had probably figured a way to get a fake passport so that even if Joe could convince the police that they needed to stop him, they would have no way of finding him in time. Joe decided he would have to do something really stupid.

"Mr. Marshall!" he yelled. The man stopped abruptly and turned, as did several other curious bystanders. Joe started walking to intercept him at the gate, and in another second Lawrence started toward that same gate. The pause had given Joe a chance to get there first, and he now stood directly in Marshall's path.

"Excuse me, but I have a plane to catch," Lawrence said to Joe and started around him.

Joe moved to block him again and yelled, "No, you don't!" Out of the corner of his vision, Joe saw one of the baggage check-in attendants at the nearest counter pick up a phone. He hoped the call would be to security.

Lawrence went again to push past Joe and again Joe moved to block him. "The police will be here any moment and they'll stop whatever plane you're on, and that will be all there is to it. It's over, Lawrence." He looked around and saw the security police arriving on the scene. Joe also saw Natalie getting out of Carolyn's car in front of the building. *It's working,* Joe thought. He was wrong.

Lawrence Marshall slowly put down his bag and reached inside his jacket and when his hand came out, it was holding a gun. A small automatic. The kind Wayne had said was used on Gloria Murphy. It had killed Gloria, Joe remembered. Lawrence reached over to Joe's left arm with his left hand and turned him to face a gasping crowd. He pressed the gun against Joe's neck and began to speak. "Dr. Nelson and I are going to get into a cab now and you police are going to put your weapons on the floor and step aside. And don't do anything to make me nervous or Dr. Nelson will be the first to regret it."

Joe didn't know what he had expected to happen, but what he saw disappointed him. Three security police took guns from holsters and placed them on the floor and backed away. Natalie was at the front of the crowd, only ten or twelve feet from him, and when the police and the crowd backed away, she was left alone, standing in front of Joe and Lawrence Marshall.

"Is this Sergeant Moore, your girlfriend, Joe?" asked Lawrence in mock surprise. "Surely she will let us pass and, in so doing, let you live, won't you now, Sergeant?" Natalie didn't move.

"Tell her I mean it, Joe," said Lawrence.

Joe looked at Natalie and finally said, "I feel like I'm in that rock fall again, with my foot trapped beneath the rock, Natalie. Back in that coal mine and about to die, *standing still.* Don't let that happen. I want to try to run."

"He's right, Sergeant. He is trapped. Don't do anything to make a man with a gun pointed at your boyfriend nervous," Lawrence Marshall said, pushing the gun into Joe's neck.

Natalie looked at Joe, who managed to nod just a little, and then she looked at Lawrence. She said nothing, just stood there for a moment. Then she looked down at the gun at her feet and nodded her head and said, "Yes, Joe."

"Now, get out of my way, all of you," Lawrence yelled. "I want a clear path to the door, do you understand?"

"Do as he says," said Natalie. "Everyone get out from behind him."

"Thank you, Sergeant," said Lawrence as the crowd cleared from behind him, leaving the way to the exit unobstructed.

Natalie looked at the gun at her feet again, and when she looked up, she stared directly at Lawrence Marshall. She knelt down and picked up the gun from the floor and stood and looked quickly to make sure there was a bullet in the next chamber of the revolver. She pointed it straight at Lawrence's head and pulled off two quick shots that blew his face away.

Later, some of the people would say they thought Lawrence started to say "No," while others swore he started to move his gun to point it at Natalie. Neither thing happened though, and Lawrence Marshall slammed backward, landing on the floor. A piece of what looked to Natalie like brain and skull continued a foot or so beyond where his head landed.

Blood poured briefly into a puddle beside his head. The air escaping from his lungs made a gurgling sound as it passed through what remained of his mouth. He never inhaled again. There was a brief twitching of his right hand. Joe would explain later that that happened because Natalie had shot him in the left side of his head, the side farthest from Joe's head. The left side of the brain controlled the right side of the body. In another minute the bleeding stopped too.

Joe had been thrown backwards as well, but had not lost his balance enough to fall. There was blood on his face and he wiped it away. It was all Marshall's blood. He was unhurt. The gun Lawrence had in his right hand had skidded across the floor and the crowd had backed away from it as if it were still a very dangerous thing. Natalie had kept her gun pointed at him until she was sure he was dead, and then, lowering it, she said to him, "There's nothing to get nervous about, Mr. Marshall." She raised her hands and showed the gun she held to the gasping crowd, with her badge in the other hand, and then she placed the gun back on the floor where she had picked it up.

State troopers ran in and Natalie saw Carolyn in the background and a SWAT team arriving. "Better put your hands in the air, Joe. These guys are all business," she said.

Chapter 46

Natalie sat and answered a state police officer's questions. The officer was a woman about Natalie's age, blond and trim and friendly, and Natalie wondered if she had been chosen for some reason that defied logic: that a woman would make her comfortable enough to "break down" or some such thing. Natalie had killed a man, and she would rather not have had to kill him, but she had no choice. Joe had told her that was what she had to do, and she had done it because ... well, because she trusted him. The first questions were about her own police status, and she knew her captain would be called soon and that everything she said would then be colored by what Andy said.

Joe was sitting with a young, blond man who had introduced himself as Sergeant Wells, Sergeant Percival Wells. Joe found humor in this though he was not sure why, given what had happened a few minutes ago, but he wondered what Reginald would think if his mother had named him Percival. He was also wondering how he could answer these questions in a way that made it clear that Lawrence Marshall intended to keep killing people until someone stopped him, and that the next one to die would have been Joe himself ... or Natalie ... or Carolyn.

"So tell me why she shot him," asked Percival Wells.

"I told her she had to," answered Joe.

Percival had an accent that said he came from a place a little farther south than where he was right then. "Now, you said that, but I don't think I understand what y'all are saying."

Joe let his own accent slip into the country style he had grown up speaking, the one that matched Percival's. "Well," he said, "Lawrence Marshall killed a four-year-old girl three years ago and a day ago shot that girl's aunt to death. He was convinced that I knew all about it, and while I had just figured out what really happened, he thought I knew all along."

Percival stretched a little and said, "But you know, his ID says he's Earl Ray."

"His fingerprints will show he's Lawrence Marshall. He was an EMT and his prints are on file, I'm sure," said Joe.

Percival Wells nodded. *Plenty of time to find out if that was, in fact, the case,* he seemed to say with that nod. "But you said you told Sergeant Moore that she had to shoot him. Why did you tell her that and I'm wondering just a bit how you told her. Plenty of witnesses heard what you said, and none heard you say 'shoot him.'"

Joe smiled. Plenty of time to work this out. "Well, Sergeant Wells, as for the why, Mr. Marshall told me he was going to kill me first chance he got. So knowing I had nothing to lose, I asked Natalie to take a chance on saving me."

"He told you he was going to kill you? Now why would he kill you? Didn't he need a hostage or something?"

"Not two hostages though—me and a cab driver or someone else—and you see, apart from the fact that he blamed me for getting him caught, he wanted a hostage with two legs. A hostage who could run if need came to that, and you see I can't." Joe pulled up his pant leg to display the prosthesis beneath it. Joe was stretching the truth here, he knew; but this young man would never believe that a man with a prosthetic leg could do anything he could do and maybe better ... except in this case Joe probably could not play basketball better.

Percival nodded. "Makes a bit of sense, that does. So how did Natalie ...? Is that her name?"

"Yes. Sergeant Natalie Moore," replied Joe.

"Sergeant of police back in your hometown, I understand."

"Yes," said Joe again.

"And you say you told her?"

"Yes," Joe said. "You see, Lawrence Marshall told me he would kill Natalie and my wife too if I said anything that would let anyone know what he was planning. He said I could die alone or with both of them, if I wanted it that way, but that he was going to kill me anyway." Joe shrugged and smiled at the state police sergeant. "I lost this leg in a mining accident, and my daddy told me then that I had to fight back. That I was better off *running than standing still* when someone was shooting at me. That's what I said to Natalie Moore, hoping she would understand. She did. She saved my life, Sergeant Wells. It's as simple as that."

Percival Wells nodded but said nothing. There was a tap on the door and Joe looked up to see a large African American state police officer motioning Percival outside. As they conferred, Joe also saw Andy and Peter come into the lobby. What were those two doing so far from home? And so quickly? Nothing good, he was sure. Joe watched all four of them converse, and then Peter came into the room with Joe and said, "It looks like you people are in big trouble here. Shooting up a fella like that. Especially Lawrence Marshall. Captain must've known you were up to no good, that's why he wanted to get down here so quick."

So Peter knew who was lying dead on the floor without looking at the body and his captain knew he would be here. How did he know? Joe looked past Peter at his captain. He had not anticipated this and was angry with himself for not realizing that these two would be down here so quickly—before he got to tell his side of the story. He was disgusted with the whole thing, but mostly with himself as he looked at the captain gesticulating at the state officers.

The captain saw Joe looking at him and smiled at him. Maybe it was a sneer, but Joe recognized it. "Sergeant Pierce. You and the captain have me and Nat nailed down pretty well. You two are pretty sharp all right, you and Captain … what's his name again?"

Peter gloated a bit and then said, "Captain Andrew Wilson. And he *is* good and you *will* remember his name, Mr. Nelson."

"I think I will," said Joe. "I have a patient by that name. Jennifer Wilson."

"That'd be the captain's niece. His half-brother's kid." Peter smiled. "You may not have her as a patient for much longer though."

Why hadn't he realized this connection before? Everyone was related in the mountains so no one, including himself, paid attention to the relationships. No one thought that it was important.

Joe stretched and said, "You think I could talk to my wife for a minute, please?" he asked. "I want to explain about Natalie a little, you know." He tried his best to put on a hang dog look.

"Guess it won't matter now," smirked Peter. "She's a good looker and will be looking for a new man, ya think? Sure. Why not?" He went and motioned to Carolyn to come into the room. "Your husband has a confession to make."

"Could I do it alone, please?" asked Joe. Peter looked over Carolyn quickly and left, the smirk on his face growing even larger.

Carolyn looked at Joe and began to speak, but Joe cut her off. "I need to call your brother without Peter Pierce interfering. Can you distract him?"

Carolyn was obviously shocked and revolted by the idea. "It's important, Joe, right? Really important? Because if it isn't, I get to kill you, okay?"

"Agreed," said Joe.

Carolyn nodded and gave Joe a look that said she was serious about that promise of death. She then unbuttoned the top button of her blouse and took a tissue out of her pocket. Joe looked at her questioningly and she said, "This will get that slug's attention better than anything I can say."

She turned and kissed Joe on the cheek. "I wouldn't really kill you, Joe, but I have to do this to make the slug pay attention properly." She then slapped Joe's recently kissed cheek and went to talk to Peter, trying not to vomit on him.

Joe watched as Carolyn began to cry softly and Peter rubbed her arm, shoulder to elbow and back again. He turned away and dialed Douglas. When he came on the phone, Douglas said, "Oh, Joseph, this is so great. Wayne and I got here before Bert had even gotten half a dozen sheets through the shredder. It's all here. He and Lawrence were in it up to their ears. Skimming the contracts and ... he's talking like crazy. Says Lawrence killed Linda Murphy while he was watching outside to make sure no one came into the room and that Lawrence shot Gloria too. Bert just won't stop talking. He refused a lawyer even. He says he's just glad it's all over and he wants to confess to everything. I think he's trying to cover his own—"

"Douglas, listen to me." Joe cut him off. "Ask him about his brother."

"Andy?" asked Douglas. "He's the chief of police. What should I ask him, Joe?" Joe shook his head. Was he the only one who hadn't realized Bert and Andy were brothers?

"Ask him how deep his brother is in all this. Did he kill anyone or just cover for the others? Ask him what his brother's share was? Those will do for starters."

"Shit, Joe. Are you serious? Andy Wilson?"

"Andy Wilson is trying to hang me out to dry right now, and your sister too, Douglas. Ask the questions and when the answers start coming, call State Police Sergeant Percival Wells direct. Percival Wells. Can you remember that? Use Reggie again if you can't get through. Ask him—"

"I told you he was on the phone!" Captain Wilson interrupted Joe. "Damn it, Peter, put him in the cruiser for Christ's sake."

The African American state police officer walked in and said, "A bit out of your jurisdiction, Captain Wilson, aren't you?"

"Listen you ... He's wanted in my jurisdiction on a murder charge and arson and ... I'll take him into custody on those charges and you can come question him up there all you want."

The state officer was unmoved. Finally, Joe said, "I'd just as soon be questioned here if that's okay with everyone. And maybe I should ask about calling an attorney?"

"You shut up," said Andy. "No lawyer can help you, so no need to call one. We'll get you one up in my jail if you still want one." He turned to the state police officer and said, "Look, murder is a whole lot more serious than anything down here."

"I'm investigating a death right here, Captain. And I don't want to drive up to your jurisdiction to do that."

They stared at each other for a moment until Percival Wells tapped on the glass and opened the door. "Hank," he said, motioning his superior out of the room. Captain Wilson scowled at Joe while the two state police officers talked outside and looked in at them occasionally.

Percival finally came back in and said to Andy, "Well now. Looks like we might be able to settle all this real quick, Captain." Nonetheless, Joe noticed he stood blocking the exit. It wasn't possible for Douglas to have gotten anything from Bert this quickly. It had only been five minutes. Joe had little time to think about it, however, as Natalie came up outside with the young, female officer.

"That one's a troublemaker too, Wells," said Andy.

"That so?" said Sergeant Wells with studied indifference.

A moment later the two state police officers came into the room with Natalie and Carolyn following them. Percival looked at Carolyn. Joe was sure she was not supposed to be there, but Percival just looked at his superior who nodded and said, "Percy, I think we can finish here pretty quickly and let Captain Wilson and these other people get on with their business. Why don't you get some specifics from the captain here while I finish with these people?"

"Glad to, Sir," said Percival Wells and opened the door for Captain Wilson.

When they left, leaving Peter and the female state police sergeant alone with Joe and Natalie and Carolyn, the state police captain turned to Natalie and rubbed his dark skin and well-trimmed, grey beard. "Now Sergeant Moore, I'm still a little unclear as to why you shot and killed that man. He had a gun pointed at Dr. Nelson, I know, but I'm not sure why you felt you had to kill him rather than … negotiate something with him. That's the standard procedure in our outfit, negotiate if you can, so I'm wondering why you didn't. Why did you think you had to kill him? I know you've already given a statement, but can you tell me?"

Peter smirked, but Natalie looked at him and smiled. Better this captain than Andy Wilson. "Joe … well, Dr. Nelson lost his leg in a mining accident twenty years ago. He told me about what happened that day and what his father said to him when they had to cut his foot off. I remember what Joe … Dr. Nelson told me like I was there myself. 'You have to fight back. It's better to be shot running than standing still.' When he said that again today, that he felt like he was in the mine again about to be shot standing still, I knew what he was telling me I had to do."

The state police captain turned to the female officer and asked, "That what she told you, Patti?"

"Yes, sir," she replied.

There was quiet for a minute until finally Carolyn could not stand it any longer, "That's what really happened to Joe, Captain."

"Oh, were you there, Miss?"

"Well no …" said Carolyn.

"I was," said the captain and smiled. "You remember me, Joe?"

Joe looked at the name on his uniform. "Morgan," it said.

"Hank. Hank Morgan. Friend of my father's. Yeah, I remember you. Sure, you came to visit me when I was in the hospital. You were going to join the state police back then." Joe paused and smiled. "Hank, I am so glad you did that. So glad."

"So am I," said Captain Hank Morgan.

Chapter 47

The tide had definitely turned and Peter saw the flood coming. "I would like to speak to you, Captain Morgan. About some unusual occurrences in my department," he said.

"Well," said Hank Morgan, "I always want to cooperate with the local departments." He turned to Patti and said, "Sergeant Burke, would you mind talking to Sergeant Pierce about his department?"

"I'll be glad to," she replied, and she looked like she would enjoy it. Had Peter been hitting on her too? Joe wondered. Had Captain Morgan purposely chosen the young, attractive, female sergeant to interview Sergeant "Slug"? He wondered if Patti would play her role as well as Carolyn had and trap him with equal ease. As if to provide an answer, Patti turned while leaving to smile and then wink; Joe thought it was at Captain Morgan, but when he looked, the captain was looking at Natalie, and when Joe looked back at Patti, she definitely winked at him.

When they exited, Patti pointed Peter toward an office well out of sight of the one Captain Wilson was in. Those two were not going to be allowed to compare stories.

The captain turned back to the three remaining and said, "So how are you doing, Joe?"

Joe smiled and said, "This day started off pretty badly, but it's turning out okay. How are you doing, Hank?"

"I'm doing pretty well, too," said Hank. "I was sorry about your dad. Sorry I didn't get to his funeral. He was a good man and he raised a good son."

"Thanks," said Joe and looked at his feet for a moment.

Hank only let that last a moment, though, before he said, "So what the hell happened here today, and where did you get these people from?" He motioned toward Natalie and Carolyn.

"Oh," replied Joe. "You know Natalie and Carolyn. Carolyn's my wife and Natalie is ..." Joe realized that the real explanation might sound a little strange.

Carolyn did not share his concern. "Joe and I are getting divorced and Joe is trying to get himself killed and Natalie is trying to interfere with that—the part where Joe gets killed, I mean."

"That's a good thing," said Hank. "The part about Joe not getting killed. Natalie seems pretty good at interfering with that, and it's none of my business, but Captain Wilson said Natalie's a 'troublemaker' and he called her your 'girlfriend,' Joe. While I'm not suggesting that it should be otherwise ... about her being your—"

"She's not my girlfriend," Joe interrupted. "And the one she's causing trouble for is Andy Wilson and he deserves—"

"She's not his girlfriend yet," said Carolyn. "Joe will take some time to get used to it, but I know Joe, and if he takes too long, I'll set him straight." After a moment, during which Hank stared at her and she became a little nervous, Carolyn added, "The divorce is not about girlfriends or anything like that. Joe and I are good friends and love each other, but we have to get divorced. For political reasons, that's all." Joe sincerely wished that Carolyn would just be quiet.

Hank continued to look at them all and finally said, "Maybe we can talk about that later. First, the simple stuff, okay? What's going on in your department, Sergeant Moore?"

"I'm not sure, but ... well, for some reason Captain Wilson and Sergeant Pierce were out to get Joe. I don't have anything solid, but—"

"I don't need any speculation," interrupted Captain Morgan. "How long have you been there, Sergeant Moore?"

"Only six months, but—"

"And is this the only thing you've noticed in that six months?"

Natalie took a deep breath. If this was going to be an investigation of her department, she may as well say it all now. She'd let one investigation fail to materialize back in the army. Not again, she decided. With a look of defiance on her face, she said, "That department sucks, Captain. Since I've been there, I've seen crimes committed and go unpunished, uninvestigated in fact, and people arrested for no crime at all. It seems that some people can do anything if they have the right friends and if they're willing to pay. And if you don't pay, anything you do is a crime. I think they're trafficking drugs and stolen property and God knows what else. Joe was shot at, and almost before the bullet hit his car window he was accused of faking the whole thing and would've been in jail now if they had had their way. He might have been dead."

"That how you see it, Sergeant?" asked Hank.

"No, Sir," replied Natalie. "That's how it is."

Hank Morgan looked at her and said, "Well, you might know better than I, but that's how it has looked to me too, and it's looked that way for quite a while now. We've been watching these people for almost two years, but they're smooth and we haven't been able to catch up with any of them. This may be the break we need to ... well, your name never came up in that investigation and seeing as you're Joe's friend ... or 'girlfriend' ... or at least his wife's friend." He smiled and chuckled. "You people are all crazy, you know that don't you?"

"Yeah, we know that," said Joe. "But a lot of our friends are crazy too. I even have this old friend on the state police force who's a bit crazy, smuggling beer into a hospital if I remember right."

"Okay. Okay. I remember that too," smiled Hank. "But y'all seem to be honest and that's not common around here today." He cast his eyes in the direction that Peter and Andy had recently gone and thought for a moment. "Maybe you can help me sort out what happened here today. First, who's that man under the blanket out there? He has a passport that says 'Earl Ray' on it."

"That's a fake," said Joe. "He's Lawrence Marshall, the CEO at the hospital."

"You're sure then?" asked Hank.

"He has a scar on his right calf that I sewed up about two years ago," said Carolyn. "It will be on his medical record."

"Well, we'll get his fingerprints too, but let me check what you say now." Hank went to the door and there was a brief conversation with a uniformed officer who looked dubiously at the covered remains of Lawrence Marshall, but he went to lift the blanket and pull up the pant leg nonetheless and then nodded to the Captain.

"Now, why did he want to kill you, Joe?" asked Hank when he was seated again.

Joe shook his head, "Three years ago he killed a four-year-old so the hospital would inherit her money, tens of millions it was. It was an impulsive act on his part, but he needed to cover up his embezzlement of funds during the building of the new ED at the hospital. Bert Wilson, that would be Captain Andrew Wilson's half-brother, was the contractor involved and he's giving all sorts of incriminating evidence right now and he's telling the police that's what happened that day. He's also saying that yesterday Marshall shot and killed that four-year-old's aunt, who was a very close friend of Bert Wilson's, because she just realized that what she saw three years ago was Lawrence Marshall murdering her niece, not trying to save her. I'm betting you'll find the bullets that killed her were fired from the gun he was going to kill me with.

"Mr. Marshall may also have killed the pathologist at the hospital, Frank Dobbs, to cover the falsification of the autopsy report." Joe looked at Carolyn's surprised face and added, "It was Lawrence that drove Frank home after he got drunk at his retirement party. Another impulsive act on his part. I don't know how he did it, but I'm guessing it was murder."

"So how does Lawrence Marshall fit into all the stuff going on in your county?" asked Hank.

"Well," said Joe. "The hospital doesn't seem to be involved with any real crime, does it?"

"No," said Hank. "Not that we have been able to find anyway."

"I think Lawrence and Bert had a little side action of their own and enlisted Bert's brother, Andy, to help when they got in over their heads. Lawrence was more a loose cannon than a builder of criminal empires," said Joe.

"And Bert?" asked Hank.

After a moment's thought Joe replied, "He builds buildings, but I think he was too timid to do much besides go along for the ride, and he seems to be relieved that it's finally over. He was willing to lie and take his share but … He was in the department when Linda Murphy, the four-year-old, was killed." He nodded toward Hank. "But Lawrence was actually in the room. The injection was probably given after Lawrence said she had arrested the second time and he sent Francine out of the room so she wouldn't see him give the intercardiac injection. That's what Bert's telling Douglas and I think he's telling the truth."

"Everyone thought it looked like artifact on the monitor," said Carolyn. "Just someone touching and moving the leads, not a real arrest. That's what it was all along, and we all thought it was a real cardiac arrest because a few seconds later Lawrence gave the injection of Lidocaine and it *was an arrest*, the bastard." Carolyn looked around at the others and added, "I'm sorry to call him a bastard since he's dead now, but it's the truth."

"Whose idea was it to embezzle the funds in the first place? Lawrence Marshall?" asked Hank.

Joe thought for a moment again and said, "I think it might have been cooked up by Lawrence and Bert, but I'd wonder if the chief of police might be someone who would naturally come up with that kind of an idea. Someone's behind more than one crime in that county, but most of that is small-time crime. This was the big one and …"

"Yes, that makes some sense," said Hank and was about to continue when Joe interrupted.

"You know, I wonder how they got down here so quickly. Andy and Peter, I mean. You didn't call them or anything did you, Hank?"

"Hell no," replied Hank.

Joe thought for a moment, "You know, Hank, maybe you should check the flights for Andy Wilson's name. I think he might have been down here to catch a flight out, not to catch us, and when the flights were all cancelled for the shooting, he thought the next best thing was to get rid of as many witnesses as possible. I doubt that I would've made it into his jail today. I would probably have just been added to the body count. He couldn't have thought he could cover anything up for long with his brother in custody, so he must have been making a run for it too, just the same as Lawrence was. He may have been meeting Lawrence, but maybe not. Maybe just making a run and decided to clear up some business when the flight was cancelled."

There was silence until Natalie said, "A man like Andy would've had the exit plan all ready to go, and he would've known Lawrence was getting ready to cut out. He would've known that time was running out with Lawrence. Andy would have known … but Peter?" She shook her head.

Joe frowned and said, "I'm not sure Peter was on the flight with him. Maybe Andy just brought Peter along to make sure he didn't start talking too much before he had a chance to disappear. What better way to keep someone quiet than to keep them with you, or bury them?"

Carolyn's face showed a mix of surprise and shock. "You mean he was going to kill Peter too? You mean you saved Peter's life today, Joe? I may never forgive you."

Percival knocked at the door and came in. "Well, Hank, I got him all set for ya. I'd give that captain three or maybe four minutes to think, enough to get a little more nervous, but not enough to realize he's in the deep weeds, and then I think you should go in for the kill. You'll get maybe seven or eight questions in before he demands an attorney."

Percival smiled like the Cheshire cat.

"I don't know about you, Percy," said Hank. "Where'd you get this stuff?"

"Well, Captain," Percy shrugged, "I watch a lot of TV crime shows."

Chapter 48

There was a short conversation between Hank and Percival, and then Hank left, still shaking his head. A minute later he was talking to Patti, who then went and got Peter Pierce and walked him quickly past the room where Captain Wilson was waiting and then back to the room he had come from, keeping him out of sight of his captain. Hank Morgan had either been watching those same TV shows or was *writing* for them. Andrew Wilson had only a minute to think about seeing his sergeant walk by with Patti before Hank went in to ask his "seven or eight questions."

"Your captain is in the deep weeds, Natalie," said Percival Wells. "And my captain thinks you're the best cop he's seen since I came along. After what you did today, I mean. You might want to get a job in another department, though, like maybe y'all should think about joining the state force?"

"Well, I haven't really thought about it, but maybe," replied Natalie.

Percival smiled broadly, a very nice smile it was, and said, "Let me give you my personal phone number in case you want to talk some more about it." He pulled an index card out of his pocket and handed it to her. His number had obviously already been written on it. "Well, back to work. Hank wants me to check some airline passenger lists," he said and went out the door, smiling still.

Carolyn looked at her and asked, "Natalie, I hope you're not thinking of calling him, are you?"

"Well, probably not, but—"

"Natalie. Are you serious? Percival?!" Carolyn looked truly horrified.

"I think he was just being friendly."

Carolyn shook her head and said, "You have been under a lot of stress, Natalie. I better hold on to this until you recover a little." She snatched the index card from her hand. "Seriously, Natalie. I mean, what if he wants your son to be named after him. Can you imagine what Reginald would be like if he'd been named 'Percival'?"

Joe smiled. He was glad that Carolyn was acting as she was, but he didn't quite know why he was glad. "Speaking of Reggie, maybe I should call and at least tell him what we have here."

"Yes," said Carolyn. "And you might want to warn him about Charles, who's telling everyone about where people are being dropped off at night."

"I'm not sure Charles told anyone anything," said Joe as he pulled out the cell phone.

"But Lawrence said Charles told him he dropped us off at your apartment last night." Natalie looked thoughtful for a moment and then said, "Lawrence said ... and, of course Lawrence ... But how did he know if Charles didn't tell him?"

Joe shrugged and said, "Someone burned out my apartment last night. I was wondering if maybe Lawrence was up there waiting for me and saw us get out of the limo. Maybe he didn't see us leave in the cab or just couldn't get down in time to follow us. Maybe he drove by the house and didn't see anything because you were sleeping in the back room, so he went back to my apartment, or maybe he never left at all. For whatever reason, he decided to burn my place down. Some of my old records were there and he may have been thinking I had some evidence, or it may have been just an impulse, the same as he did everything else. By then he must have known he was going to have to get what money he could and get out fast, so he needed me out of the way for what, another day or so?"

Someone spoke in the phone. "Hello Reggie," said Joe. "Just wanted to call and bring you up to speed."

Joe went over to the corner of the room to talk quietly and Natalie looked at Carolyn. "Maybe you should keep Percival's card, Carolyn." She was quiet for another minute and then said, "He's an amazing man, Carolyn. Are you sure you want to give him up?"

Joe looked over at them and he could be heard saying, "… it's just that she was thin and so is …" He turned away and they could no longer hear what he said. He didn't appear to have heard what they had been saying.

"Only to the right woman, Natalie, and I think I've found her," Carolyn smiled. "He's still going to be my friend, probably my best friend." She seemed only a little sad at this. They were hugging each other when Joe came over.

"So Reggie had some news," he said. "It seems Gloria mailed him a letter the night she was killed. She gave it to Rose, my secretary, to mail, as a matter of fact. I even heard her tell Rose to mail something but didn't think to ask what it was." He seemed embarrassed to admit the oversight. "She probably wrote it in my office while she was waiting for me. It was on my stationary." He shrugged again. "Whatever, she didn't put a stamp on it, so Rose stamped it and wrote a note on the back of the envelope, asking Gloria to send her a stamp. I guess she was annoyed at Gloria for assuming that she would stamp her mail for her. Reggie asked me to make sure I gave Rose her stamp back.

"He also asked if he could take care of Rose's holiday bonus this year too. I think he's considering giving her a small country somewhere. Anyway, he had just opened the letter when I called and he read it to me. It said about what we have already figured out."

What you've figured out, Joseph Nelson, thought Natalie. And it was your idea to sleep in the back room too, which may have kept Lawrence from killing us all last night.

Joe was still speaking. "The letter said that Lawrence gave the intercardiac Lidocaine when Francine left the room, but

Lawrence told her he was trying to save Linda," continued Joe, "and Gloria didn't realize what she was seeing until I had that conversation with Walter. She thought I knew all about it and couldn't figure out why I didn't tell Walter right then, but she speculated that I didn't trust Walter, which is at least a little true.

"She said that she was going to meet Bert that night to tell him he was a jerk and their relationship was over. It didn't sound like she realized Bert was in it with Lawrence. Maybe it was Lawrence she met, or maybe it was both Bert and Lawrence who showed up. I don't think she would have trusted Lawrence enough to let him get that close to her, but maybe if Bert were there. I somehow can't see Bert having the courage to shoot her three times, and I can't see Lawrence trusting him to do it without being there himself. I also kind of think that by this time Lawrence was … well, enjoying the slaughter too much to let Bert steal his fun." Both Carolyn and Natalie shivered at this thought.

"Oh," he added, "Reggie offered to give us a reward too, but I turned him down." There was a little disappointment evident on the countenance of the ladies on this last point. "I did suggest that he look after his remaining niece and nephew."

"Lucinda's other children?" asked Carolyn. "Why?"

"Oh, it's just that Linda was awfully thin and so is her mother and … well, I just thought there might be a problem. I also think Reggie would be happier if he had something to do with his otherwise meaningless life," said Joe.

"A genetic thing, you mean?" asked Carolyn.

"If anorexia is genetic, then yes," replied Joe.

"Anorexia?" asked Natalie. "Maybe inherited if not genetic, 'learned' from her mother. Reggie said his mother never fed him enough, and that's why he's short. Could she really have starved her children, and could her daughter be doing that to her own children?"

Joe just shrugged.

"I'm kind of sorry you turned down the 'reward.'" said Carolyn. "The 'devil's excrement' he called his money. 'Drowning in it,' he said. I might like to try swimming in it for a while."

"Well, Reggie called it that because he doesn't know how to swim in it. Someone just needs to point him toward the shore," said Joe. "Saving his niece and nephew may be the life preserver he needs."

"The metaphor is collapsing, Joe," said Carolyn.

"'The devil's excrement,'" said Natalie. "Did he think that up himself, do you suppose?"

"No," said Joe. Both women looked at him and he added, "Juan Pablo Perez Alfonzo, an economist from Venezuela, said it about that nation's oil. He predicted that Venezuela would drown in the 'devil's excrement,' just as Reggie predicted that the Murphys would drown in their money.

"Gloria said that her mother was responsible for it all when she told me to meet her in Murphy Park. 'This is her fault too,' she said." Joe frowned.

Natalie thought for a moment. "Reggie said that. Whatever was the reason, and whoever was the assassin, it was 'money' that killed them both. He was right, wasn't he?"

Patti came into the room at that point and nodded to them all. "Ohhhh," she said, "that Peter Pierce is such a slime ball. He actually thinks he can charm his way out of all this, as if he has any charm at all. That, along with giving every incriminating detail about his captain that he can think of and some that he's just imagining." She shook her head and added, "Oh, and Hank asked me to tell you that only Andy Wilson's name was on the passenger list. Just Andy's, he said. Apparently he couldn't stand Peter either. It's all over except the details."

There were expressions of surprise and some satisfaction too. No one would be sorry to see Peter Pierce get his just desserts. Patti smiled and went over to Joe. "You were really very courageous, Dr. Nelson," she said. She ran her hand down his arm and added, "and Captain Morgan said you're very intelligent as well. Putting everything together for him." She smiled at him for a moment and then started to leave, turning at the door to wink and say, "I just wanted you to know that. That I think you're a remarkable man."

There was silence for a moment after she left until Carolyn said, "Joseph, you had better tell her that you're already taken, don't you think? Or should I tell her?"

"Oh," said Joe. "I don't think—"

"That's a problem, Joe," said Carolyn. "You don't think, but fortunately Natalie and I are here to think for you, and we've decided that it won't be Patti." She nodded toward Natalie, who had the grace to blush a little.

"Do I get a say in it?" asked Joe.

Carolyn looked at Natalie who looked back. "No," they both said together and then giggled.

"You do prefer Natalie, don't you, Joe?" asked Carolyn.

Joe shrugged and then had to nod. "Well, yes."

"I have to warn you about Joe, Natalie. He has this problem with fidelity," said Carolyn.

It was Joe's turn to blush, "I ..."

Natalie's face took on a look of concern.

"Admit it, Joe," said Carolyn. She turned to face Natalie and continued, "We've been married for almost ten years and this divorce has been going on for six months, and I don't think you've been unfaithful to me even once have you, Joe?"

"Well, no ..." replied Joe.

"That's just not natural, Joe," said Carolyn, shaking her head. "It's an endearing quality, and I'm sure Natalie will appreciate it as much as I do, but men aren't supposed to be that way."

"Well, did you—" asked Joe.

"No, of course not, but ... well, it's different. You know that," said Carolyn.

Joe was saved from further embarrassment when Hank came back into the room. "Ah, that fool, Percival. I got *eleven* questions in before Captain Wilson asked for a lawyer. And the answer to number ten will hang him out to dry. Oh, and your lawyer is here if you want to see him."

Chapter 49

"Our lawyer?" asked Joe.

"Yeah," replied Hank. "I think he's your brother, Dr. Prentiss. Is that right? Douglas his name is."

"Douglas?" said Carolyn.

They looked out the glass partition and saw not only Douglas, but Carl Summers. Hank motioned them into the room.

"Hank," said Joe as he was leaving, "I'd like you to meet two men you'll probably be hearing from for some time to come. This is Carl Summers in operations at the hospital, and he'll be able to provide information about the contracts you'll be investigating, and this is Douglas Prentiss who will be running for governor soon." If Douglas was surprised, he hid it well.

"This is Hank Morgan, a friend of my father's and of mine and a state police captain and general savior of us all today. And Douglas and Carl, I don't think you've met Sergeant Natalie Moore of our local police and savior of me specifically today." Joe's arm slipped over her shoulder as he drew her forward to meet the new arrivals and it dropped slowly as they shook hands all around.

"Well, I'm glad to meet you both, and I'm sure glad to meet a potential governor. I'll be talking to you all, but I still need to gather a little information today," said Hank and turned to leave.

"Douglas has also been very instrumental in the interrogation of Andrew Wilson's brother, Bert," said Joe.

"Oh," said Hank, stopping in the doorway. "I *will* need to speak to you, Mr. Prentiss. Was it you that called Percival about the connection with Andy?"

"Ah, yes," answered Douglas, who seemed a bit nervous.

"That was quite helpful," said Hank. "I'll be back in just a few minutes, Mr. Prentiss." He left, looking back at them as he did.

It was Carolyn who looked most surprised. "Carl, what are you doing here?"

"Well," he said, "I was concerned about you, Carolyn. I mean, when Joe called about the contract this morning, I looked into it and found that the check had already cleared. Very unusual. Almost impossible unless someone had submitted it days ago. So then I called Douglas to tell him that the check had already cleared, since you seemed so interested," he nodded toward Joe. "And he said something about you being in some sort of ... well, I asked if he'd mind letting me ride down and make sure you ..."

There was silence as Carolyn stared at Carl, and Carl became more nervous. Finally Joe said, "And I'm sure Carolyn's very glad you were concerned enough to leave the hospital, especially at a time when things must be in some upheaval."

"Oh ... yes ... of course I am," stammered Carolyn. "Of course."

"Well, it's not really ..." began Carl. "I mean, they're impounding all the records at the hospital." He nodded toward Douglas. "And no one, especially administrators like myself, is allowed to even enter the building at this point. Not for a week or so probably."

Joe shook his head: the perfect opportunity to act like a hero and Carl had to be honest instead. "Yes," said Joe. "But still very thoughtful on your part and I'm sure Carolyn appreciates it."

"Yes, of course," said Carolyn again.

"Don't worry," said Carl. "The health care function of the hospital will proceed relatively unimpeded."

"Yes," Joe said. "With the lack of administrators, it's likely to show some benefit."

The silence was finally broken when Douglas asked, "So who's under the blanket out in the lobby? Was there an accident here or something?"

Joe realized that despite the feeling that it had been ages ago, it had probably only been two hours since Lawrence had died and that if it was on the news at all, it would be the very minimal information the police would feel compelled to provide. "That's Lawrence Marshall. He was killed while trying to kill me."

"Lawrence?" said both Douglas and Carl at once. "Killed?"

"Did you say he was trying to kill you, Joe?" asked Douglas.

Joe nodded as Hank poked his head in again to say, "Perhaps I can have a quick word with you, Mr. Summers? That shouldn't take long and then if you have a few minutes, Mr. Prentiss? Oh, and the hospital records were able to confirm that scar, Dr. Prentiss. The marvels of the electronic record. It may not help medicine but it sure helps the police. The fingerprints will be back in a day or sooner maybe, but I think we can presume the identity of the dead man."

Carl left the room and Carolyn turned to Joe to say, "Carl Summers? He wanted to make sure I was all right?"

"A very nice thought," offered Joe.

"I don't think I could survive a 'concerned' Carl Summers. I mean, I'm not sure I'm ready for any relationship."

Joe frowned slightly as he said, "I think you're looking at this the wrong way around, Carolyn."

"I'm looking at Carl Summers, Joe. Any way is the wrong way around."

"No," said Joe. "You should be thinking of him as a partner in the career part of your life, not the personal part. It's always good to have a friend in 'operations.' Think of him as a potential 'undersecretary to the surgeon general.'" He smiled at her and continued. "If more comes of it … well, then that's good, but he'd be an asset in your campaign, don't you think?"

"I don't know, Joe," said Carolyn.

Joe took a deep breath and put his arm around her shoulder. "I'm not saying that you're lacking in charm, especially since your demonstration with Peter just now, but … well, Carl leads a boring life. I think that you may have been more an excuse than a reason for him to come down here."

Natalie nodded and said, "I think Joe may be right, Carolyn. Carl might just crave a little excitement. He might see you as an exciting person to be around. Not romantically, just a dynamic person."

Carolyn and her brother looked dubious. Joe went on, "I think that Carl may have wanted to be 'in on the action' as they say. Why would he have taken the time to look up the check and all that? Certainly not to impress you or me."

Carl came back into the room looking very angry. "This is very upsetting, Joe." He looked even angrier as he stared at Joe with his arm still around Carolyn. "It's very … immoral," he said and shook his finger at Joe, frowning even more severely.

Joe looked back and Carl continued, "Someone had to have submitted that check days ago for it to be clearing today. That captain doesn't seem to understand the implication of that. No reputable institution would allow a draft of that size to clear without time to process it. Lawrence did that without any authorization, and I'll find out how he did that and what else is going on here!"

Joe's arm slowly dropped from Carolyn's shoulder. She seemed to be the only one who noticed. He thought for a moment and said, "Of course. It must have been in the works when the trial started, even before. That's why Lawrence was so anxious to keep things from being discovered. He couldn't afford to have anyone looking into the contracts or the work on the new ED, or at Bert at all. Once the check was submitted, once the 'end game' was started, if anyone started questioning any of it, it would all have come undone. He had to drag out the trial. All he needed was a few more days, but the trial was threatening it all."

"This is serious, Joe," said Carl. "Very serious. I mean, this isn't just about the money. This is about people's health too. It's about their lives." He seemed appalled. "Lawrence must be brought to task for this."

"I think he has been," said Carolyn.

"Oh. I'm sorry, Carolyn," said Carl with surprise. "I didn't notice you standing there. I hope I didn't frighten you with all that coarse language." After a pause he added, "Yes, I suppose Lawrence has been punished, hasn't he?" He cast a look at the lobby again, but if it was possible, he seemed disappointed that Lawrence would not be "properly" punished by having his assets seized or his salary garnished.

"Carl," said Carolyn. "I'm going to interview for a director-ship of a department in Las Vegas, if I ever get there, and ... well, I'm going to ask to fill some positions there as part of accepting the directorship. I was wondering if I could talk to you about maybe coming out there to work with me?"

"Well, I don't know," replied Carl. "I hadn't thought about leaving, but—"

"It would be a really good thing to do," said Carolyn. "I would like very much to have your help with this, Carl. I think we could have a really good professional partnership, and you could help significantly." After a pause she added, "I was very impressed with the passion you showed when you talked about the damage Lawrence had done to people's lives and health."

"Oh," said Carl. "That aspect of the health care system deserves attention too, Carolyn. It's not just a financial problem, you know."

Carolyn smiled and nodded.

"Maybe you could help me too, Carl? With my campaign, I mean," said Douglas.

"You are *not* running for governor, Douglas, and that's final," said Carolyn.

"Well, I thought I might," he replied sheepishly.

"I'll think seriously about that, Carolyn," said Carl, seemingly oblivious to Douglas and his plans and disappointments.

There was a pause until Joe asked, "One question, Douglas. How on earth did you get Bert to implicate his brother so quickly? I mean, it was only five minutes between my call to you and when Percival called Hank out of the room. There was hardly enough time for you to make the call, let alone get Bert to talk."

"Oh," said Douglas, growing nervous again as he said, "You were doing so well predicting things today that I kind of ... well, I assumed that you were right and ... well, I just told Percival I had the confession I knew Bert was going to make. You know, you can tell when they're going to spill their guts. They start looking real nervous and turning pale," Douglas shrugged.

Sort of the way you look right now, Douglas, thought Joe. "But there was a confession wasn't there? He did 'spill his guts,' I mean."

"Oh yeah," said Douglas. "It took a few minutes, but Bert rolled right over on his brother without a second thought." He turned to his sister. "Not like our family, Sis. When Joe said you might be in trouble, I ... well ..."

Carolyn smiled as beautifully as Joe had ever seen her smile, saying, "You lied for me, Douglas? That's the sweetest thing you've ever done." She hugged him and added, "Okay, okay. You can run for governor if you really want to." She hugged him again until they were both embarrassed.

Patti came back in and cleared her throat. "Could I get you to sign your statement, Sergeant Moore? Just a formality now. That dead guy was a real bastard, they say." She shook her head and added, "Killed a four-year-old girl? Is that true? And told you he was going to kill you too, Dr. Nelson? Because you couldn't run with a prosthetic leg? And threatened to kill your wife and ...?" She nodded toward Natalie.

"Yeah," said Joe. "He said he'd kill them both unless I went with him quietly and didn't try to say anything to let them know what he planned to do with me."

Patti shook her head again. "And putting up with Peter Pierce on top of it all, Sergeant Moore." This last seemed to be the worst. "You're a remarkable woman. Anyway, can I get your signature? You can just read through it in the other room if you want."

"Yeah, sure," said Natalie, and they went out to the room where a few moments before she was being interviewed. Patti did not stay behind to chat with Joe this time.

Carl and Douglas began a conversation about either the finances involved at the hospital or possibly Douglas' run for governor. Carolyn came over to Joe and asked, "Lawrence told you all that, Joe? Now, it seems to me that he didn't have time to say that much, and you can run with that leg of yours as well as anyone can and Lawrence knew that."

Joe shrugged and said, "I knew what he could do ... would do. He didn't have to tell me all of it."

"But you said he did tell you. Not like you, Joe, to say something that isn't one hundred percent true ... unless it was for Natalie. Unless it was so she wouldn't think she might not have had to kill him. So she wouldn't think that there might have been another way out without killing him. Is that why you said it? Or was it so that no one would ask why and make trouble for her over the scum's death?"

"Well," said Joe, "I knew she had to or ... well, it wasn't just me. Lawrence would keep killing until ... I mean, I'm sorry he died, but—"

Carolyn put her hand over Joe's mouth. "Let's start with one thing we both can agree upon, shall we? I don't know what a person has to do to deserve to die, but whatever that is, Lawrence Marshall did it. He killed poor four-year-old Linda Murphy on an impulse when he thought her death might get him out of a jam. He wasn't even sure it would work but figured taking away her life might help him a little, so why not? Then he killed Frank Dobbs on the night of his retirement party to cover things up a little. He shot Gloria to death and … and it could've been your brains on the floor out there for all he cared.

"So," she said, "you … well, maybe you lied a little. To make Natalie and the police believe she had no other choice. And you know what I think? I think she had no other choice. Lawrence would've killed you and maybe a dozen others if she didn't stop him. If she feels better thinking he told you he was going to kill you, well that's okay. She still had no choice, and if she hadn't killed him, I would have. She's just a better shot than I am, that's all. So what does that make you? A liar? Well, what I think that makes you is a 'really courageous person,' just like Sergeant Patti said. And, after standing very still while Natalie blew Lawrence away, telling the police that Lawrence told you he would kill us all and that Natalie had to stop him, that was the best thing you've done all day today, Joe Nelson."

"I had to hold still," smiled Joe. "I think it would've bothered Natalie if she had shot me by mistake. And besides, you know I think that God has a plan for me. Ever since that day in the mine I've believed there was a reason I'm alive, and I didn't want to screw that up either." He smiled at her and she smiled back.

"No," she said. "You don't want to screw up God's plans. I would've been upset too if you'd gotten shot, Joe. You're very courageous and you deserve this." She then pulled his face to hers and kissed his lips with a passion that surprised them both. When they parted, not too quickly, they were both embarrassed by what had happened, but Douglas and Carl were speechless.

Chapter 50

Hank came in, in time to be a little embarrassed himself, and cleared his throat. There were a lot of troublesome throats around today. Natalie followed him in too late to see any of it, though. Hank cleared his throat again and said, "I'd like to ask you some questions, Mr. Prentiss. It's not 'Governor' yet, is it?" Hank smiled at them and went on. "I'll need to get the specifics on all this from you. We're chasing the rabbits down right now and they're running hard to get cover. It would be real helpful if we knew which way they were going to run, if ya know what I mean. So's we can get there first. You were the one that got the records impounded up there, weren't you, Mr. Prentiss?"

Joe smiled at Hank's language. He was enjoying this, Joe thought, this final success after watching for two years. What Joe wasn't prepared for was Douglas. "Well, yeah, Chief. I was," he said, putting his arm over Captain Hank Morgan's shoulder. That it was Joe who had insisted Douglas do that might not get mentioned just yet, if it was ever mentioned at all. "The rabbits are running for cover all right, but they're also trying to cover their tracks, if ya know what I mean. There's a paper trail and an electronic trail that'll bury these suckers for sure, and we need to get that before they have a chance to bury it. I can help ya there."

"I thought a gubernatorial candidate like yourself might be the one to do that," said Hank, smiling. "Maybe we should get you some special status or something; 'investigator' or something like that. I wonder if a judge could be convinced to hustle that through real quick?"

Carolyn smiled and then asked, "So where's the money?"

"What?" asked Joe.

"Yes," said Carolyn. "If this was all about the money, where is it?"

Carl had sat quietly puzzled throughout the conversation, but now found his voice. "Granada," he said.

"What?" replied a collective voice from the others.

Carl seemed startled and began to fumble his words. "The money," he said. "It's in an offshore account in Granada. Strange, I thought, that Bert would want it in that sort of an account. Non-interest bearing, I mean. And another strange thing," Carl relaxed more now, "it's in Lawrence's name. An oversight, I was sure, although my friend in the bank in Cincinnati seemed to think it might be some sort of criminal activity. She was the one that looked up the transfer information for me. She really shouldn't have, of course, so I better not mention her name."

"Well," said Douglas, "do you think Lawrence was trying to skip out on Bert and Andy too? He was definitely not a nice person … and not very smart either. We can get all that information and maybe get the money back, but it will involve getting the federal people involved."

Hank seemed slightly distressed at this. "Well, they were bound to get involved eventually. Yeah, that account in Granada can be frozen, and you might eventually get the money back," he said to Carl.

"Or," offered Natalie. Hank looked at her and she continued, "You could suggest the federal boys watch that account to see who tries to scoop up the cash. Andy was into drug trafficking and stolen property and all kinds of stuff we may not even know about, so seeing who knows the money is there and who tries to get it might be a clue as to which way the money usually flowed."

Hank smiled at her and said, "Now, Nat'ly might have a good idea there."

"And you could score one on the feds, too, Captain Morgan," *Nat'ly* said.

Hank smiled. "Now, I wouldn't mind that either, but if you and I are going to work together, you're going to have to call me Hank. Hate being called 'Captain Morgan.' Terrible name for a good Baptist boy like myself. It's been twenty years since I've had even a beer." He smiled now at Joe.

"Not quite twenty," said Joe. "I think *Nat'ly* can learn to call you 'Hank.' I also think Walter is involved in all of this too. He tried to commit suicide today and is in the ICU back home."

"Walter?" asked Douglas. "Suicide?" He shook his head. "I'm not surprised. He's got more problems than all of us together, starting with the unfortunate fact that he didn't marry someone as nice as my sister."

"What?" Joe asked.

"Oh," shrugged Douglas, "it's just his divorce. His wife is dragging everything out: the property, fund concealment and mismanagement, and, of course, Walter's extramarital stuff." He seemed embarrassed to be so forthcoming. "Anyway, he's strapped for money and generally a pariah in the profession. I told Carolyn to warn you, Joe."

"I did," said Carolyn. "Remember, Joe, I told you he was a loser?"

Joe smiled at her and said, "But not why he was a loser."

"When you're a loser, it doesn't matter why," responded Carolyn.

"But it would explain why he ... well, he was very interested in postponing the trial," Joe shook his head. "I wonder ..."

"Wonder what?" asked Douglas.

"Well," said Joe, "Stevens, the judge, was awfully willing to delay the trial too. I just wonder if—"

"The judge?!" said Carolyn.

Douglas looked first shocked and then amazed and finally enlightened as he gazed first at Carolyn, then at Joe, and finally at Hank, who frowned a bit and then nodded his head, that kind of nod that says, *I'll find out.*

After a minute Joe continued, "I can call Reggie if you want, about the 'special investigator' thing, I mean," offered Joe. "He can pull some weight."

"Reggie?" said Hank.

"Reginald Murphy," said Joe.

Hank looked at him and whistled. "You *are* amazing, Joe. I haven't heard anyone call that guy 'Reggie' before. You two good friends, are ya?"

"Since last night," replied Joe.

Hank smiled for a moment and then said, "You know this thing could go pretty deep, and I'm going to need to talk some more to y'all, but it might be better, and safer, if you were out of sight for the next week or so. 'Til we round them up, I mean." He paused and then continued. "There's a paper trail, I'm sure, and probably a bigger electronic one." He nodded toward Douglas and continued again, "But there are a few people these folks might want to see buried too. I think it would be nice to make it difficult for them to find y'all, if ya know what I mean."

Joe nodded. "I'll call Reggie and see if he can get a judge to give you 'special investigator' status, Douglas, and Hank … we'll be around if you need us, but not too close maybe. You have the cell numbers for Natalie and Carolyn. Captain Andy has mine, so I'll have to stay close to them, I guess."

Hank just smiled and nodded. "I'll get that back for ya, Joe," he said and then left, talking intently to Douglas.

When they were gone, Natalie said to Joe, "Walter was the one that … well, it was his office that Lawrence used to shoot at you."

"Walter was an accomplice maybe, but I don't think he knew what Lawrence had done or what he had planned. He acted pretty surprised when I told him. Lawrence sent Bert to his office after he overheard me say I was going there with the Lidocaine from the ED, and Bert got Walter to go over to that bar on Somerset.

"When I picked up the Lidocaine, Lawrence got nervous. He probably thought that I was figuring it all out, so he went over to the house, broke in, and took the gun. He shot at me and put the gun back so it would look like I'd faked the whole thing. Then he called Andy to alert him to what had happened, and that's how Andy and Peter knew it was my gun and that it was in the house."

"The door to the office wasn't broken in or anything. You think Bert managed to leave it unlocked for Lawrence or something?" asked Natalie

"Yes, that's possible," he replied.

She paused again and then asked, "Why didn't they just arrest you instead of that whole thing with stealing your gun and shooting at you?"

Joe thought for a moment and then said, "These guys aren't acting logically, at least not our logic. Killing a four-year-old ... It's just not something you or I could ever do. Maybe they were playing Gloria and Reginald too. I mean, they were already using Gloria to get the contracts and to discourage any investigation of Bert and the ED work. Maybe they had to be a little subtle to keep them from suspecting that it was all about the work at the hospital. Reggie already questioned 'the adequacy of the police,' so arresting me might have been more of a 'clue' than a solution. Discrediting me, on the other hand, would make Reggie think he'd picked the wrong guy to investigate his niece's death. I'd just be a crazy doctor that no one would pay any attention to. Remember, all they needed was ... well, another couple of hours when it came down to it. Lawrence, or Earl Ray I should say, almost got on a flight out of here today."

"Andy Wilson backed away from Reggie pretty quickly, didn't he?" said Carolyn.

"I think Andy was afraid of Reggie," said Joe. "Not his money."

"Not his money?" asked Natalie.

"Yeah," said Joe. "When we were rescued in the ED last night, I thought they were just afraid of the Murphy money, but Andy was probably more afraid that if he didn't accommodate Reggie, he would start looking into the whole thing himself and would find that a check had been submitted for final payment. Reggie's good at the financial things, so he would have known that was an irregularity and stopped it even if he didn't know it had anything to do with the death of his sister or his niece. Andy couldn't take any chances on that check not clearing."

"But how did you figure out it was Lawrence?" asked Natalie.

"I kept coming up against the same problem every time I tried," said Joe. "What possible reason could anyone have to want Linda Murphy dead? Finally, I just looked at it the other way around. Who could have done it? Killed Linda, killed Gloria, shot at me, and probably killed Frank Dobbs?

"It seemed to me that all the murders had to have been done by the same person, and Lawrence was the only one who could have done all three and shot at me too. Bert and Walter had an alibi. Andy didn't fit, and besides, he was at the police station when you brought me in that night, not returning my gun to the desk drawer. I was his alibi.

"Once I figured that Lawrence was that one person, it all came back to the ED contracts and back to Bert and Walter and Andy too, but as accomplices. Douglas confirmed that there had been 'irregularities' in the ED work, but that Linda Murphy's death had stopped the investigation. That explained why Lawrence had killed her. Lawrence had said he was leaving today, and Stacy and then Carl confirmed that. Carl confirmed that the check had been issued and so it had to be today. Only one flight out of the country matched the timing."

"I told you he was a prick," said Carolyn.

Natalie shook her head. "Walter too? Your own lawyer?"

"I don't think Walter really knew what was going on. He just needed the money. Lawrence was the bad actor all along. Bert and Walter were just players. Lawrence, and Andy too of course, were the movers," said Joe.

Natalie smiled. "You *are* a remarkable man, just as Patti said, and I'm going to fight her for you, Joe Nelson." She reached up, pulling him to her and kissing his lips long and hard. When she finished, she turned to Carolyn and said, "I'll get Carolyn to tell her that."

Carolyn smiled and nodded. "It's time to straighten this all out."

Natalie smiled too and shook her head. "I hope they nail Andy."

"I hope they nail Peter Pierce," added Carolyn, rubbing the arm Peter had been rubbing an hour earlier.

Joe smiled at them: Natalie, Carl, and Carolyn. "You're missing your interview in Las Vegas, aren't you, Carolyn? You and Carl both. That seems a shame. But what bothers me most is Hank Morgan."

"What about Hank Morgan?" asked Natalie.

"Did you hear him say we couldn't go to Las Vegas?" asked Joe.

"No," said Natalie.

"I didn't hear anything about that either, Joe," said Carolyn.

"Neither did I," said Joe and pulled out the cell phone. "Let me see if Reggie has a private jet and a condo or something in Vegas that he'll loan us."

About the Author

Paul Janson spent five years practicing as a physician in the coal mining, Appalachian region of Eastern Kentucky.

He now lives on a small farm in rural Massachusetts with his wife and children and practices medicine in an emergency department.

He is the author of a children's picture book about the adoption of his two daughters. *Mal Practice* is his first published novel.

CPSIA information can be obtained at www.ICGtesting.com
Printed in the USA
BVOW01s0054141013

333547BV00001BB/1/P

9 780988 515727